a FALL *of* SPARROWS

By

Paul J. Bennett

Published by

ATHANATOS
PUBLISHING GROUP

a FALL of SPARROWS

By

Paul J. Bennett

Published by

ATHANATOS
PUBLISHING GROUP

A Fall of Sparrows
   by Paul J. Bennett

   Website: www.fallofsparrows.com

ISBN: 978-1936830718

Published by **Athanatos Publishing Group**

   Website: www.athanatosministries.org

CHAPTER I

A single blade of broom straw, stirred by the afternoon breeze, brushed gently against the smoky gray woolen coat and its motionless occupant. Other bodies similarly clad lay strewn about and would have otherwise appeared identical save for the rhythmic rising and falling of that single chest. In the center of the ring of bodies lay a ragged wound in the grass-covered hillside, out of which rose thin wisps of white, acrid smoke that curled delicately above the jagged orifice before being whisked away. Distant thunder as from a passing storm wafted across the open space, rising at times in a crescendo that made the individual noises blend into a single ominous chorus.

Initially, any attempt of the broom straw was fruitless in awakening the soldier. Then, a faint tremor appeared in the blackened right hand. First, the movement remained confined to the fingers as they groped blindly among the blades of grass. Next, the left hand began to move and, in concert with the right, made a united effort to push the gray-clad soldier over onto his back. As he lay still, bathed in the warmth of the late afternoon sun, his mind fought desperately to free itself from the same murky white haze which clung tenaciously to the field of battle. His name? His name? What was his name?

"Will," the parched lips responded into empty air. "I remember now. William Mark Seymour."

The distant thunder of cannon reached his ears and brought back vivid images of the conflict in which he had struggled for what seemed an eternity.

"And where are you from, William Mark Seymour?" came the rhetorical question.

"Georgia. That's it. Bainbridge, Georgia, I believe."

Will inhaled deeply as he recalled peaceful scenes of a swift river lined with cypress and long-needled pines.

"I remember the Flint River."

Summoning all his strength, Will sat up and examined his uniform systematically. With great relief, he discovered no evidence of any major wound and was especially proud to learn that his abdomen had survived the ordeal unscathed.

"That's right, Will," he continued to converse with himself. "You're just an ordinary Georgia volunteer. And you've lived to fight another day."

After rubbing his hands over his face in a further attempt to clear the haze from his mind, Will looked about him at his comrades and realized instantly that he alone had survived. The smoking, jagged defect in the hillside was the only remaining evidence of the explosive shell that had burst among his group of sharpshooters as they harassed the enemy's movements. Will's last recollections before losing consciousness were the white puff from the enemy cannon, a brief whistling sound, and a blinding flash of light. The sorrow he felt over the expressionless faces lying about him was a familiar one, having become his nearly constant companion since the war began.

As his mind continued to clear, Will realized that he had no idea where the lines of battle were, or for that matter, where his own army was. He could hear the continuing noise of battle but knew that striking off in the general direction of the conflict would very likely get him killed or captured. Having already narrowly escaped death and having no desire to become a prisoner, Will decided to adopt a stealthy approach. Immediately, he began to search the ground for his prized Whitworth rifle, as he was one of only a few in Lee's entire army to be awarded the coveted English rifle. His heart sank as his gaze fell upon the weapon, its stock splintered and smashed by shrapnel. The long, distinctive Davidson scope had likewise been twisted near its proximal end into shattered, useless metal. Almost as if saying farewell to a loved one, Will gently touched the weapon that had bought his life with its own. His companion's rifles were the two-banded Enfields, which seemed to be in good repair. Will lifted one of the weapons from the tall grass and ran his arm through the sling. With great respect, he gingerly slipped the cartridge box from the arm of one of the bodies and placed it over his other shoulder.

"I'm sorry, Jack," Will whispered. "I'll take good care of it for you."

Rising to his full height, Will felt the landscape spin about him and remained motionless while he regained his balance. Turning his back to the distant conflict, he slipped away from the top of the hill and stole down the slope toward the woods from which he had emerged earlier that day. As he entered the forest, he was greeted with the welcome sound of silence, although many of the trees bore the unmistakable scars of heated gunfire. Will stopped for a moment to listen for the sounds of soldiers' voices or the rustle of feet in the underbrush, but he detected none. His keen eyes, now much clearer than when he first regained consciousness, searched for anything out of the ordinary, but he saw only the occasional flutter of a bird. He proceeded to push further into the forest, the lengthening shadows testifying to the age of the day. As a veteran soldier, Will knew that hostilities would cease after sundown and that it would be impossible for him to find the Confederate lines before then. Traveling after dark would only increase the likelihood of his capture or worse. With that in mind, Will searched for a secure place to spend the night and hoped that the sunrise would bring better fortunes with it.

Will soon found that his stamina was not what it had been and that the concussion from the explosive shell had taken more of a toll on him than he realized. Taking a rest beneath a Virginia maple tree, Will made a closer inspection of his new weapon. As before, he noticed no damage. The nipple was uncapped and the hammer rested firmly upon it, but Will did not know whether a charge was present in the barrel of the muzzleloader. Drawing the ramrod, he passed it down the barrel and heard the distinct sound of metal upon metal as the ramrod contacted the breech. That sound, combined with the distance that the ramrod passed down the barrel, assured him that the rifle was unloaded. Reaching back into his cartridge box, Will pulled one of the paper cartridges from its holding place and tore off one end with his teeth. He then poured the black powder down the barrel and seated the .58 caliber bullet in the end of the muzzle. Using the ramrod once more, he pushed the bullet down until it came to rest firmly on top of the powder. Leaving the percussion cap off for the moment, Will resumed his trek.

On the far side of the forest, Will saw a field of corn illuminated by the evening light. The crop remained, for the most part, in good order, but there was evidence of a fair amount of trampling as some of the stalks had been trodden underfoot and snapped off at ground level. Still, the remaining stalks provided adequate cover and Will slipped silently into their midst. Once completely surrounded by the lofty crop, he immediately knelt down to listen. Only a slight evening breeze rustled the coarse green leave, but there was still no evidence of another human. Trusting his instincts, Will reached back on his belt and lifted the lid on the smaller leather container of percussion caps. Nimbly sorting out one of the copper caps, he quickly placed the hammer of his rifle on half-cock and slipped the cap down onto the nipple underneath. He then fully cocked the hammer and advanced, his rifle at the ready.

As he approached the final row of corn, Will was able to make out structures silhouetted by the failing light. In the far distance, with no lights illuminating the windows, was a farmhouse. Closer, and of greater interest, was a barn without evidence of battle damage. He watched intently, but no activity was evident. In fact, the entire place had an eerie blanket of desertion draped over it, and at that moment Will could have easily believed that he was the last survivor viewing the remaining skeleton of a long-dead civilization. Leaving the cornfield behind and staying low to the ground, Will advanced until he came against the closest barn wall. Pressing his ear against the rough wood, he listened intently but heard no voices within. Still gripping his rifle, Will made his way to the front of the barn. Leaning out, he peered around the corner and saw that one of the barn doors had been left slightly ajar. Silently, Will rounded the corner and approached the door. Will removed his brown slouch hat and placed it on the tip of the ramrod. Slowly, he advanced the slender instrument until just the tip of the hat projected in front of the opening. No movement. No whispered orders. No gunshots. Will replaced his hat and ramrod and opened the door fully with the muzzle of his rifle.

The barn was as silent on the inside as the entire farm had been outside. All was dark at first, but as Will's eyes adjusted he was able to see that very little remained inside. Most likely, the owners had heard about the advancing armies and had taken their possessions to safer locations before the battle was fully engaged. Because of the orderly nature of the barn and the grounds, it seemed less likely that its barren state was produced by pillaging. Only a small stack of hay remained in the back left corner, but there were no signs of any livestock. Will made a quick survey of all four corners and found nothing out of the ordinary. With a sigh of relief, he carefully returned the rifle's hammer to half-cock.

Will, becoming more aware of his fatigue, sat down against the back wall and listened to the silence punctuated by only an occasional distant rumble. As the darkness deepened, the rumbling became less frequent and then disappeared altogether. In the solitude of that hiding place, Will missed his companions more than ever, but he also became acutely aware of another familiar sensation. Since joining the army, Will had become accustomed to shortages in all basic necessities, but perhaps none so glaring as the shortage of food. He had had nothing to eat since that morning, as it was the custom of many of the soldiers to eat all of their daily rations, consisting mostly of corn meal and a little pork, prior to a battle. Will vaguely remembered seeing an apple tree near the barn, and he rose from the dusty floor to see if any fruit remained before the darkness became too thick. As he passed through the open doors, he could see the form of the tree outlined against the western sky. The tree was still full of apples, but Will had difficulty telling if any were ripe. However, underneath the tree were many apples which had already ripened and fallen to the ground. Never letting go of his rifle, Will knelt down and picked up one of the better specimens, polished it on the front of his coat, and took a bite. Gratefully, he was greeted with the sweet taste of a ripe Virginia apple and then began to stuff his pockets with similar specimens. He then rose to his feet and swiftly reentered the barn, pulling the doors together behind him and lowering the wooden crossbar.

Once back in his dark corner, Will decided to make a small fire, if only temporarily. Over to his left he found a few small scraps of wood, and he assembled these in a teepee formation over a mound of dry straw taken from the nearby stack. Retrieving his flint and steel from his pack, Will struck them together briskly over the straw. The momentary flashes of light illuminated the center of the barn and the gray-clad soldier like diminutive bolts of lightning. One of the sparks fell directly into the midst of the straw, and Will blew gently on the glowing ember. Soon, yellow flames burst from the straw and began to lick at the wood above. Will leaned back and continued to eat some of the apples while sipping water from his canteen.

With his stomach full, he watched the dancing flames as his mind wandered to his Georgia home and the countless fires that he had enjoyed in his own hearth. How distant those times and the faces of his wife and children felt. And yet, it was not they who had changed. The man he was when he enlisted in the army no longer existed, a man whose very nature had been scored and hardened by the fires of war essentially into a killing machine replaced the former. How innocent and satisfying were his skills of marksmanship as a boy, yet now he could snuff out a man's life 1000 yards away with hardly a thought. He was by far the best marksman in his unit, but those triumphs were meaningless, and he would have given everything to

5

return to the way things used to be. Perhaps his greatest fear was that he would actually survive the war only to return to his family a complete stranger. As sleep overtook him, the flames dwindled, leaving only glowing embers.

*****

When Will awoke, the ashes before him lay cold and gray, illuminated by the early morning light pushing through the cracks in the barn door. Remembering where he was, he began to listen intently for any sounds of activity but heard only sparse, distant gunshots. As he slowly recalled the events of the previous day, Will did not look forward to the dangerous journey ahead, but he also knew that he would feel relieved once he was back among his own. He reached over to his left and felt the stock of his rifle exactly where he had left it and then sat up to gather his meager belongings.

Even in the low light, Will's keen eyes detected something out of place. In the dusty earth of the barn floor, Will could see the prints of his own worn Brogan shoes, but they were no longer the only prints visible. Scattered among his own were multiple new imprints of bare feet which traveled right up to where he had been sleeping. Horrified, Will realized that someone had walked up to him and stood beside him while he slept. Sliding his hand down to his belt, Will found his Bowie knife still strapped in place. The large blade slipped from its sheath. Turning around slowly, Will saw no one. Studying the prints once more, he saw that the tracks led directly to the haystack. Silently, as if stalking dangerous prey, he stood up and followed the tracks to their origin. The light from the sunrise was gradually increasing, and Will could see the dark shape lying just underneath an inadequate layer of straw. Burning with rage after having been caught off guard by this intruder, he gripped the Bowie knife tightly and felt the muscles of his legs tighten as he prepared to strike.

With all of his energy focused into a single action, Will pounced. He landed squarely on top of the body and felt it jerk away from him in an attempt to escape, but Will's reaction was swift and he quickly grasped the still unseen enemy at the base of the neck. Almost immediately, Will noticed that the person beneath him reacted differently than the battle-hardened opponents to which he was accustomed. The skin too was more delicate and lacked the rough texture of a man's unshaven face. A scream exploded from beneath the hay, and Will pulled his arm swiftly up from beneath him. Staring back into his face were the terrified features of a young Negro woman.

"Don't hurt me!" she gasped as the large blade stood poised to strike. "I don't mean you no harm!"

"Who are you?" Will yelled back. "And what were you doing standing over me last night?"

"Nothin'!" the terrified woman screamed as she struggled for air. Will relaxed his grip only slightly.

"You were going for this knife, weren't you? Or maybe my rifle? You stole in here and then were going to make short work of me, weren't you?"

"No, sir! I...I been in here all along since before you came. I done tried to leave, but I couldn't get da door open."

"That's a lie!"

"No, sir! It was dark, and I was scared I was gonna wake you. I was just hopin' you'd pass me on by."

Will, his soldier's mind in perpetual motion, grasped the woman's arm and jerked her to her feet in the shifting straw. Disregarding her gender, Will began to search her for any signs of a weapon. He then turned her sharply, and the tattered dress fell from one shoulder to reveal linear stripes across her back, but Will was undeterred.

"Who else is with you?"

"Nobody."

Will shook her slightly.

"I said who's with you?"

"Nobody!"

Will sensed that the terrified woman was telling him the truth. The rage which had momentarily blinded him began to subside, and only then did Will realize the force of his grasp. Exhaling through pursed lips, Will released his grip and let the menacing blade fall to his side. Even through the brown skin Will could see the crimson mark of his fingers upon the base of her throat and arm. He took a few steps back and sat upon the dusty earth.

"You've been here all the time?"

"Yes, sir," the woman replied while a trembling hand replaced the dress across her shoulder.

"There's only one reason you're here, so I'm not going to insult you by asking," Will began as his eyes initially remained focused on the ground. He then gazed intently into her eyes.

"You're a runaway."

"I's just lost, dat's all."

"Never heard of a lost slave, unless they ran away first."

The woman didn't answer, her gaze never rising above the dusty floor.

"If you're lost, tell me where you're from."

Still, no response came from the woman. Will sighed and replaced the Bowie knife in its sheath.

"Listen, there's no need for us to dance around what both of us know is true. You're running from something, and I'm trying to get back to something."

The woman still remained silent.

"You don't have anything to say? You're not going to talk to me?"

"Jus' not much to say."

As simple as her statement was, Will recognized how true it was. She knew as well as he the Confederate position on runaways, and no amount of words could change that. Nevertheless, she brought with her an unwelcome problem for the Confederate. Will knew that his strict orders were to turn in all runaways. Yet taking an unwilling slave with him, especially a woman, behind enemy lines was not appealing.

"Sit," Will commanded. "And don't move."

She obeyed immediately and sat in the straw. Will turned and picked up his Enfield as he moved to the door of the barn. Removing the stiff wooden crossbar, he gingerly opened the door slightly before risking a glance outside. As he gazed at the farm, he saw that nothing had changed from the night before, and he saw no evidence of another human. Turning around, he saw the woman had remained obediently in her place as if she had accepted her fate. Will returned to his captive and knelt close by.

"What's your name?"

"Evaline."

Will inhaled deeply and leaned heavily on his Enfield.

"Well, Evaline, it would appear that you have gotten us both into a predicament. You've done something that you shouldn't, and I've got my orders to take runaways to the proper authorities. The only problem is that I've gotten separated from my unit. Finding them with you will be much more difficult."

"Ain't no need for you to trouble yourself with me," she responded softly.

"Orders are orders, and I don't take them lightly," Will answered sternly. "Following orders is what has kept me alive for this long, and I don't plan to make exception now."

Will looked about him and saw a stretch of rope near the haystack. With little thought, he snatched the rope from the dusty floor and approached Evaline.

"Hold out your hands."

She obeyed without opposition, and Will wrapped the rope securely around her wrists. As the gray-clad soldier stood above her, Evaline raised her eyes to him, her expression pleading with him where words would have failed miserably. Will's eyes met hers for a moment as he towered above her, but he quickly turned away and filled his mind with the daunting task ahead.

"Come on. We have to go."

*****

A more unlikely pair could not have been imagined as the two stepped through the barn door and into the early morning sunlight. The tall, lean soldier led the way, his Enfield at the ready. Behind him came a smaller, humbled human whose tattered clothes and bound hands only added outwardly to her inner destitution. Before departing, Will made one last trip to the apple tree and filled his pockets with as much of the fruit as he could.

Will's brogan shoes, barely holding together themselves, surpassed the bare feet behind him, the brown skin showing the wear and tear of a long journey over uneven ground. The difference, however, had gone unnoticed by Will, his mind occupied by far more pressing matters. He could still hear distant gunfire, but nothing on the scale of the previous day. Although he couldn't be sure, Will felt that this likely meant that the main battle was over and that the two armies had settled down to skirmishing. Still, he had no idea where the battle lines were and what the outcome of the conflict had been. Having been in that part of Virginia for some time, Will was familiar with the general layout of the land and the surrounding roads. After some time the silence became oppressive, and Will was the first to risk conversation.

"How far have you come?" he asked without turning around.

"How do you mean?"

"In running away. How far have you traveled?"

"Not sure."

"Where are you from?"

"Round about Lynchburg."

"I know where that is. Beautiful country."

"Not so pretty from the slave quarters."

"Come to think of it, it wasn't so pretty from camp, either."

Just as he spoke the words, it suddenly dawned upon Will that although he had suffered many hardships in the army, they had all been undertaken by choice, whereas Evaline endured her torment through forced enslavement. Evaline, unsure of the repercussions she would suffer, never uttered those sentiments.

"I'm not from here," Will continued.

"I thought so."

"Why is that?"

"You talks different."

"Strange, huh?"

"No, jus' different."

"Where were you trying to go?"

"Away."

"I know that. I mean where were you trying to get to?"

Evaline didn't answer, and Will sensed her hesitation.

"Listen, I'm not asking you these questions to try to capture your companions or arrest those who might help you. I don't even know if you have any companions. That's not why I'm here."

There was still no answer, and Will didn't push the issue any further. In all honesty, he knew that given her present situation, he would have had no answers if their roles were reversed. She had no reason to trust him.

*****

The sun was almost directly overhead, but Will had still seen no sign of another soldier. The gunfire still resounded in the distance, but he seemed to be making little progress in reaching it. He traveled with some trepidation, fearing that he would suddenly emerge from the wilderness into a brigade of bluecoats. The sensations of hunger and thirst reappeared, and Will realized that he had been marching like a soldier, indifferent to the needs of the one behind him. His time in the army had taught him to endure or ignore his most basic longings, but Evaline had no such training. Still, she uttered no protests and plodded forward under the watchful eye of her new master. Will realized, with some embarrassment, that it must have been some time since she had had anything to eat or drink, and he had never even thought to ask.

A shady white oak soon presented itself, and Will motioned for Evaline to sit underneath. The polished blade of the Bowie knife made a smooth metallic sound as he drew it from its sheath and approached the young woman.

"Let me see your hands."

In obedience, Evaline slowly raised her hands. Will carefully slid the tip of the honed blade underneath the rope in the groove where her wrists lay. With a twist of his hand, the ropes were severed and fell to the ground.

"I don't think you'll need those anymore."

Will then removed his canteen from across his shoulder and sloshed the meager amount of water. He then removed the cork and offered it to Evaline.

"There's not much, but take some. Hopefully we'll find a well or a creek soon."

At first Evaline did not move, almost as if she expected the offer to be a mere hoax and for her burning thirst to remain unquenched. The Confederate's offer remained firm, however, and Evaline reached for the canteen. As she took her first few sips, Will produced one of the apples and sliced it in two with his knife.

"Here," Will stated as he offered half to Evaline. Will could see the spark in her gaze as she saw the apple, but her actions never betrayed the depth of her hunger. She slowly reached and took the piece of fruit and handed the canteen back to Will. Quietly she ate as Will sat close by. He had almost brought the canteen to his lips when he remembered Evaline drinking from it. When he was sure she wasn't looking, he quickly wiped the opening on his sleeve before taking a drink.

*****

While they were resting, Evaline cast several brief glances at her captor. He was tall and thin, his lack of adequate food and the rigors of campaigning making his cheekbones even more prominent than usual. From underneath his slouch hat fell locks of straight chestnut brown hair in desperate need of trimming. His face was long and thin and marred with black streaks from burnt powder. The thin mouth was surrounded by a goatee, and the piercing blue eyes scrutinized every detail of their surroundings searching for the slightest deviation. He was in many respects a distinguished looking man and, at first glance, did not at all appear unkind. However, like a bloom beneath the snow, the beauty of the man had been subdued beneath the icy covering of war.

*****

Will ate a little of the fruit but gave most of it to Evaline. After a few moments of enjoying the respite, he realized that it was time to move on. As Evaline stood, Will for the first time noticed the condition of her feet, but there was little he could do even if he wished to try. He comforted himself with the possibility of finding some footwear at one of the nearby farms.

"Hopefully it won't be much further," Will stated as the sun continued to descend.

"Much farther where?"

"We'll need to find a place to stay tonight."

"You don't 'spect to find your folks tonight?"

"No. I don't seem to be making much progress in that area."

Silence followed.

"What you plans to do with me when you finds 'em?"

"Turn you in."

"And den what?"

"Then they'll decide what to do with you."

A pause followed.

"Who's 'they'?"

"My superiors in the army."

"Dey is just gonna send me back."

"I don't have any say over what they do."

"Guess not. But you has a say now."

CHAPTER II

Evening had come when the pair emerged from the forest and gazed out over an open field. A single split rail fence separated them from a white farmhouse in the distance. Will motioned for Evaline to stop, and he scrutinized the scene for several minutes. He saw no activity or movement at all except for the billowing waves of grass in the evening breeze. The sun was making long shadows across the field, and Will knew that they would need shelter for the night. Having seen nothing ominous, he stood before turning to the young woman behind him.

"Let's go," he stated, motioning toward the distant house.

The white farmhouse grew steadily larger as the pair approached. Nothing moved, but Will, nonetheless, felt a sense of unease, and he stopped just short of the split rail fence.

"Stay close to me," he instructed as he turned to face Evaline. "It's a little too quiet here for my liking."

"I can wait here until you checks it out," the young woman offered. "Ain't no need to slow yoself down on account o' me."

"Nice try, but you're coming with me."

"Why?"

"I always look out for whoever is with me."

"Look out for me now and turn me in later?"

Will didn't answer.

"Looks like you on the wrong side to be lookin' after me," Evaline continued, feeling bolder.

"You might be surprised," Will responded without turning around.

"Why is dat?"

"All I'm saying is that men are men, no matter the color of their uniform. Many men in gray are not as low as you believe, nor are the ideals of those in blue always as lofty as they might have you believe."

"You talks real proper."

"I was a teacher in my former life."

"Former?"

"Yes. The one I no longer know how to live."

As the two spoke, they crossed the rail fence and approached the rear of the house. Will turned and motioned for Evaline to keep quiet as they made their way to the back entrance. Nearby was a well with a serpentine pump handle. The house itself was not like one of the great plantation houses, but neither was it the house of an impoverished man. Will climbed the steps up onto the back porch, making certain that Evaline stayed with him. He knocked on the back door, but there was no answer. He tried the lock, but the doorknob would not turn.

"Dey ain't here," Evaline observed.

"No," came the slow reply. "Most folks in this area have cleared out a long time ago. Too much fighting to keep a family around here."

Will moved around to one of the windows and peered inside and was shocked to see the ambiguous shapes of covered furniture in the dim light. The house had not been vandalized.

"Must still be behind Confederate lines," Will mumbled half to himself. "The Yanks would have carted off anything worthwhile and burned the rest."

Will returned to the back door and studied it carefully, as if he were searching for a weakness or perhaps another solution to the problem which faced him. Seeming to have come to a satisfactory conclusion, he squared his shoulders against the door and drove himself against the wood. Almost as if it had no will to resist, the door made a splintering sound before swinging open in front of them. He then turned to Evaline.

"You first," he ordered, motioning toward the open doorway. Sheepishly she obeyed, the thick, gray light swallowing her as she entered. Will followed and allowed his eyes to adjust to the gloom. The rear entrance opened into a hallway, which ran straight through the house to the front door. To the right off the hallway was a sitting room, while a small library was off to the left. A staircase, the steps facing away from them toward the front door, led to the upstairs. The floors were oak and in good repair, but there was little furniture save for the pieces that Will had seen through the window. The walls were bare and nothing of value was visible, all indicating to Will that the owners had adequate time to prepare for their retreat. The house had a dry, stagnant odor as one would expect in one sealed and unoccupied for some time. The gentle evening breeze wafted through the back door, and the house inhaled it as a man starved for air.

"Move to the left," Will ordered. "And stay ahead of me where I can see you."

The two moved into the library and Will was amazed to see that many of the books remained on the shelves, the absence of their more valuable siblings marked by the gaping spaces between some of the volumes. Keeping one hand on Evaline's arm, he moved over to the bookcases, scanning each spine and drinking in their titles as if refreshing acquaintances with old friends. In the middle of the bookshelves, Will noticed a collection of the McGuffey Readers, which had taught more of his students than he could remember the basics of reading and grammar. Inexplicably, he picked up the first reader and placed it in his haversack, but not before placing a small Confederate bill in its vacancy. Next to the Readers was a much thicker and more lavishly decorated volume.

"Shakespeare," he whispered. "Now that's been quite a while."

Never letting go of Evaline, he placed the strap of his Enfield over his shoulder and took the book from its place with his free hand. The worn volume fell open in his hand and his eyes gazed over the familiar lines of Hamlet, the words conjuring up vivid images of a small schoolroom in Southwest Georgia. The young faces of his students, some of them having been lost to the conflict, reappeared, and he recalled with accurate detail where they sat, what they wore, and what they brought each day for lunch. The laughter, sights and sounds of a now dead world burst upon his senses and, unable to bear it, Will snapped the book shut. A small puff of dust wafted in the air as the pages fluttered together. Suddenly, all was silent.

"Somethin' da matter?"

"No. Let's move on."

On the far side of the library on the front wall was a door leading to a room which would have been to a guest's right if they entered through the front door. It was very similar in appearance to the others, square with little furnishings and a single fireplace. Two other nearly identical rooms were across the hallway on the far side of the stairs, and Will found nothing worthy of his attention. With Evaline still to his front, he then made his way back to the stairs. The pair then stood at the bottom of the flight looking up, almost as if they questioned the safety of ascending.

"You go first," Evaline asked.

"No."

"I don't know what's up dere."

"Nothing's up there."

15

"Den why we gots to go?"

"To make sure."

"I feels pretty sure dat I don't want to go up dere."

"Listen, you're not my shield. It's the only way I can keep an eye on you and make sure you don't run. Of course, I could bind you hand and foot and leave you down here if you want."

Evaline didn't respond, but instead turned back to face the stairs. With a gentle nudge from Will, they began their ascent.

The stairs creaked beneath them as they climbed. Evaline led the way with Will, his Enfield now in his hands, close behind. At the top of the stairs, two large rooms were visible, one to the right and to the left. A quick look into the rooms revealed them to be vacant except for the stripped skeletons of two four post beds. Will first directed Evaline into the room on the right, and noted a closet door on the front wall. Moving over to the portal, Will turned the knob and opened the door with the muzzle of his rifle. Peering cautiously inside, only emptiness stared back at the soldier, and he closed the door. Moving on to the other room they saw a similar closet, but again found nothing inside. Evaline seemed to breathe a sigh of relief.

"Told you there was nothing up here," Will stated.

"Had to be sure," came the response.

The pair returned down the stairs the way they had come. Will directed Evaline toward the back door.

"I saw some wood outside. It looked old but dry, so we should be able to have a fire. I'm going to fill my canteen from the well. Come with me."

Again Will motioned for Evaline to move ahead of him, and they exited the rear of the house the same way they had entered. The wood stack was nearby, but Will passed it by and made straight for the well. The sun had just set behind the woods to the west, but Will was still able to make out clearly the forms ahead of him. Upon reaching the well, Will grasped the handle and pumped it a few times until water flowed freely from the spout with each cycle. He then slipped the canteen from his shoulder and, after opening it, held it underneath the stream of water until it overflowed. Will stared at the full container and stopped pumping, the stream of water gushing from the well's spout trailing off to only a trickle. He then handed the canteen to Evaline.

"Here."

Evaline did not hesitate as she had earlier but stepped forward more eagerly and accepted the gift of fresh water from the soldier's hand. Having finished, she passed it back to him. Will immediately began to pump the handle once more and, as discreetly as possible, made sure that he thoroughly washed the tin spout and placed fresh water in the canteen before drinking from it himself. Having finished, the pair returned to the house and the stack of firewood. Upon reaching it, Evaline, as if acting on some innate protocol, began to grab logs and pile them onto her arms. Will watched at first, but something inside him made him uneasy, and he found himself unable to simply stand and watch.

"Wait," he commanded as he stepped forward. He then slipped the canteen once more from his shoulder. "You take this. I'll take the wood."

Evaline stopped piling the wood and stared at the Confederate for a moment as if what he was saying was some type of cruel, sarcastic insult. Perhaps she had moved too slowly, or perhaps he was displeased with the amount of wood that she could carry. However, as she studied him, his expression did not change and, without hint of displeasure, he gently took the wood from her arms after slipping the linen canteen strap over her head.

"You first," he motioned with his head toward the back door. Evaline obeyed, and soon the two were back inside the house. In the rapidly thickening darkness, Will led Evaline into the library to the left of the hallway after closing the door to the house behind them. As the door closed, each had his own reservations regarding the evening. Evaline, although her companion had shown no obvious ill will, was uneasy about being forced to spend the night with this strange soldier. Will, on the other hand, was unsure of how to deal with his unusual prisoner. The obvious, and safest, solution was to bind her for the night, but throughout the day he had become inexplicably less comfortable with that approach. Nevertheless, he could not have her roaming about completely unfettered.

Will reached into his knapsack once more and retrieved his flint and steel. Utilizing some dry straw he had brought in from outside, he soon had a small fire going and began to pile on smaller splinters of wood before adding the larger pieces.

"I miss fatwood," the Confederate spoke out loud as the growing flames from the fireplace cast an orange glow across his features.

"Miss what?"

17

"Fatwood."

"What's dat?"

"Back home some of the pines will make this wood that has a lot of sap. You can cut it from older branches and make splinters from it. The wood has a nice smell to it, and if you light it, then it immediately catches fire, and it'll burn for some time. We use it back home to start our fireplaces and stoves. The pines here in Virginia don't make it, or at least I haven't seen it."

Will then stood and leaned his Enfield close by in the corner, nestled among the shadows.

"Anyway, there's not much to eat. I have only a couple of apples left, but you can have them."

"You don't want one?"

Will shrugged his shoulders.

"Not hungry."

He then motioned for her to rise.

"Come with me. Just once more. I left the apples with my bedroll. We'll get them and then try to rest."

Evaline obeyed and once again led Will out of the room and into the hallway. The fire was now robust and some of the light from its flames stretched its fingers beyond the room and into the hallway. As soon as Will left the room, he immediately realized that the back door was not as he had left it. He had made certain earlier that it was closed completely, but now it stood slightly ajar and creaked back and forth ever so slightly in the night breeze. He had no way of knowing factually, but every fiber of his being told him that this new finding was not by accident nor was it of benign origins. The dark shadow that suddenly materialized from beneath the stairs only confirmed his suspicions. The click of a gun hammer echoed in the vacant halls and the cold steel of a Colt pistol pressed against his temple before he had any chance to react.

"Don't move, Dixie boy," the raspy voice exhaled through clenched teeth. Evaline, shocked by the sudden appearance of this intruder, gasped and instinctively recoiled toward Will.

"You can just stay where you are too," he growled, motioning toward Evaline. Will did not respond verbally and showed no sign of external distress. Without moving his head, Will looked to his extreme left and noted a bearded, burly man dressed in the typical blue coat of a Union soldier. He lacked Will's stature, but his physique was more muscular, either by inheritance or better nutrition. He was not at all an inviting creature, nor did he strike Will as an honest one. Will had little doubt that this soldier's reasons for being separated from his unit, if indeed that was the case, were more dubious than his own.

"What's your unit?" the gruff voice demanded.

"Third Georgia sharpshooters."

The muzzle of the pistol pressed more intensely against the side of Will's head, pushing it to the right.

"I ought to kill you where you are!" the voice boomed into Will's ear. "You have any idea how many friends I've lost to cowards like you?"

"No more than I have."

The man's left fist shot forward and hit Will in the pit of his stomach, knocking the wind out of him. Will leaned forward only slightly, then resumed his upright posture.

"Smart off at me again and I'll blow your brains out!"

"What unit are you from?" Will gasped.

"None of your business!"

"You asked me first."

"Yeah, cause I'm the one with the gun."

"There's no need to be uncivil. I've got some…"

"You got nothin' I want!" the voice shot back, his eyes diverting swiftly and surreptitiously to Evaline. "Now, shut your mouth! You and your little friend can get back in that room and sit down."

With little choice in the matter, Will gently touched Evaline's arm and backed into the library. The flickering orange light from the fireplace fully illuminated the Union soldier as he entered, and Will's initial impression seemed to be verified in the greater illumination. In fact, the hardened features and the cold blue eyes were far more sinister than he first imagined.

"Even if I shot you right now, boy, you'd be getting no worse treatment from me than you would be your own. The Rebs shoot deserters just like we do."

"I didn't desert."

"Yeah, I'll bet. Just out having a little fun with your little Negro princess? Maybe just showing her a good time?"

Will ignored the comment.

"She's a runaway. Simple as that."

"Uh-huh," came the sarcastic reply, the Colt pistol never wavering. "Probably just running from her other white boyfriend and figured she'd try you out for a while."

Will again ignored the comment, but became aware of Evaline trembling beside him.

"Where's your weapon?"

Will resisted the strong urge to look toward the Enfield still hidden in the shadows off to the Federal's right.

"I don't have one."

"Bull."

"A cannonball took care of my Whitfield. Blew it to pieces. When I woke up, there was no one around."

The Union soldier did not respond immediately but began to study the Confederate more closely.

"Throw me your haversack," he commanded, pointing toward the pouch slung around Will's neck by a linen strap. Will obeyed and tossed the haversack to him. The Federal caught the bag in midair and immediately dropped down on one knee while keeping the pistol leveled at Will. He then turned the haversack over and dumped its meager contents onto the floor. A tin mess plate with fork and spoon clattered onto the wood along with a tintype photograph, a cup, comb, Bible and the McGuffey Reader. The Federal picked up the picture first and studied it for a moment before looking back at Will.

"This your wife and kids?"

"That's right."

His gaze returned to the photograph momentarily before a sadistic smile curled upon his face.

"You're in trouble now, boy, when your lady finds out what you been up to!"

Will again ignored the accusation.

"How you think she's gonna feel, you laid up here with her like this?"

Will remained silent. The Federal suddenly seemed to grow weary of the Confederate's silence, and he snapped the pistol up and pointed it menacingly at Will's head.

"I asked you a question! Answer me!"

"What would you have me say?" Will responded. "Tell you the truth once more only to be accused of being a liar? Or fabricate what you believe would be a more reasonable story only for you to find out that I *am* lying?"

It was the Federal's turn to be silent and, after studying Will for a moment longer, he returned to sifting through Will's belongings. He picked up the McGuffey Reader and thumbed clumsily through its pages.

"What are you carrying this around for?"

"Nothing."

"You some kind of teacher or something?"

"Not anymore."

The Federal then dropped the book and seemed to stare about the room as if looking for something or searching for the right words. He glanced over once more at Evaline and then back at Will, pointing the barrel of the colt at one and then the other.

"Got any food?" came the raspy question.

"No."

"Any whiskey?"

"No."

The Federal's head dropped momentarily as if to indicate his frustration with Will's answers. A growing sense of dread swelled within Will's chest, and he, ever so cautiously, moved his feet underneath him.

"You see, Reb," the Federal began again. "The way I see it you've proved yourself to be of no help to me at all. You've got no food, no weapon, and you're not even carrying anything of value. Now, you know there's no way that I can take both of you back with me single-handedly. So as I see it, I've got no choice but to lighten my load."

Will's legs coiled up beneath him like a viper as he awaited the opportune time. If he waited much longer, he knew what the outcome would be.

"So you see, you've got no value really."

The Federal motioned toward Evaline.

"It seems a whole lot more reasonable to get rid of you and take someone with me that I can have a little fun with…"

Will's attack was sudden and vicious as his legs drove him forward, his right hand drawing the Bowie from its sheath as he hurled himself at the Federal. The Colt bellowed flame and smoke, but Will twisted his body as he flew to avoid the deadly projectile. He slammed full force into the Federal, knocking the pistol from his hand and pushing him over backward. The two then fell into a writhing heap, each trying to gain the upper hand, only to kick the pistol to the far side of the room in the process. Evaline, stunned by

21

the sudden attack and the boom of the gunshot, came to her senses only to realize that the struggling men barred her way out. She quickly ran to the rear door which exited to the front room but realized that it had been locked from the other side. She then attempted to open the windows, but to no avail. She looked frantically for another escape route, feeling very much like a trapped animal.

The Federal was a stalwart man, but he found in his tall, lean opponent a ferocious fighter and a hardened veteran of many Southern brawls. The Bowie was knocked from Will's hand, but he continued to use his elbows, fists, and knees as weapons of great efficiency. The Federal was taking the worst of it. As the two struggled, the Federal searched for something to use to his advantage, and his groping hand found the lip of Will's tin mess plate. Swinging it up with all his might, it connected full force against Will's face, causing the Confederate to stumble backward. Evaline, seeing her chance, attempted to run past the now separated men to the freedom beyond. Just as she was about to pass the Federal, his hand shot out and grasped her ankle, tripping her and causing her to fall viciously to the floor just short of the door.

"Where do you think you're going?"

The Federal, Bowie now in hand, crawled up and snatched the terrified young woman up to his chest and placed the deadly blade against her throat, his face just behind and to the side of hers.

But Will was already in motion. As soon as he had fallen backward, he began to stretch toward the Enfield in the shadows. Almost as if it knew its owner's need, the rifle jumped into Will's hands, and the two began to move as one. Will rolled to the side and, coming to rest on his knees, he felt the familiar feel of the rifle as it bonded with his shoulder. In one fluid motion, Will cocked the hammer and swung the rifle until the exact moment the sights lined up evenly with the Federal's head. Then, he pulled the trigger.

The roar of the Enfield shook the entire house as the plume of white smoke erupted from the muzzle and engulfed both Evaline and the Federal. The force of the large caliber bullet shoved the Federal flat onto the wooden floor, where he lay motionless. Suddenly, there fell an eerie calm and the only movement was the drifting of the acrid smoke, the only sound the ringing in Will's ears. The Confederate initially remained motionless, but then he slowly lowered the Enfield as the smoke cleared enough to reveal Evaline, staring ahead in a trance-like state. She remained in the same position as previously, the dead Federal sprawled out behind her. The brown skin of her left cheek showed the ebony markings of the powder residue mixed with a crimson color of a more grisly nature. In fact, her entire left face and hair were covered with the results of his pinpoint shot.

"Evaline!" Will called as he placed the Enfield on the floor and moved to her side. There was no response. He touched her on the arm and repeated her name, but she continued to stare directly ahead.

"Evaline, I'm sorry," he spoke as he looked about frantically for something with which to clean her face. The pitiful contents of his haversack remained scattered on the floor, but there was nothing there to assist him. Reaching into his pocket, he retrieved an old, yellowed handkerchief and without any thought for security, he stood and raced outside to the well. With a few sturdy pumps, the water again flowed freely from the spout and Will washed and rinsed the handkerchief multiple times before wringing it out. He then rushed back inside to find Evaline unmoved from her position and staring ahead. He once again knelt beside her and gently began to clean her face. The cool sensation from the cloth caused her to wince, but she otherwise did not respond.

"Evaline, I'm sorry," he stated repeatedly as his guilt for traumatizing the young woman grew. And yet, he could not explain why he felt as he did, for it was certainly not the first time he had been forced to kill. In addition, his actions had been in pure self-defense, not for some murderous objective. Still, he had dragged this young woman unwillingly into his world, a violent world whose realities shocked even one calloused by a life of slavery, and for that he found his conscience to be most unforgiving.

"Evaline, can you hear me?" Will spoke to her as he moved her face to his. "Evaline, we have to go. We can't stay here."

Slowly, and ever so slightly, her head and eyes turned to meet his, but there still seemed to be no light of comprehension. Quickly replacing his haversack and Bowie knife and swinging the Enfield across his shoulder, Will then gently placed his arms underneath Evaline and lifted her from the floor.

"I'm sorry, Evaline," he repeated. "But if anyone is close enough to have heard those shots, they'll be here in no time at all. We have to go outside."

Without looking back, Will moved out of the library and through the back door. There was no light to illumine the back steps, so Will made a cautious descent using his feet as guides. His feet finally touched ground and he made off for the black woods, still carrying Evaline in his arms.

*****

It was midnight before Will could settle down enough to rest. He had found a small clearing out of sight of the house and had tried to make Evaline as comfortable as possible. She still did not speak, although Will found no evidence of injury. He offered her water, but she would have none. Feeling generally useless, Will had reloaded his rifle and placed his back against a tree, listening intently for any sound of movement. None came and the silence, having a hypnotic effect on the weary Confederate, lulled him to sleep.

*****

He was awakened by a sudden, terrifying cry, and it took him a moment to orient himself and remember where he was. Gripping his Enfield in a vice-like grip, he suddenly realized that it was Evaline who was screaming. But his eyes, having adjusted to the gloom, saw no attacker. She was sitting upright and staring straight ahead into the darkness. Half out of concern for her and half out of fear of being discovered, Will quickly moved in front of her and grasped her by the arms.

"Evaline, stop!" he whispered gently but firmly. "There's no one here but me. You've had a bad dream. There's nothing here."

The screaming stopped, but Evaline continued to shake uncontrollably as her eyes stared off into the night. Realizing that she was still suffering from the earlier trauma, Will instinctively pulled her closer as he would have one of his own children. The trembling slowed and then eventually stopped altogether as her head came to rest against his shoulder. Will remained motionless for a moment until he felt assured that she was asleep. Supporting her head, he allowed her to slowly recline onto the forest floor. He then unwrapped his bedroll and placed it over her all the while wishing that he had something cleaner. He then resumed his position against the tree, placed the rifle across his lap, and drifted back to sleep.

*****

As Will slept, he began to dream. His usual dreams during the

24

war were very rarely pleasant, or if they were they consisted of nostalgic visions of home and his wife that left him more depressed upon awakening than he ever felt on the battlefield. But this dream was different, and none of his surroundings were familiar. Will was in a home, but not a stately or modest Southern home. Instead, it was a foreign dwelling where many men lay on their sides with their heads and upper bodies toward a low table which cleared the floor by only a few inches. The men reclined upon their left arm and reached over to eat food from the table with their right hand. In his vision, Will was not at the table but had his back against the wall observing all that transpired. Other than the obvious foreign nature of the room and the meal, Will's attention was drawn to one Man in particular reclining at the table. There was nothing about the Man's appearance which captured Will's gaze, for He seemed an ordinary fellow. However, a woman was present at His feet as they lay away from the table, and she was continually weeping and wiping the Man's feet with her hair which fell unfettered around her shoulders. Many of the men at the table stared at the woman with expressions of disdain, but the Man whose feet she washed did not forbid her and was, in fact, speaking to a wealthy-appearing man at the table.

"Simon, do you see this woman?" the Man asked.

"Yes," came the curt reply from the wealthy man.

"Simon, when I came to your house today, you gave Me no greeting kiss, but this woman has not stopped kissing my feet. You did not offer to wash my feet, but this woman has washed my feet with her tears and has wiped them with her hair. You gave Me none of the usual greetings that you would usually extend to a guest, but she has given Me all that she has. So you see, Simon, I promise you that this woman's many sins are forgiven. You, Simon, are just as much a sinner as she; you just don't see it. The more you see your own sin and what it takes to forgive it, the more you love others. So, I ask you again, Simon. Do you really *see* her?"

Suddenly, the Man ended his conversation with the one called Simon and turned unexpectedly to Will, allowing the soldier to see His face for the first time. Facing Will was a Man with olive skin, similar to pictures that Will had seen of men from the Middle East. His head, similar to all the others, was covered in a turban and His clothes were simple robes which reached almost to His feet. His eyes were piercing, seeing past the superficial exterior and penetrating deeply into the very soul.

"And you, Will," the Man spoke directly to the Confederate without notice of the others at the table. "Do *you* see her?"

Glancing quickly at the woman once again, Will saw that her image had changed dramatically and that in place of the previous Jewish woman was the unmistakable form of Evaline.

"Do you *see* her?"

*****

The sun was just beginning to peek over the horizon when Will finally stirred from his position, the night's vision still prevalent in his thoughts. His gaze then fell upon Evaline, and a new sense of compassion flooded his emotions. Evaline had not moved from beneath the blanket and as of yet had shown no signs of awakening. Will stood and stretched, again listening intently for any signs of activity, but he was only greeted by the early morning sounds of the forest. Will was used to being hungry, but the emptiness in the pit of his stomach was worse now than it had been in quite some time, and he knew that he would have to find food soon. He no longer heard the distant gunfire and so his proximity to the army was now in question, although the appearance of the Federal reassured him that the distance was likely not great. As he leaned over to pick up the Enfield, Evaline began to stir underneath the blanket and suddenly sat up with a gasp as she looked about her to regain her bearings.

"It's all right," Will stated softly. "You're safe."

Will could see that Evaline's faculties had returned and that she no longer stared off into the distance.

"Do you remember anything?" Will asked.

Evaline did not respond immediately but seemed to sort out the memories from the previous evening. Suddenly recalling Will's deadly struggle with the Federal, she looked up at the Confederate with an expression of terror.

"I'm sorry," Will began. "I had no choice."

Evaline responded by touching her left ear.

"I can't hardly hear out of dis ear."

"I figured so. You were very close to the gun."

Evaline continued to examine her ear with her fingers.

"I'm going to build us a fire, and then I've got to get us some food. It shouldn't take long."

"You knows where to find some?"

"I've got a pretty good idea."

26

Evaline nodded in response.

"You can stay here if you want. In fact, where I'm going I'd recommend you stay."

Evaline nodded in understanding.

"You goin' back to the house, ain't you?"

"Yes."

Will then proceeded to gather kindling and in a very short time he had a warm fire going. Evaline moved closer and held out her hands to the growing flames.

"I'm leaving the canteen with you. It's full. As soon as I do what needs to be done, I'll come back here. I'll try not to be too long."

He then looked at Evaline and spoke with words of true concern.

"Are you going to be all right?"

The young woman nodded.

"Stay here."

Will then turned and was swallowed by the forest. As Evaline watched him disappear into the foliage, she felt a sense of loneliness return. As strange as it was to her, she could not deny the sense of security that surrounded the lean Confederate wherever he went. She then turned back to the flames and continued to warm her hands.

*****

Will remained concealed in the edge of the woods, carefully watching the house for any signs of movement. Satisfied that all was still, he made his way swiftly across the yard to the back door. He was relieved that, at least superficially, all was as he had left it. He quickly climbed the rear steps and entered the still gaping back door but halted in the hallway. He knew what awaited him in the library, for he had seen it over and over on the battlefield until his mind had almost become numb to the suffering of others. This time was somehow different, but his sense of duty drove him forward and through the library door.

The Federal lay undisturbed exactly as he had fallen the previous night. The rest of the room remained unchanged except for the gray ashes present in the fireplace. Will immediately moved to the far side of the room and picked up the Colt revolver. As a sharpshooter, he had little need for a sidearm, but he felt much safer with the weapon in his possession. Making sure the hammer still rested on the empty chamber, he stuck the weapon into his belt. As he rose, his attention was caught by a round dark defect in the far wall of the library. Will moved over and rubbed his hand over the ragged .58 caliber hole about waist high and just to the left of the window. He then turned around and looked back at the dead Federal, perfectly in line with the defect in the wall. Moving over to the body, Will knelt down beside him and removed the oilcloth haversack from the stiff arm. Opening the bag, Will saw contents similar to his own. However, inside the haversack were also two square, hard, cracker-like items which Will quickly placed in his own haversack along with the tin cup. A small bag made out of linen and tied off with a bit of twine fell out of the Federal's haversack, and as Will picked it up, he detected a fragrance that he had not smelled in quite some time. Opening the twine, Will poured the coffee beans into his palm. Holding them closer to his nose, he inhaled deeply before placing them back in the bag. Realizing the value of the waterproof oilcloth, he folded the Federal's haversack and placed the entire pouch in his haversack as well.

As Will rose, he glanced down at the Federal's feet and noticed the shoes of much better quality than his own. Will's shoes were not in the best of condition, but suddenly Evaline's bare feet came to mind, and the Confederate felt a twinge of guilt. Moving to the dead soldier's feet, Will slipped the shoes off and held them out to gauge the size.

"Too big," Will said out loud as he thought of the petite woman. Will drew his Bowie knife and, with swift precision, cut some cloth from the hem of the Federal's trousers. He then shoved the woolen fabric deep into the toes of the shoes.

"Maybe that will help."

Will took one more glance around the room but, seeing nothing of any further value, looked once more at the Federal. He seemed mesmerized, almost as if the gravity of the deed and the senselessness of the act suddenly descended upon him.

"It didn't have to be this way," he stated softly.

Realizing that he at least owed the man a proper burial, Will pulled one of the curtains from the closest window and used it to wrap the shattered head. He then resolutely pulled the man out the back door toward his final resting place.

*****

It was late morning before Will returned to find Evaline just as he had left her. Even in their short time together, Evaline knew the cadence of his footsteps and there was never any doubt that it was her Confederate guardian that approached through the woods. Will found her continued presence puzzling, having expected her to make her escape while he was away. Nevertheless, after his ordeal of burying the Federal, he found her company welcome.

"Found something you may like," Will stated as he knelt by the fire. He removed the bag of coffee beans from his haversack and poured some out in his hand.

"Coffee," Will stated. "Real coffee, too. Not that chickory stuff."

"Dat from the dead man?" Evaline asked.

Will nodded in response.

"You want some?"

It was Evaline's turn to nod her approval. First, Will filled both of the tin cups with water from his canteen and set them over the fire. Will searched the ground and soon spotted a nearby flat-topped stone. He retrieved it and brushed off the surface. Then, he placed it on a level section of earth and put some of the beans on top. Using the butt of his rifle stock, Will rolled over the beans repeatedly, crushing them into smaller and smaller pieces. He then retrieved the tin cups and set them away from the fire to cool. Then using the makeshift coffee grounds, Will had soon produced a potent brew.

"Sorry, I don't have any sugar. Haven't had any in a long time."

"Dat's all right," Evaline responded. "I likes mine strong and black. Same as I like my menfolks."

Will chuckled at Evaline's comment, and he felt great relief that she was feeling better.

"Here," Will stated as he handed one of the square crackers to her. "You'll want this too."

"What's dis?"

"Hardtack."

"What's dat?"

"It's what the Yankees eat when they're on the march. It's made out of the same things as biscuits, but they make it really hard so it'll last a long time and not spoil. You'll want to let it soak in your coffee first, though, to soften it. Believe me, it lives up to its name."

Evaline did as she was instructed and let one of the corners of the square biscuit soak in her coffee. She then removed it and broke off the corner. However, just as she was about to sample this new food, her attention was diverted by movement on the surface of her coffee.

"What's the matter?" Will asked, observing her scrutiny of her coffee.

"Dey's something in my coffee."

Will glanced over the rim of her cup.

"Oh, right. Those are like meal worms."

"What?"

"I forgot to tell you. The hardtack can be full of them. Don't worry though, I've eaten these things many times and you can't really taste them at all."

"I suddenly ain't hungry."

"Here, have my coffee; it doesn't have anything in it. You need something to eat. I'll try to break up one of these and clean it out for you."

Will took the hardtack from Evaline and began the slow process of ridding it of its elongated inhabitants. As he did so, Evaline took a few tentative sips from her coffee.

"Where to, now? We soon leavin' to find your friends?"

Will continued his work and answered without looking up.

"No."

Initially, Evaline did not believe what she had heard and felt that this must have been some cruel joke and yet, she could not deny the fluttering of hope.

"No?"

"No."

"Den where we goin'?"

"Home."

"You goin' all the way back to Georgia?"

"No, I'm not going home. You are."

Fear suddenly swept across Evaline's heart."

"Please don't take me back to Lynchburg."

Will looked up from his work.

"I'm not. I'm taking you to a new home."

Suddenly, the realization of what Will was saying dawned upon the young woman.

"You mean..." she hesitated to say what was on her mind for fear that it might only be a dream and that speaking it openly might rouse her. "You mean you gonna help me?"

"You're lost. And you can't make it through these armies without me. As you've seen, you can't trust anyone."

"Is dat legal?"

Will chuckled.

"Depends on who you ask."

Evaline remained silent, unable to grasp all that was happening.

"What made da change?" she asked.

"I was reprimanded."

"By who?"

"A Jewish Carpenter."

Evaline smiled. She then studied at her coffee again and with her free hand reached up and touched her injured ear.

"You know, you almost hit me back der."

"No, no, I didn't," Will stated as he continued working. "Not even close."

Evaline contemplated what the Confederate was saying and realized that he was not speaking out of arrogance, but merely reassuring her that his shot had been placed precisely where it should have.

"I'm sorry, Evaline. I had no choice. He wasn't right."

"I know. It's okay."

Evaline studied her coffee for another moment.

"What's your name?"

A wave of embarrassment swept over Will as he realized that he had not even introduced himself to the young woman.

"Forgive me. My name is William. William Mark Seymour. My friends call me Will."

A pause followed.

"What you wants *me* to call you?"

Will ceased his labor and gazed back with a sincere expression.

"I want you to call me Will."

CHAPTER III

The following morning, after extinguishing the fire, Will and Evaline resumed their journey. After their earlier conversation, the Confederate found his companion to be a much more willing traveler. Will knew the dangers inherent in the journey, but he did not speak openly of them, realizing that their encounter with the Federal had likely erased the last remnants of the young woman's innocence. Will had given her the modified shoes and, although a little awkward, they provided much better protection from the rough terrain. Disregarding the possible position of his army, Will turned northeast to cover the shortest distance to the Rappahannock River.

"Will, how far you thinks it is?"

"What do you mean?"

"I means, how far is it to wherever we's going?"

"That's complicated."

"How?"

"For you to be completely safe, I'm afraid you're going to have to go all the way to Canada. Slavery is outlawed there, and, as you've seen, even things in the North are not always favorable to you. But, before all of that, I have to get you out of the war zone. Then, your chances will be better."

Will paused for a moment.

"By the way, how did you ever end up in this place? I mean, in the middle of the war hiding in a barn?"

"I gots lost."

"Easy to do when you're not used to navigating. Especially in the Virginia wilderness."

"I didn't come dis way last time..." Evaline's voice trailed off.

"I see," Will replied. "You've done this before."

Evaline nodded.

"Tried to."

"That would explain the stripes on your back."

"Yes, sir."

"Just Will is okay. No sir needed. You're not in the army."

"I'll try to remember. Ain't never called no white man by his first name."

"There's a first time for everything."

*****

Traveling the roads would have been much easier for the pair, but Will was also aware that this was the route most likely to get them discovered, and so he continued cross country. The sun monitored their progress from its lofty perspective, beating down on their shoulders as they pressed onward. They continued to drink water sparingly from the canteen and eat whatever food Will could scavenge from the land about them. The occasional wild fruit or wild onion was about all there was. Yet, neither of the two complained, each resolved to the task before them.

As they pressed on, Will knew that they would inevitably come across units from one army or the other, although he desperately wished that fate would not befall them. He was, all at once, an enemy to all and he knew that he must at all cost avoid prolonged entanglements. Discovery by his own would mean court martial and return of Evaline to her owners, while capture by the Federals meant prison camp for him and an uncertain future for Evaline. Who else could be trusted with the fate of this most precious of souls? And what if, as Esther of old, he had come to the kingdom for no other purpose than the one that now lay before him?

*****

"How long you been married?" Evaline asked as Will closely inspected an abandoned barn. Will turned and pressed his finger over his lips, not yet satisfied with the barn's apparently vacant status. The farmhouse, gutted and lifeless, stood nearby as a silent sentry watching them through its black windows. Will slowly opened the door, but saw only gray, heavy light inside. He then turned and motioned Evaline through the door. Will let the Enfield fall to his side as he followed her.

"Ten years," came Will's belated answer.

"You mean you been married ten years?"

"That's right."

"Good years?"

"Very. Except for the ones I've spent here."

Evaline nodded.

"What about you? Are you married?"

Evaline paused, sat on the dirt floor, and pulled the tattered remains of the hem of her dress between her fingers.

"Dat's hard to say."

"Really? How so?"

33

Evaline continued to study her hem, trying to patch the impossible tears.

"'Bout a year ago, he run off. He tried to get me to go. Said there was a place where we could go and start new. Do what we wants to do. Be who we wants to be. I jus' thought he was wishin'. I never paid it much mind. Den I wakes up one morning, and he ain't nowhere to be found. The massa went into a big rage and dey look for him all over the place. I can still hear dem dogs barking far off. I know dey never found him 'cause they never brought him back. Dead or alive, dey would have brung him back. Dey asked me what I knew, but I told dem the truth. I didn't know anything."

Evaline stopped for a moment and Will, intent upon listening, silently sat upon the floor.

"I know why he left, but after he was gone it was terrible lonesome. All I could do was think about what he tried to tell me before he left. He wanted me to go too, but I never paid him any mind. Now, he was out dere all by hisself, dem dogs chasin' after him. No food, no water, and nobody who was goin' to help him. I was mad at him for leavin', but I was more sad that he was alone. Everything felt empty, like he was dead."

Evaline paused once more, letting the tattered hem fall from her fingers.

"Den, when I couldn't stand it no more, I left. I didn't have any idea where he was, but I knew he went north. I didn't think about what would happen if I got caught. I was just tired of bein' alone. When I heard dem dogs comin', I knew dey was gonna catch me. I ain't never been so scared as when all dem dogs came at me and all the men came yellin' through the woods. It didn't matter that I was cryin' and telling them I was sorry. They dragged me back anyway. Made an example out of me."

The Confederate remained silent, his concept of the young woman constantly evolving as he remained mesmerized by her account.

"Now's da time you supposed to tell me dat you never owned no slaves," Evaline continued. "Dat you's a good Christian man and dat you never looked down on the colored folks. Whether it's true or not, dat's what you supposed to tell me."

Will remained silent, his only response the slow rhythmic nodding of his head.

"All dat's true, ain't it?" Evaline asked, amazed at the composure of the man in front of her.

"It is."

It was Evaline's turn to listen.

"But my silence gave consent to all that was about me. Perhaps my greatest sin is not what I did, but the fact that I did nothing at all."

Will paused for a moment.

"I love my home and would gladly give my life for it. That is why I am here. But that in no way means that it is a home without blemish. Still, for me, there is no other place like it in all of the world, and I do not wish to see it in flames."

Silence then descended between the two and both stared at the dusty ground between them. Will broke the stalemate and removed the haversack from his shoulder.

"Let me show you something."

He reached into the linen pouch and removed the McGuffey Reader.

"Can you write your name?"

"No."

"Have you ever seen it written?"

"Not dat I can remember."

Will moved over next to Evaline and opened the book to its first page.

"That's about to change."

"You gonna teach me to write my name?"

"More than that if I can."

"I ain't able to learn to read and write."

"Who told you that? I've taught some of the most pitiful souls in Decatur County how to read and write, and you are certainly more able than they."

Evaline leaned toward Will and looked over at the pages of the book with their strange ink markings and complicated arrangements. Will seemed to sense her apprehension, for he had certainly seen the expression among his former pupils.

"You don't have to learn it all at once," Will encouraged. "You just take one step at a time."

Will leaned forward and smoothed an area in the dirt floor with his hand. Then, using his index finger he traced a capital letter "E" into the makeshift slate and followed this with each succeeding letter until the young woman's entire name was spelled.

"That's it."

Evaline stared in disbelief.

"That's my name?"

"Yes. Yours and yours alone."

The young woman continued to gaze at the letters as if her entire essence rested within their borders.

"What's your name look like?"

Will wrote the name "William" in the earth beneath Evaline's.

"You gonna teach me what all these mean?"

"Yes. One step at a time."

*****

Will was awakened near sundown by the rhythmic beating of raindrops on the tin roof. He lay there momentarily, listening to the cadence and remembering the similar sound of rain on his own roof at home. As he lay listening, he suddenly became aware of a different rhythm buried within the sounds of the raindrops. Dread suddenly filled him, and he arose quickly and crept to the door. Pushing it open slightly, he gazed out into the storm, the splashes of rain stinging his face. The darkness had descended heavily upon the landscape, and at first Will could see nothing through the gloom. A sudden flash of lightning brought brief clarity to the features, and Will was able to discern the movements of several mounted figures closer to the farmhouse. Will recoiled immediately from the door and grabbed his Enfield.

"Evaline!" he spoke to the sleeping figure nearby. "Evaline! Quickly! We have to go!"

The young woman stirred slowly, the fatigue from the day's journey still weighing heavily upon her. Realizing the value of each passing second, Will quickly wrapped the Colt revolver and his cartridge box in the oilcloth haversack to protect the black powder from being fouled by the driving rain.

"Come on, quickly!" Will commanded as he grabbed her by the arm. "They're here! We have to go now!"

"Who's here?" came the groggy response.

"Soldiers. One side or the other. It doesn't really matter. Come on!"

Will pulled her to the door and, after taking a brief look outside, charged outside into the deluge, veering off to the right away from the farmhouse.

"Stay low," he commanded as he ran forward, his back arched forward.

"Where we goin'?"

"Not sure. Away from here."

Will paused at the edge of the field and looked back toward the farmhouse. The flashes were more frequent now, and Will could see more movement in the vicinity of the farmhouse and closer to the barn.

"We've got to get some distance between us and them," Will explained as he resumed his stealthy escape. Grasping Evaline's hand, he raced forward toward the edge of the forest when another flash illuminated movement directly ahead, the soldiers' silhouettes outlined against the jagged streaks in the sky behind them. Will immediately dropped to the ground, pulling Evaline with him.

"Stay down!" he hissed through the driving rain. Peering ahead through the palpable gloom, Will could still see that no one barred the way to his left between him and the farmhouse, but he also knew instinctively that this would not remain the case for long. Waiting for the next flash to pass, Will rose quickly to his feet.

"Run!" he ordered as he pulled Evaline up, pointing in the desired direction as he did so. The two ran forward through the field, the mud sucking their feet and hindering their progress. They crested the top of a small hill and immediately began to descend, when another flash illuminated a small creek nestled at the bottom of the hill and a simple bridge spanning its narrow breadth with more mounted soldiers approaching it from the far side. With no time to explain, Will headed directly for the bridge. Reaching the rocky bank, Will entered the water without hesitation, pulling Evaline behind him.

"Get under! Quickly!" he ordered as he pointed underneath the wooden structure. Will then removed his cartridge box and held it over his head and out of the water as he dived under the bridge.

*****

The pounding rain drowned out all outside noise until the horses were upon them, their hooves drumming upon the wooden planks overhead. The pair remained motionless, panting with their faces only inches above the water and even closer to the underside of the bridge. Will tried at first to count the number of horses that passed, but soon lost count. He was not even sure if the troops were Federal or Confederate, although he realized that the distinction really made little difference.

Evaline was terrified and shook both from her fear and the cold, which was seeping into her arms and legs. Will was sympathetic but had little to offer except his presence while he remained completely motionless. As he stared up through the narrow space between the planks, Will became aware that at least two of the animals stopped directly overhead.

"Wilson!" a voice suddenly boomed over the downpour. "How many behind you?"

"Two," came the response.

"You see anything?"

The accent was definitely northern, thought Will, possibly from New York.

"Are you kidding? There's nothing moving in this weather."

"All the same, keep your eyes open. We're awfully close to the Rebel lines and moving at night like this makes me nervous."

"You're always nervous."

"That's why you're still alive."

Will remained motionless as the trooper above him wheeled his animal about and drove toward the farmhouse. The momentary pause was then followed by the deafening thunder of three more sets of hooves as they pounded the wooden planks. An uneasy silence followed, but Will quickly ducked from underneath the bridge and saw no one on the creek side opposite the farmhouse. He reached under the bridge and grasped Evaline's hand.

"Now!"

Like two lumbering sloths, the pair emerged from the creek water amid the driving rain, their slow deliberate movements pushing them onward through the gloom. Will drove straight ahead, the intermittent flashes revealing nothing in his path. Evaline held tightly onto his hand, the cumbersome shoes now waterlogged and cumbersome as ever. A line of trees appeared ahead of them, and Will dived inside, not stopping until they were well within its borders and swallowed completely by the darkness.

All was silent save for the driving rain as it beat out a random cadence upon the foliage around them. The two sat shivering beneath a sycamore, but Evaline's suffering was worse, as Will had spent many such nights in similar circumstances. Still, the suffering of his companion nullified what little comfort he found in his own experience.

"I's cold," Evaline stated through chattering teeth.

"Here," Will replied as he removed his outer coat and wrapped it around her shoulders. "It's wool, and it'll help keep you warm regardless of whether it's wet or dry."

"You think we okay?"

"They didn't see us. In the morning I can get my bearings better and see where we need to go. We just need to stay put for now."

Evaline nodded, pulling the gray coat tighter around her as she continued to shiver. Will remained close by, his shoulder pressed up against the quivering form next to him.

*****

The rain stopped during the night, leaving behind only the leaden gray skies and the continual dripping from the saturated forest. Will removed the charge in his Enfield and replaced the fouled powder with a fresh load. He then dozed intermittently but found his proximity to the enemy disconcerting, and his guard would not allow him to rest fully. Evaline fell asleep, but as she rested, Will noticed the development of a cough and a deep rattling within her chest. She would awaken but, even with Will's urging, found herself unable to stand and walk for any significant distance.

"I don't feel so good," she finally confessed as she rested with her back against an oak, her breathing more labored.

"What's wrong?"

"Can't breathe so good."

"We haven't had much to eat. We'll rest a while. You're tired."

"I thinks it's more than dat."

Will reached out and placed his hand against her cheek and felt the burning skin beneath.

"You've got fever."

"Told you I didn't feel so good."

"Will instinctively looked about him as if searching for a cure. He suddenly felt very vulnerable, as he felt quite responsible for Evaline's well-being. He realized, however, that he was totally inadequate for the task. He had no food, much less any medications which might offer some benefit.

"Evaline, I don't know if there are shelters of any kind around here. Even if there were, they may all be occupied by the Yankees."

Evaline raised her hand.

"Don't matter. Couldn't make it der no way."

Will's gaze fell to the ground as he mused through his limited options. As a schoolteacher, his mind was a logical one, and choices that he would normally not have considered raised and presented themselves as being the most likely to succeed.

"Evaline, I need you to listen to me."

Evaline's eyes opened, and she focused her gaze on Will.

"You're ill. I have nothing that will help you. We've been running from everyone until now, but you have to consider that someone else may be able to help you better than I."

Evaline's gaze never faltered.

"The Yankees will have medicine. I know what happened back at the house, but all are not like that. I can't provide you with shelter or food, and it would be unfair of me to keep you here when they could offer you so much more."

Before he had finished speaking, Evaline began to wave her hand.

"No, Will, you can't leave me."

"I'm not going to leave you. I don't want you to go, either. I'm only trying to do what's best for you."

"I ain't got nobody, Will," Evaline responded, her voice growing weaker. "Nobody. I don't know any of those people. But I knows that you sees me different. You looks out for me. Will, with you I's safe."

The silence that settled between the two did nothing to conceal the understanding that bonded them together.

"All right, Evaline."

A withered smile broke across Evaline's face as her eyelids fluttered together and remained there.

*****

Evaline's condition only worsened as the day waned and darkness took its place. Will remained by her side, watching helplessly as the pneumonia took its toll. He covered her with both his shell jacket and blanket, but she, nonetheless, continued to suffer from shaking chills. Fully realizing the risk of an open fire, Will gathered the driest wood he could find and was able to kindle a flame among the branches. The orange glow reached out and caressed the face of the ill woman and her concerned companion, illuminating the deep lines of worry that crossed the soldier's brow.

As he waited, the silence became unbearable, and the loneliness that often plagued the gray warrior reappeared and fell upon him almost as a predator that had been sulking in the shadows. He had seen the faces of death upon his companions, but never had he sat and faced the great darkness as it slowly robbed the life of someone so innocent. Was she to come all this way only to meet this end? To die, here in the woods like an animal? Was his conscience, already heavy laden with the deaths of so many, to be scarred further by this unbearable failure?

As he waited, Will moved closer to Evaline's side and studied her features in the amber glow. How many times he had seen his own children with fever and had held and rocked them amid the glow of the hearth and the cracking of the firewood. She was so young, and in so many ways no different than his own. An ebony facsimile of everything he cared for. She and her kind had been about him his entire existence. And he had never noticed.

*****

Sleep finally overcame him and he suddenly felt the warmth of the Georgia sun upon him as he wandered the pine forests of home. The wiregrass brushed his legs amid the sounds of the blue jay and mockingbird. He turned his face to the crystal sky and closed his eyes. All was familiar and warm and safe. And mixed within the musical sounds of the breeze in the evergreen needles, he heard the wind whisper his name.

*****

When Will awoke, the darkness was still heavy upon the forest, and he realized that his slumber had been short lived. The fire had died down but still sent yellow slivers up into the night. He looked over at Evaline and was relieved at the rising and falling of her chest, although her breathing remained raspy. As he gazed at her, clarity suddenly swept across his troubled mind, and he became keenly aware of what he had to do. No longer would he sit and wait. He had nothing to offer her. No supplies, no food, no medicine. Yet somewhere close were the men in blue, and Will knew that to him and his starved comrades the supplies of the Yankees seemed inexhaustible. He removed the Colt revolver from the oilcloth and studied the weapon for a moment before rotating the cylinder to assure that the next primed chamber was in position. In spite of the rain and the creek, Will had been able to keep the pistol and his cartridges wrapped in the oilcloth, and all had remained dry and unspoiled. He moved closer to Evaline.

"Evaline," he called softly. There was no response except for the continued breathing. He reached out and placed his hand on her shoulder. She awoke with a start and stared at the man beside her with eyes that held the blank stare of the unrecognized.

"Evaline, it's me," Will continued. "I have to go now, but only for a little while. I have to go and find us some food and supplies, and maybe some medicine for you. I promise you I will return. You keep this."

Will placed the revolver next to her.

"I will return."

Evaline looked at the pistol but made no move to touch it.

"All right, Sam," she spoke out of her delirium. "You go if you gots to. But you best remember to unhitch dem mules. Da massa didn't like at all what you done last time."

"No, I suppose not," Will responded as he contemplated her words upon a different level. "But perhaps because of what I do this time, in the Master's presence I will no longer feel so ashamed."

*****

The darkness was almost palpable as Will made his way through the forest. There was no moon, but the clouds had vanished altogether, leaving behind the glittering patterns of stars overhead. Will soon found the familiar shapes of the Big Dipper and Cassiopeia, and he knew that he was traveling west toward the farmhouse. Heading back into the very camp of the enemy seemed the most foolhardy of choices, yet Will remained amazed at his confidence that his current course was leading him directly where he needed to be.

Will stopped periodically in the darkness and knelt down on one knee among the leaves of the forest floor. Closing his eyes, he strained every nerve to hear the slightest hint of voices or the crackling of the flames of campfires. Hearing nothing and realizing that he remained alone, he rose and continued on.

*****

The Georgian had always been amazed at how the coming of night transformed benign objects of daylight into their sinister counterparts. Objects that in the daylight were warm and welcoming became cold and foreboding once the shroud of night fell upon them. Even more so in this foreign land. Something deep inside him had always told him that Virginia tolerated his presence only as a necessity, and the beauty of the landscapes that he had observed was never to be knitted into the fabric of his soul. Or perhaps the smell of gunpowder and the shrieks of the dying had scarred him beyond all hope. Whatever the reason, nothing would ever love him as Georgia had.

*****

Will saw the flickers of the campfires through the trunks of the trees long before any voices were audible. He waited just within the line of timber and observed the dark shapes of the soldiers as they moved in front of the flames, most involved with cooking their rations. Several horses were tied nearby and he quickly recognized the unit as cavalry. With that designation, Will knew that they would be involved with reconnoitering and could be well removed from the main Union force. They would also travel lightly when doing so but would still carry sufficient supplies for Will's needs. Even a couple of haversacks would go a long way, especially if he could supplement their contents with some salt pork or other rations. Will wasn't sure of the best treatment for pneumonia, but quinine had been given for just about everything else, and if he could find some of the bitter liquid he felt that it would, in the very least, improve Evaline's chances.

Will knelt down and leaned upon his Enfield as he would have a staff. As he saw it, two options presented themselves. He could wait until most of the men had retired to sleep and deal only with the sentries, or seize the current opportunity and get what he could while the men were distracted by their activities and conversations with one another. After a moment of contemplation, Will decided to make the most of the current situation and hasten his return to Evaline. The horses were tied away from the men, and Will felt certain that at least one of them would still have a haversack still slung across its pommel.

*****

Will remained crouched in the shadows as he observed the camp in front of him. He would have given anything to have had a pair of the field glasses that he had been issued for skirmishing, but these were lost somewhere on the battlefield. As he looked to his right, he could see the row of Federal horses. Upon their flanks, Will knew he would find at least a few haversacks and possibly enough provisions to supply his needs. Without further debate in his own mind, Will began to make his way under the cover of darkness to a position closer to the horses.

Stealth was his lifeblood as a sharpshooter, and Will employed the skill to its fullest as he swept around the camp's flank to where the animals were tied. He had always been able to move silently through the tangled forests of South Georgia, and the open woods of Virginia were even more suitable to a man of his talents. The horses, their keener senses undoubtedly alerted to his presence, sounded no alarm as they practiced no particular prejudice between blue and gray. Still, there was far too much activity within the camp for Will to proceed, and he nestled himself into the murky edges of the forest and continued to observe from a distance.

After some time, a hush fell over the camp. Will was aware only of an occasional murmur as the men drifted off to sleep. From his position, Will could not see all of the sentries, but he knew they were there, nonetheless. He would have to pick out their positions as he approached. Will then took a deep breath, checked the Enfield upon his back and the Bowie in its sheath, and began his slow and intrepid undertaking.

The glow from the campfires stretched out a short distance from the camp but lost its illuminating warmth long before it reached the approaching Confederate. Will crawled forward through the grass and mud one short distance at a time, stopping briefly between advances to make certain that he had not been detected. The sentries that he could see remained steadfast and silent, peering into the thick gloom in front of them. One was posted far away in front of the farmhouse that he and Evaline had seen earlier, while another was closer to the horses. Their Spencer carbines glowed coldly in the shimmering firelight. Oddly enough, the barn in which the pair had hidden earlier appeared only as a murky outline, apparently completely ignored and unguarded. The horses continued to show no concern, their tails flicking haphazardly in the night air. Will crawled to his left, placing the line of horses between himself and the closest sentry. Looking beneath the animals' legs, he detected no movement nor did the shuffling of feet reach his ears. He then looked over both shoulders, but his investigations were greeted only by darkness.

The closest horse had nothing on his flanks, but the second in line had a haversack slung over its pommel. With this as his goal, Will moved forward in a slightly more upright position in view of the horses as not to startle them. Will passed the first horse without disruption and approached the second. Reaching its side, Will paused but still heard nothing of concern. Rising up to a crouched position, he stretched his arms above his head and opened the flap of the oilcloth haversack. The darkness provided no opportunity to see what was inside, but his investigating fingers quickly detected three squares of hardtack, and Will removed these and placed them in his own haversack. There was nothing else of use to him. He knew time was against him, yet an inner drive pushed him onward. Evaline needed him, and he had given her his word.

Will moved on to the next horse but was disappointed to find nothing of use hanging from the saddle. Taking a deep but noiseless breath, he moved onward knowing that each step brought him closer to the sentry. As he reached the next horse and felt along its flanks, his fingers encountered saddlebags at the rear of the saddle: possibly an officer's mount. Without the slightest noise, Will opened the bag and again gingerly investigated its contents. At first, he felt only the cold metal of eating utensils, but his fingers then detected a rectangular metallic bottle with a cork stopper firmly sealing its mouth. Perhaps it was only contraband liquor, but Will removed it, nonetheless. Wrapping the tinned iron container firmly in the bend of his left arm, he grasped the cork with his right and slowly twisted it free. He passed the opening beneath his nostrils and detected no hint of alcohol. Replacing the cork and tilting the bottle slightly to catch the faintest rays of firelight, he was able to see the paper label which read *Quiniae Sulphatis.*

"Quinine," Will whispered silently before checking the cork once again and placing the bottle in his haversack. Will reached into the second saddlebag but initially found nothing. Convinced that he was missing something, Will reached further and found an inner pouch similar to what was found in haversacks for carrying food. Inside the pouch, he felt something soft and fleshy, yet almost leathery in texture. Removing his hand, he moved his fingers to his mouth to confirm his suspicions. It was salty: most likely salt pork or beef. This too was quickly transferred to his own haversack.

45

As he removed the last of the supplies, a feeling of guilt for his thievery swept over him, almost as a visitor from a previous existence. He found himself tempted to leave a few of his Confederate bills in the saddlebags, but he realized that these would be worthless to the Federals and would only alert them even more to the identity of the perpetrator. The sensation of chivalry soon passed and left in its wake only the realization of reality as it had become.

No sooner had he placed the salted meat in his own haversack than he heard the sounds of approaching footsteps. Terror gripped his iron nerve as he realized that the sentry was walking down the line of horses. Gritting his teeth, Will's mind raced swiftly but methodically for an answer. The footsteps were not rushed or hurried so it was doubtful that his presence had been detected. Making a run would likely get him shot, or in the least, alert the whole camp to his presence. The sound of the trooper's boots was coming from in front of the horses, so Will quickly slid to the horse's rear just as the sentry reached his animal and then silently slid to the opposite side as he passed. As in so many other times, the sentry was not expecting anything out of the ordinary, and Will's clandestine movements went undetected. He could hear the Federal coughing only a short distance away, and Will was amazed that he was completely unaware of the proximity of the enemy. The horses snorted as the sentry returned, and Will simply reversed his movements as the Federal approached. Feeling suddenly quite vulnerable and having pushed his fortune to its limits, Will snatched a tin canteen from one of the horses and crawled back the way he had come. Peering back over his shoulder, the camp remained as it had been previously, completely unaware that he had ever been there.

Once again immersed in the gloom of the forest, Will took a bearing from the stars and headed back toward Evaline. Her condition and his being forced to leave her unattended concerned him, and he whispered a prayer that he might find her well. He was encouraged by his success at the Federal camp and finding the quinine gave him hope. Yet hope, in so many ways, was a stranger to Will.

*****

Will came upon Evaline much as he had left her. She was shaking beneath the blanket, yet he found the movement a welcome sign. Will knelt beside her and placed his hand on her shoulder, but there was no acknowledgment. He then placed all of his equipment on the ground and rekindled the fire. Looking through his haversack, he found his cup and washed it out with water from the canteen. Taking the bottle of quinine, he searched the label for some kind of instructions but found none. He laughed to himself as he poured some of the bitter liquid into the bottom of his cup. He reasoned that if the army physicians had not yet killed him with a toxic dose of the medicine, then it was unlikely that he would do any harm either. He replaced the cork and again knelt beside Evaline. Speaking softly to her, he lifted her head. Her eyes fluttered open but were still hazed with the fog of delirium.

"It tastes bad, but it'll get you better."

Evaline took the liquid as Will lifted the cup to her lips, the scowl upon her face indicating the accuracy of his warning. Will then gave her a drink from his canteen and placed her head back where it had been. Watching her breathe for a moment, he then moved away and sat close to the fire, his thoughts drifting away to a time and place far away.

*****

Several hours had passed when a sudden movement from Evaline's direction caught Will's attention. He turned to see her sitting up, obviously confused but attempting desperately to gain her bearings.

"Sam?" she called out in desperation.

"No," Will responded. "It's just me."

Her eyes moved to Will, and her gaze seemed to focus steadily on him as the firelight illuminated his concerned expression.

"Will?"

"I'm here."

CHAPTER IV

The sun rose like a lethargic dreamer above the eastern horizon, but Will could see none of its golden rays until it ascended high enough for its light to filter down through the branches of the forest. Evaline was still sleeping, but Will was encouraged to see that she was no longer shivering. Perhaps it was only his imagination, but the ebony skin of her forehead did not seem as feverish as previously. Will did not wake her but set forth to preparing the food that he had been fortunate enough to acquire. Reaching into his haversack, he was relieved to find that the events of the previous evening were not figments of his imagination. He knew that Evaline had been the main reason for his acquiring the supplies, but in all fairness to himself, salt beef and hardtack represented the most diverse nutrition that he had seen in sometime, and he looked forward to the temporary change of diet.

It was not Will's first encounter with salt beef, as he had chances to sample it from captured Federal supplies, and he was well aware of its reputation. Fresh meat of any kind was a treat even for the Federals, and to preserve what meat they did receive, the quartermasters pickled it with enough salt as to make it inedible. To work around this obstacle, the men would soak the meat in water before cooking to leach out as much of the salt as possible. Running water worked the best and Will made his way through the forest to the nearby stream that eventually ran to the farm. The brook was shallow and swift there and appeared as clear as crystal. Will investigated upstream and found nothing contaminating. Close to his bank of the creek was a deeper bowl-shaped area with a smooth, rocky bottom. Realizing that no self-respecting animal would eat the stuff, Will tied a string around the beef and allowed it to settle to the bottom. He tied a similar knot around two of the hardtack biscuits and placed them in the flowing water. Stabbing a sharpened poplar branch deep into the muddy earth, Will then secured the ends of both strings.

Back at camp, Will occupied himself by collecting more wood and keeping the fire going. He gave Evaline another dose of quinine and allowed her to rest. He was not at all comfortable with his proximity to the robbed Federals, and he knew that he could be easily tracked if the effort was expended. Yet, Evaline could not travel; therefore, Will made the best out his situation and frequently rechecked the status of his Enfield.

Around mid-morning, Will returned to the creek and retrieved the beef and the hardtack. He carried his skillet with him and placed all of the food in its bottom. Upon returning to camp, he stoked the fire with fresh wood and placed several stones in the middle of the flames to act as a cooking surface. He then placed the pan on the stones and began to fry the beef, leaving the hardtack out for the time being. The soggy meat soon began to sizzle and Will methodically turned the beef to make sure all sides were evenly cooked. Satisfied with the results, he removed the beef and placed the soaked and softened hardtack in the grease remaining in the bottom of the pan and cooked the mixture as he stirred. It was a pathetic meal; yet Will knew that many times he had marched to battle sustained by far less, and he was thankful for what he had.

Will took his creation and moved over to Evaline. Her eyes fluttered open before he spoke and he could tell that she was still ill, but the haze of delirium seemed to have passed.

"How are you?" Will asked cautiously.

"I don't feel so good," came the weak response.

"You remember me?"

Evaline nodded.

"What's my name?"

"Robert E. Lee."

"Close enough. Do you think you can eat? You have to keep your strength up."

"I'll try."

Will helped her up slowly to a sitting position while keeping his hand on her back, fearing that at any moment she would fall. He put the plate of cooked hardtack before her and scooped some of it up with the fork from his haversack.

"Try this first. If you can handle this, we'll try some of the beef."

Evaline tentatively tried some of the hardtack, and Will saw no change of expression to indicate that she found the food unpalatable.

"If you feel sick, go ahead and stop. Take just a little at a time."

Evaline nodded her head as she continued to eat.

"What's dis stuff called anyway?"

"The Yanks have a name for it, but I won't repeat it in mixed company."

"I see."

Evaline paused momentarily as she strained to recall the events from the previous few days.

"What's been wrong with me?"

"Pneumonia, I think."

"I's gettin' better?"

"I hope so. I think the medicine is helping."

"Where'd you get medicine?"

"Borrowed it from friends."

"What friends?" Evaline asked as she looked about her surroundings.

"The kind that wear blue coats."

Evaline nodded, not fully understanding all that the Confederate had risked for her. She suddenly began to appear very fatigued, and Will set the plate down as he assisted her back to a supine position.

"That's enough for now," he stated softly. "Now get some rest."

Evaline nodded as her eyes grew heavy with exhaustion.

"You got younguns, ain't you Will?"

"Yes," Will responded as he turned to get his Enfield.

"I can tell."

*****

Will sat for what seemed like hours, his back toward Evaline as the young woman slept. He too was exhausted, and his head continually fell forward as he struggled to remain awake. Eventually, his head drifted back against the tree behind him as the forest around him faded away.

The sound of approaching footsteps fell upon Will's ears, but he could not determine at first if the steps coming toward him were merely a dream or the product of a harsher reality. His instincts brought him fully awake, but he remained motionless except for the opening of his eyelids. Listening intently, his ears confirmed approaching footsteps methodically advancing through the leaves. Will could only discern one set of footfalls; nonetheless, he swiftly moved behind the tree and leveled the Enfield at the approaching disturbance. Carefully aligning the sights, Will peered down the barrel and felt the throbbing of his heartbeat quicken as he waited. Nothing was visible at first through the underbrush, when suddenly Will caught a glimpse of blue coming from his front and slightly to his left. Will adjusted his rifle and remained as still and silent as the dead, his aim never more true.

The soldier that emerged into his full view was a young man, younger than Will, and reminiscent of a hundred other young men who wore the gray. He was dressed in the typical uniform of the Federal cavalry, and he gripped his Spencer carbine tightly. He approached cautiously, staring at the ground periodically as he tracked. He came to within thirty yards of Will when he suddenly stopped and looked about him, almost as if he sensed that he was being watched. Will was camouflaged against the forest background and shielded by the tree as the young man's gaze passed over him and onward to where Evaline slept. Seeing the trace of smoke from the fire and the shape huddled near it, the trooper took one step to investigate before Will called out his challenge.

"You can turn around and walk out the same way you came, or I can assure you that the war will end for you right here."

The Federal was startled by the sudden boom of Will's voice among the trees, and he immediately froze. His head turned slowly in Will's direction, and his eyes were finally able to discern the Confederate and the muzzle of the Enfield leveled at him.

"If you fire, everyone will know where you are."

"True, but it won't really matter to you at that point, will it? Now, get out of here."

"Why didn't you shoot?"

"You caught me in a generous mood. I won't ask you again."

"Wait. I know you've got to be the one who took some of our supplies last night, and anyone that brave at least deserves some slack."

"You know it was me? It could have been any of the others in my regiment."

"There's nobody with you."

"How do you know that there aren't a hundred other rifles pointed at you right now?"

Will's response seemed to catch the Federal off guard, and his nervous glance quickly searched the woods behind Will. Instead of finding an accompanying regiment, the young man's gaze once again fell on the huddled figure lying next to the fire. As he observed her, Evaline stirred beneath the blankets and revealed her face as she turned toward the pair.

"Who is that?"

"None of your business."

"It's a woman," the Federal stated in astonishment. "And a Negro at that!"

51

Will did not respond. His silence, instead of casting a shadow upon his character, spoke volumes to the Federal. He saw in the unflinching gray warrior a dedication that he had long thought extinct. The billowing of compassion that welled from behind the menacing rifle was unmistakable.

"Is she yours?"

"I don't have slaves."

"Whose is she, then?"

"God's."

In spite of Will's evasive answers, the Federal began to place all of the pieces together.

"Is she ill?"

"Not so now as she was."

"And that's why you came to our camp last night. The food and the medicine were for her."

There was no response.

"What do you need?"

The question caught Will completely off guard, and he found himself at first speechless.

"Leave your Spencer and cartridges on the ground."

The Federal laughed.

"You know I can't do that. Besides, it would cause too many questions when I got back."

"You're going to tell them where I am anyway."

"No, I'm not."

"I don't believe you."

Suddenly, as the two were conversing, a low rumble from behind the Federal wafted between the trees of the forest and fell upon their ears. Each soldier recognized the deep bellows of the cannons far in the distance and the onset of bloodshed heralded by those ominous sounds.

"It would appear that your services are needed elsewhere," Will commented somberly.

"Yours as well."

"For the moment, mine are needed right here."

"Here," the Federal responded as he placed the Spencer on the ground. "It's not much, but I do have some coffee, hardtack and salt beef. You're welcome to it. As I said before, any man brave enough to break into camp deserves some payment for his deeds, especially since you risked it all for her."

The unarmed Federal reached into his haversack and retrieved the few remaining pieces of hardtack and held them out to Will. Reluctantly at first, Will let the Enfield drop and rose to meet the Federal. He took the hardtack and was then given the coffee and beef.

"You sure that you don't want to keep some of this for yourself?"

"I'll be fine. You need it more than I do."

"Thank you."

"Don't mention it. Take care of her."

"I will."

"Where will you go from here?"

"North across the Rappahannock when she's able to travel."

"Go as quickly as you can. The fighting is moving this way. The countryside is going to be crawling with soldiers soon."

"I understand."

Will turned to leave and took a few steps toward Evaline, when he turned to thank the young man once more. Instead, he caught only a faint glimpse of the blue coat as he rushed through the forest to join his unit. Will then turned back to the camp, the portentous booming still echoing in the distance.

*****

Will listened to the distant conflict for the remainder of that day until the advancing nightfall ceased the slaughter. As the silence fell, Will leaned back against a tree and pondered through the images of the battlefield that he knew existed beyond the reach of his senses. He need not have been there to know the carnage of blue and gray that once again tarnished the fields of Virginia, for the images were etched deeply into his memory and would never be erased. How many dead this time? How many more towns and boroughs gleaned of their youth? And was the Federal trooper that he had met only a few hours earlier now numbered among the sleeping?

*****

Will saw her that night as he slept. She was as authentic in his mind as when he had last seen her standing with the folds of her summer dress billowing in the breeze. She was much less somber than when he had left, and she reached out to clasp his hands in hers. Her hands were warm and her skin soft, as his eyes traced every detail of his wife's beautiful face.

"Come home to me," she whispered into the morning air.

"I will return," the words rushed forth without a thought to the long road ahead. "As God is my witness, I will come back to you. But she needs me, and I will see it through. I must."

His wife's kind expression was one of painful understanding.

"Do not forget us."

"Have I been gone so long?" he asked, the pain of separation welling within. She smiled as the breeze played with a strand of hair across her forehead.

"You never truly left."

*****

Evaline awoke the next morning without fever. Looking about her with the fog of delirium completely lifted, she saw Will steadfastly watching her as a father would an ill child. He remained motionless, except for the smile that slowly broke the stoic unwavering of his features.

"It's about time you got up. I thought I was going to have to leave without you."

"How long we been here?"

"About two days. Are you hungry?"

Will then produced some more of the mixture of salt beef and hardtack.

"I know it's not much variety, but it will keep your stomach full. There's not a chicken to be had for miles, and I didn't see much in the way of fish in the stream."

"Dat's all right," Evaline responded as she accepted the meal. "Beggars can't be choosers."

"How do you feel?"

"Weak as water."

"I imagine so."

Evaline stared back at Will's expression for a moment.

"You gots dat look in yo' eye."

"What look?" asked Will, amazed that the young woman could discern his intentions merely from his expression after such a short time of acquaintance.

"Da look what says we gonna be movin' soon."

Will nodded as he looked at the earth between his feet.

"You're right."

The booming, closer than it had been the day before, suddenly resumed and interrupted the conversation.

"And that's why," Will explained as he motioned in the direction of the cannons. Evaline's expression fell visibly as she understood the danger inherent within the distant roar.

"And it's coming this way."

"How long before dey gets here?"

"Hard to say, but the sooner we leave the better. Eat first, and then let's see how you walk."

Evaline obeyed and quickly finished the meal, urged on by the fear of being overwhelmed by what was lumbering toward them. After packing his meager belongings and checking his Enfield, Will offered his hand to Evaline and assisted her in standing.

"Legs weak?" Will asked as he observed her unsteady gait.

"Sho' is. But I'll be all right."

"I'll go as slow as I can. We'd stay here if we could. Make sure you drink plenty of water."

"All right."

"Let's go."

Instead of assuming a position in the lead, Will settled in step beside Evaline, watching her closely as she gingerly picked her path unsteadily through the forest.

"I'm gonna have to stop every now and then to catch my breath."

"I know. Just let me know when you need to."

*****

The progress they made through the forest was slow, but steady. As she promised, Evaline had to stop frequently to rest, her breathing interrupted occasionally by spasms of cough. Yet the fear of the fighting overtaking them was greater than her physical frailty, and she plodded onward. Will led her on in a direction away from the fighting, but he knew that it was quite likely that the armies' movements would outpace theirs, and they would be overrun. What was he to do if that were to happen? He couldn't bear the thought of failure. He wouldn't allow it. There had to be a way.

The sun continued its ascent as the pair trekked across the deserted countryside. For lack of a more elaborate plan, Will continued on in a direction away from the growing threat. The thought crossed his mind to try to backtrack and possibly flank the armies, but the noises seemed to come from multiple directions. He stopped numerous times to try to make some sense out of where the fighting was taking place, but he always resumed his previous course, staying just ahead of the advancing guards. Evaline grew more weary while every fiber within Will told him to run. But he would never leave her behind. Never.

The forests seemed to increase in tangled underbrush almost as if the vegetation itself decided to spread before their very eyes. Will was thankful for the added cover, but it made the way almost impossible for Evaline. Will stared at her expression and saw the unmistakable signs of exhaustion.

"Will," she gasped between rasps of air. "I's sorry."

"Nonsense, I shouldn't have pushed you so hard. Let's rest. Up ahead it seems to be getting lighter, so I think we're coming up on a clearing. We'll stay here where there's more cover."

Will cleared out an area in front of a large oak and placed his blanket down for Evaline. Once she was seated, Will sat nearby looking off into the thick underbrush.

"Will?"

"Yes?"

"You still got dat book?"

"You mean the reader we looked at before? When I showed you your name?"

"Uh-huh. Can we look at it?"

Will felt around his left hip and removed the McGuffey Reader from his haversack.

"Sure."

Evaline was leaning back against the tree, and she sat up more so that Will could sit next to her. He sat down and opened the book to the first page.

"Now, be straight with me," Evaline began. "I wants you to teach me jus' like one of yo' students. What would you teach me first?"

"Well, before you can read you really have to know your letters. Otherwise, the words don't make sense. If words are locks, then letters are the keys. The letters make sounds, and when you put them together, the sounds make words."

"How many letters is der?"

"Twenty-six."

"Dat's all?"

"That's it. But believe me they can add up to a lot of words."

"Den let's get started. I ain't getting' any younger."

Will stared at her for a moment before responding.

"Did you order your husband around like that?"

"Sho' did."

"That's what I thought."

Evaline stifled her smile only momentarily.

"You's a mean man."

"Couldn't resist. Let's get started."

*****

The apparitions appeared and faded as Will taught the afternoon away: visions from a faraway schoolroom, sights and sounds from an existence that had died long ago and lay buried beneath the Virginia soil. Each ghost was more vivid and tangible than the last, and each stared in disbelief at the conflicted human before them. He was at once both a peaceful man of knowledge and a devastating warrior, each irreconcilable with the other and yet a distinct ingredient of the man who now desperately sought to reawaken the soul that died the day the war began. Each face Will saw and did not see, resolving to focus on the features of his newest student, finding some semblance of peace in the child-like joy that beamed from her eyes.

*****

The tumult of war came upon them without warning. Will heard movement through the forest, clandestine at first, and he quickly closed the book and motioned for Evaline to be silent. His options were few as he knew that Evaline could not travel far, and his progress would be further impeded by the thick underbrush. Looking about him, Will sighted a large oak that he had noticed earlier. The trunk was massive, but age and the elements had formed a cavity in the trunk large enough for one person to squeeze into. At that same instant, a tremendous roar erupted from the west side of the forest, and Will quickly recognized it as a volley of musket fire. Will quickly grabbed Evaline's wrist as he pulled her to her feet.

"Come on, quickly!" he commanded. "They're almost on us!"

"What's happening?" Evaline asked as she forced her legs to move.

"Come on!" Will responded. "Quickly, go to that tree!"

The pair swiftly ran to the oak as more and more gunshots and shouting echoed through the woods. Will pushed Evaline inside and filled the opening with his own lean frame.

57

"Stay quiet," Will instructed. "I'll cover the opening. Our only hope is that they pass us by. It will be nightfall soon. Cover your eyes and ears if you must. I don't know what will happen. Above all stay silent."

Evaline did as Will instructed and pressed herself against the back of the tree, covering her ears and closing her eyes in an attempt to shut out the coming storm. Yet, no amount of effort could drown out the roar outside. Will, huddled against Evaline in an attempt to make himself as small as possible, saw the acrid white smoke drifting through the trees. A zipping sound, followed by the invisible severing of leaves and branches, announced the passing of the Minie balls as they sliced through the underbrush. One thudded into the back of the oak, and the vibration stirred the dust on the inside.

A tremendous roar erupted, and Will could almost feel the shock wave pass over him like a tangible wind. The cannon ball followed and tore a gaping hole in the forest underbrush and splintered the trunk of a maple tree about twenty yards to Will's left. The tree groaned momentarily as the shattered trunk tried desperately to right itself. As Will looked upward, the top of the tree painfully swayed toward him before it began its deliberate earthly plunge. There was nowhere to run, and Will watched helplessly as the hissing of the air through its thick green foliage drew rapidly near. The sea of green washed over him and obscured his vision as the boom of the trunk propelled leaves and dust in all directions. To his surprise, only the tender, green ends of the branches brushed him and did no more damage than to brush off his slouch hat. The musket fire and artillery fire continued unabated, but the pair's hiding place was completely hidden by the foliage of the felled maple.

"Will!" Evaline called above the roar. "Will, is you hurt?"

"I'm fine," Will called back. "We're better off than we were. Stay where you are."

The roar outside intensified.

"Will…"

"I know. Hold on. It will pass soon."

*****

Many times had Will heard the cadence of battle but never from the viewpoint of a spectator. As he closed his eyes, the battle's roar seem to enlist a life of its own as it drew breath from the very lips of those it slew. It seemed to rise from the bowels of the earth itself and

58

to lumber through the forest with massive slumped shoulders consuming all in its path. Forced to listen to every rattle of its foul breath, Will hung his head and prayed that the canopy about him would solidify and never reopen.

*****

The lead pierced the air relentlessly and continued to strike the thick hide of the oak, but Evaline, terrified and huddled against its back, remained silent. The voices were now all about them, shouting and screaming amid the roar. Soon, the noise became so intense that Will no longer heard individual sounds but a conglomeration of every ominous noise known to man. The very earth seemed to tear itself apart. Will heard innumerable soldiers running over the trunk as they fled through the forest, but his presence went unnoticed. Dusk was falling, and Will prayed again that the deepening gloom would swiftly cover them. As the darkness crept onward, the noise of battle shifted away from them and to the north, toward the clearing that Will had noted earlier when he and Evaline had rested. He turned around and through the murk could make out the quivering, huddled figure, her hands still pressed firmly over her ears. He reached out and gently touched her arm. She was startled by the contact, but, recognizing Will, she slowly lowered her arms.

"We're okay. It's moving away."

"It's over?"

"For now."

"We gonna be goin' now?"

"Let's wait just a minute."

Will handed his canteen to Evaline, and she took it with trembling hands. She drank slowly and sat still in the darkness as if contemplating something far beyond her understanding.

"Will?"

"Yes?"

"Is it always dat bad?"

"Worse sometimes."

"I can't stand it."

"I know. It's all right."

*****

There remained so much unanswered, but the young woman found herself at a loss for words to accurately pose her questions. So many times had she imagined the struggle within her own nation. Her mind had conjured images of grand splendor in which brave young men marched unfaltering beneath their fluttering banners toward their fates. Yet the small sample of the conflict that she had endured revealed none of the characteristics that she had so vividly imagined. And the gray-clad man who sat hunched in the opening in front of her was the antithesis of everything she had imagined a Confederate to be. He sat there like a reed before the wind, the weight of the world upon his shoulders. His frailty had become her only hope. Perhaps it was for the best that she found no utterance for her questions, for the deep sadness which draped itself across him like a shawl would have produced no answers.

*****

Will remained motionless as the sun completely disappeared from sight and left the sky to the dominion of its smaller siblings. The noise of battle completely died away, but Will knew that the soldiers could not be far off and that the better part of valor would be to stay exactly where they were. Will's personality was one of action, and he found waiting difficult. Yet if he had been taught anything, it was that sometimes the best course of action was no action at all.

"We's gonna stay here a little longer?" Evaline whispered.

"Just for a little while. Let's let things settle down a bit. Do you think you can travel some?"

"Tonight?"

"It'll be better if we can move out of this area before they get started back up in the morning."

"I'll do what I gots to do, Will. I don't never want to go through dis again."

Will nodded in the darkness and resumed his silent vigil. As he sat there concealed by the maple leaves, a pungent but familiar odor reached his nostrils. Straining his ears, he could hear a distant crackle which seemed to grow in intensity as time passed. Even concealed in the foliage, he became aware of a shimmering orange glow penetrating the canopy. Deciding to risk a look, Will motioned for Evaline to stay where she was as he slowly rose to his feet. He pushed his way through the branches, the glow growing steadily brighter as he did so. As his head finally emerged and he gulped the unrestrained air, Will's attention was drawn to his left where an ominous line of orange was advancing in their direction. The flames were growing in intensity and constantly shrank and grew as their fingers stretched out into the blackness. Will immediately retreated below the leaves.

"Come on, Evaline. We have to leave now," Will stated calmly.

"What's da matter?"

"The woods are on fire. We have to go."

"Who done that?"

"No one in particular. The powder and shells set things on fire by themselves."

Will reached out his hand and, after she had established a proper grip, helped Evaline to a standing position. The roar of the flames was growing louder, and as Will peered out from the canopy, he saw deep orange tongues of flame erupt skyward as the fire found better substrate. He could almost feel the heat as his face was bathed in the flickering light.

"Follow me," Will stated as he parted the green foliage for Evaline.

"Will, dey still gonna be soldiers out here."

"I know. We're going to make it."

"You knows where dey are?"

"No, but God does."

The light from the fire made navigation simple at first, but Will was very uncomfortable being silhouetted against the glow, and he wanted to get away as fast as possible. He followed the trunk of the maple toward its shattered base, all the while looking for movement amid the darkness. Perceiving nothing but the flickering flames, Will proceeded north toward the clearing that he had seen earlier, hoping that the open terrain would provide an opportunity to find the best path.

A sudden eruption of noise from their left stopped them, and Evaline's eyes widened at the horror of the noise. It was a shrill scream, almost inhuman, that rose quickly in pitch and intensity, repeated itself, and then was gone as suddenly as it had begun. Will's grip tightened on Evaline's wrist as he renewed his effort to pull her forward.

"Quickly!"

"Will, what was dat?"

"Evaline, please…"

"Tell me, Will!"

Will's expression was one of profound sadness, very similar to a parent who has discovered that he can no longer protect the innocence of his child from the cruelty of the world and is forced to face that cruelty himself.

"It's the wounded."

The full magnitude of Will's statement, chilling in its simplicity, weighed fully on Evaline as her mind conjured pictures of wounded soldiers, unable to move, caught in the flames. She attempted to pull away from Will, but the Confederate's grip tightened.

"Will, we can't leave 'em! Will, we gots to help!"

"Evaline, stop! You don't understand! If you go wandering through these woods, you'll be captured, killed, or caught in the flames yourself!"

"How does you know?"

"Because I've tried!"

Evaline stopped struggling.

"You can't begin to understand the magnitude of death and suffering that's out there," Will continued as he pointed toward the flames. "I'm not being cruel. Believe me when I tell you that I've tried. When the war began, it was all that I could do to stay at my post and ignore the cries for help and water. War is ugly business, Evaline. Nothing is as it should be. I have to save those that I can."

"So, you don't even hear dem anymore?"

"Evaline," Will began, his face appearing ready to fracture under the strain. "I hear them all. Always. There is no rest for me, and there never will be."

Will inhaled deeply, and then let the breath go as he regained his composure.

"We'll help those we meet along the way. Now, let me help you."

Evaline's resistance relaxed, and she followed Will's lead toward the clearing.

*****

No moonlight illuminated their path as they made their way as best as they could through the darkness. As they approached the clearing, the orange glow seemed to grow in intensity; the roar of it was different from the one it made as it consumed the forest. They could see the flames stretching high into the night sky through the branches. Will still saw no evidence of movement, but he knew that soldiers were likely all about him. In spite of that, Will's curiosity got the best of him; he proceeded forward to get a better look at what was burning. As his view improved, Will was able to see a square-framed structure engulfed in flames, the unmistakable sounds of breaking glass evident amid the roar.

"Farmhouse," Evaline whispered as she looked over Will's shoulder. The Confederate nodded in agreement but seemed mesmerized by the scene before him. The house creaked and groaned as the flames devoured it, calling for a help that would never come. Will sighed deeply before turning away.

"Will, dey's bodies out in the yard. I can see 'em by da light of da fire."

"I know. I have a feeling we're going to see a whole lot more before we make our way out of here. Come on."

The two small shapes rose and, silhouetted against the fire, made their way to the right, this time Will swinging much farther out to avoid getting too close to the structure. The house sat on the edge of the clearing, and as the pair approached, they could almost sense the open air fill their lungs after their stagnant confinement in the forest. But instead of rushing ahead, Will stopped suddenly and held his hand back toward Evaline, motioning for her to stop. Before them stretched an open expanse with only the closest of its edges revealed by the flames. Even in that dim lighting, Will could see that the ground was littered with the bodies of the dead and dying, some of them still trying to move pitifully amid the destruction. Evaline saw the scene at the same moment, and her horror was evident on her face. Will turned quickly to face her and pulled her gaze away from the battlefield.

"Evaline, we have no choice but to cross here. You've got to try to focus on what has to be done. This will all be over soon."

"Will, dey ain't no way," she responded, her voice filled with trepidation. "I can't shut all dis out like you."

"I never told you that I could shut this out. Watch my back. Don't look around you. Focus on staying behind me and doing as I do. Can you do that?"

"I don't know, Will."

"We have no choice."

Evaline nodded in understanding.

"Watch me closely. If I see soldiers, I'm going to stop. You can do this."

Evaline was shaking, seeming ready to break at any moment.

"I won't leave you. I'm right here."

With those words, Will turned and began to make his way across the field, stepping carefully as he did so. He turned to look over his shoulder and saw Evaline following him, slowly but steadily, her eyes fixed on the smoky gray of his jacket. Will believed and hoped that the battle lines had moved further east and that their movement would go unnoticed, but he was also keenly aware that for all he knew they were now marching in no man's land between the very armies themselves.

The sounds that greeted the pair were all too familiar to Will, and he was eternally grateful that the darkness hid most of the horror from Evaline. The darkness, however, did nothing to dampen the calls for help coming from those still clinging to life. The cries for water or for a mother or wife were the most grueling to endure, and Will had listened on many similar nights, unable to help, as the cries degenerated into agonizing groans before being swallowed by the darkness. He had always prayed that if he met his fate on the battlefield, it would be a swift end instead of his suffering from some mortal wound from which he would linger for hours before his soul departed.

Will continued to select his path carefully among the bodies as the cries intensified toward the middle of the field. Evaline, covering her ears, followed behind silently as she sought to duplicate Will's steps. Evaline's right foot caught something on the ground and she stumbled forward onto her knees. Looking back for the cause of her fall, she was greeted by the agonized expression of a wounded Confederate who had reached out to grasp her ankle as she passed.

"Please," he rasped. "Please, ma'am. Water… please."

Instinctively, Evaline recoiled. But as she crawled backwards, she was greeted by the presence of more bodies. Trapped and unable to move from fear, she began to shake uncontrollably, and unquenchable sobs welled up in her throat. Suddenly, she felt a presence next to her and a hand on her shoulder as Will arrived at her side.

"It's all right," he whispered as if out of reverence. "He doesn't mean any harm. The thirst is unbelievable when you're wounded."

Will pulled his canteen from across his shoulder and removed the lid. Moving over to the wounded soldier, Will knelt beside him and cradled his head in his arm.

"Here you go, son. Just a little at a time."

As Evaline watched the scene before her, she felt her fear suddenly vanish as fog in the morning. In its place remained something unexpected as she felt all enmity suddenly die away. She moved next to Will and studied the face of the young soldier. Twisted by the agony of pain and war, he nonetheless maintained the look of many young sons who had left home never to return. As she observed, she was suddenly struck by the realization that it could have just as easily been Will lying mortally wounded on that field, and the thought of him dying alone without even the comfort of an enemy soldier brought a profound change upon her. She moved closer and reached out to grasp the canteen. Will's gaze turned toward her, no words being necessary to express his emotion.

"Will, let me."

With a nod, Will let go of the canteen and Evaline raised the canteen to the young man's lips. He took a few halting sips, some of the water running in small streams down his cheeks. Even in the darkness, Evaline could see the hint of a smile as it was all the young man had to offer in return.

"Thank you."

Evaline nodded. The young man's gaze then shifted to Will, who still held the young man's head in the bend of his arm. He spoke no words, but he stared at Will almost as if awaiting permission. Will seemed to understand, the bond between soldiers surpassing any need for words. Will nodded and smiled as he replied to the unspoken question.

"You've done all you could. You can go home now."

Satisfied, the man smiled once more and closed his eyes. His breathing eased, slowed and then stopped altogether.

"You can go home."

With great tenderness, Will placed his head upon the ground. He then looked about him and saw several wounded Federals nearby.

"Grab a canteen and come with me."

Evaline suddenly found herself completely drained, but she obeyed, nonetheless, and took a nearby canteen from one of the fallen and followed Will's example as he set about giving water to those he could. The pair could hear voices in the distance, but on this occasion Will, being aware of the activity about him, seemed bent on some new purpose from which he would not be deterred. Finally, the stir of voices became so close that Will could no longer ignore it, and he turned to Evaline.

"We have to go. We've stayed as long as we can. Come follow me."

Evaline nodded, but on trying to comply, she found her legs utterly spent and regardless of her effort they would no longer support her. Her recent illness, poor nutrition, and the physical and emotional strains had exacted their toll.

"Will, I can't."

"Can you move at all?"

"Will, I can't go no more."

"It's okay," Will stated calmly. "It's okay. We'll get through this."

Shifting his Enfield over his shoulder, Will reached underneath her. Placing one arm under her knees and one behind her back, the lean Confederate slowly lifted her from the ground, ignoring the screams of his own hunger and fatigue. With a slow and deliberate pace, Will again picked his way through the battlefield making certain that he took every precaution to keep his balance, his unsteady gait making a fall a constant possibility.

"I's so sorry, Will."

"My goodness, child, whatever for?"

Amid the darkness of the battlefield, the pair pushed on, the Confederate carrying the slave in his arms. As they moved through the night, the two remained silent except for an occasional sob from Evaline and the repetitive, whispered reassurance from Will:

"Though I walk through the valley of the shadow of death.
I will fear no evil
For Thou art with me."

Chapter V

Will knew his exhausted form could not carry Evaline far, yet he strove onward undaunted until he had cleared the main battlefield. There, concealed by a stand of heavy growth, he collapsed and slept until the first light of dawn illuminated the killing fields. Raising himself up on his elbows, he found Evaline sleeping peacefully nearby. He closed his eyes and strained his ears once more. Although he could hear movement in the distance, he could detect none close at hand and, surprisingly, he heard no gunfire. He sat fully upright and gathered his meager supplies about him. As he had carried Evaline the previous evening, he had been able to stoop down with some difficulty and retrieve some of the fallen canteens and haversacks, and he had slung these over his shoulder. He had tried to retrieve only the Federal ones as he knew that most of the Confederate haversacks would be devoid of food. As he sorted through the supplies, he was relieved to find at least some hardtack, but sadness soon followed as he sorted through personal effects of the fallen men, all of whom would never see home again. Most of the items in the haversacks were very similar to his own, and it was a chilling realization that at any moment another soldier could find himself sorting through his. Death was his constant reality.

Will picked up the next haversack and a tin type photograph tumbled out onto the forest floor. He lifted the picture from the leaves and turned it over in his hand. On the other side was the image of a young man and his family. Roughly the same age as Will, the young Federal was dressed in what was likely the best clothes that he owned. As was the custom, no emotion was expressed upon his handsome features, but Will could discern a deep sense of peace and fulfillment beaming from his eyes. But, oh, what those eyes had seen since then. Horrors that he could never have imagined at the time of the photograph. Seated next to him was his fair wife, her dark hair parted neatly in the middle with curls flowing over her shoulders and down her back. How she would weep when the news of her fallen husband stabbed through her trembling heart, and how she would despise the gray-clad soldier who sat sifting through her husband's most personal items in an attempt to save himself and a runaway slave. And how could he blame her? Standing to either side of the pair were two young boys, nearly the same age as Will's own. As he studied their features, his keen eye noticed that one son, apparently the older of the two, had the distinct features of his father, while the younger displayed the softer features of his mother. Who would care for them now? Who would teach them their father's trade, take them fishing, or speak to them of the things of God?

God. How the very mention of His name struck fear in Will's heart whereas before the war it brought only peace. Fear of the judgment to come. The fact that the guilt which layered itself heavily upon his soul was mostly self imposed did little to ease his conscience. Perhaps it was the harsh reality that every time he pulled the trigger, he deprived some bride of her husband, a son of his father and a mother of her son. The idea of his efforts shortening the war brought no comfort, and his deeds had become the stuff of nightmares. Such things were not redeemable. Such things could not be forgotten.

Will placed the photograph gently back in its haversack and reached for the next. He unlatched the flap and stretched the bag open to examine its contents. His attention was caught immediately by a book, which Will quickly removed as he placed the bag on the ground beside him. In his hand rested a copy of the Bible that was overall similar to his own. As his fingers passed over the front cover, Will noted that the paper and leather were torn and ragged. He turned the book over in his hand, where he noticed a jagged hole in the center of the book. The hole penetrated the book halfway through but then stopped abruptly. Will had seen this effect before and immediately recognized the damage as the work of a .58 caliber Minie ball. Once before, the owner had been in the midst of battle, and his life had been saved by this Bible. It was not so now. Will's fingers silently flipped the pages as a sense of frustration swept over him. Why save a man only to take his life later? Why give him false hope that he may return to his loved ones and then cut him down?

The sound of the flipping pages wafted gently beneath the forest trees as Will searched for the last page that the bullet penetrated. The words passed by unread as his thoughts remained miles away and mired in heavier things. The damage stopped and Will placed his finger on the first intact page. His finger arbitrarily fell upon the eleventh chapter of John, and his mind, drawn from its darker musings, read the words as they leapt off the page.

"I am the Resurrection and the Life
He that believeth in me, though he were dead, yet shall he live."

The words came alive and swirled about Will almost as if they had been spoken as an audible answer to his previous questions. Suddenly, for the first time in years, the horrors of battle were swept away by the bright reality of the Carpenter from Galilee. All of the earth and everyone in it, including Will's beloved Georgia, were passing away even though they gave the illusion of life. Death, though it may come early and at the hands of man's foolishness, was certain, and there remained only one hope. Will felt sorrow as never before. Not merely a sorrow over the suffering of his fellow man, but grief for those who died alone. For those who never knew the Carpenter.

Will's head spun with the weight of his thoughts, but the return of distant gunfire brought him back to reality. The noise of battle was now farther away and to his right, but the distance gave Will little comfort. He knew that the armies were still likely swirling around him, and he could already hear some of the burial parties as they searched out the dead. In any case, he and Evaline were no closer to safety than they had been days before, and the temporary shelter of the forest would not protect them forever.

Will's gaze then fell upon Evaline as she continued to sleep. She had not stirred since collapsing the previous night, but her breathing remained slow and unlabored. It would be of little use to wake her and compel her to march onward, for she had reached the limits of human stamina. She had no time to recover from her illness before having to move on. Will had pushed her too hard, but he had done so for her protection. He had become so accustomed to the rigors of a soldier's life that adjusting those demands to someone unused to the strain had not even crossed his mind. With nothing else to do at the moment, Will rested his head back against the tree behind him and drifted off into an uneasy sleep.

*****

Will's mind continued to work feverishly as he slept, and his dreams once again took him home. The scene that surrounded him was familiar, and he recognized that he had been taken back to a day many years before his marriage. One that he would never forget. The season was summer and his family was out in the fields tending

69

the cotton. Nothing had seemed out of the ordinary initially, but as Will walked back to the wagon, movement from the far edge of the woods caught his attention. He saw nothing at first except for his sister working nearby. Although he could see nothing to account for it, a chilling sensation told him, nonetheless, that all was not as it should be, and he quickened his pace. Upon reaching the wagon, his gaze fell upon his father's rifle and he quickly picked it up. Turning around, he still saw nothing but began to make his way toward his sister.

In the years since that day, Will had replayed that scene over and over in his mind, and he had memorized each detail. He recalled the way the afternoon sun was behind him and cast elongated shadows in his path. He remembered the snow white appearance of the cotton bolls as the fibers burst out into compact bundles ready for picking. So, it was no surprise in his dream when the dog burst out of the woods and darted directly for his sister. At a glance, Will knew that the dog was feral and rabid, for it had none of the characteristics of the domesticated breeds. Snarling and frothing, it seemed at once to hate all that was around it and became intent on destroying the closest living thing. Will knew that he could never reach his sister in time and his frantic warnings would be in vain. In reality, Will had swung the rifle up to his shoulder and dropped the dog at a full run at his sister's feet one hundred yards away. But this was not reality. As Will swung the rifle to his shoulder, the dog turned sharply and headed directly for him, its snarls intensifying as the distance closed. Will dropped to his knee for a better shot, and at the last possible moment pulled the trigger. The hammer fell on the percussion cap underneath, but there followed no recoil or plume of white smoke as the gun misfired. The dog leapt at him, and Will could smell its hideous breath as its jaws lunged for his throat.

*****

Will awoke with a start, his pulse pounding in his ears. He quickly looked over to see Evaline's sleep undisturbed. He saw no one else around him, and he took several deep breaths. His pulse slowed as the terrifying dream slowly faded into the temporary calm of reality. Will laid his head back once again and closed his eyes, but the dream lingered. He had never been one to place much emphasis on dreams and their interpretations, but this one was somehow different. Why had he dreamed it? Perhaps it was the fact that he had experienced the events in real life, or perhaps it was the vibrancy of the dream itself. Or, most of all, perhaps it was the lingering sound of the impotent fall of the gun's hammer.

"Something must be coming," Will whispered almost inaudibly.

The Enfield. His eyes opened and immediately fixed on the nearby weapon where it remained exactly where he had left it. Nothing was out of place, yet the dream would not give him any peace. He had not changed out the rifle's charge in over a day, and the thought of fouled powder or a faulty percussion cap suddenly plagued him mercilessly. Without hesitation, Will reached for the weapon and removed his sergeant's tool from his belt. The tool contained everything needed for cleaning the rifle and for removing fouled or unfired charges. Quickly exposing the needed attachments, Will removed the nipple from under the hammer and thoroughly cleaned the flash hole. He then removed the ball-puller and secured it to the end of the ramrod. Passing the rod down the barrel, he stabbed the instrument into the soft lead of the Minie ball and gave the ramrod a few tightening twists. He then stood and, with the rifle in front of him, pulled the ramrod and its attached bullet out of the barrel. The black powder that poured from the barrel superficially looked fine, but Will took no chances. After passing a dry cloth patch down the barrel, Will was satisfied and retrieved a fresh cartridge from his box. Will completed his task by reloading the rifle, replacing the nipple, and attaching a new percussion cap. The primed rifle was placed nearby as a peaceful sensation replaced his previous apprehension. Nibbling on a piece of hardtack, Will resumed his previous position and looked out upon the temporarily calm countryside as one would look upon a thief.

Will once again fell asleep and when he awoke, the sun had sunk below the western horizon. The crimson glow still clung to the edge of the earth, but the forest was already black, and Will could see shimmering points of light in the sky overhead between the branches. Evaline's position had changed very little, and she still rested comfortably. The idea of sleeping an entire day away did not sit well with Will's work ethic or even with his plan for the most efficient use of time, yet Will was thankful for the rest. He could not remember when he had last slept so much, as drilling, marching and fighting usually occupied the greater portions of his time.

Will had gathered some wood earlier in the day, but with the onset of the darkness, he thought better of making an open fire and decided that it would only serve to reveal their position. Will studied the prostrate figure nearby and closely monitored the rhythmic rising and falling of her back. He hated to wake her, but they would need to move soon if possible, for the darkness would provide the best cover. The tattered dress had fallen from her shoulder and Will could just see the uppermost lashes upon her back. He sat there in the fading light and studied the marks as if he expected to find his own answers among the road map of scars. Taking a deep breath, he reached out and touched her upon the clothed shoulder. To his surprise, his touch didn't startle her as she rolled toward him, one eye open and the other unwilling to awaken from its slumber.

"You still here?" she asked as her gaze focused on Will.

"Now, exactly where else would I be?"

"I don't know. Savin' Georgia or somethin' like dat."

"One thing at a time."

"Well, den let me guess. It's time to go."

"How'd you know?" Will responded with a smile.

"If you anything at all, you's predictable."

Will shrugged his shoulders.

"We don't have to leave right away. We've got time for you to get your bearings and have a little to eat. You can guess what kind of food I've got."

"Sho' can."

"It's better than nothing."

"Sho' is."

Will passed her some hardtack and a canteen.

"How long I been sleepin'?"

"You slept all day today."

"Dey still fightin'?"

"As far as I can tell, they've moved on for the moment. There are still some folks around, but not the main body of soldiers. Mainly just burial parties and such."

"But we's probably gonna run into 'em again, ain't we?"

Will nodded his head.

"More likely than not."

Evaline asked no more questions as she ate in silence, but Will knew well the anxieties that must have plagued her thoughts. At first, he was tempted to offer words of encouragement, but as his own thoughts settled on the daunting task ahead, he merely settled in close by and allowed his presence to offer assurance where words would have provided only hollow promises.

After Evaline was finished, Will stood to his feet and gathered his limited supplies. The Enfield rested against a nearby trunk, and he once again slung the long weapon over his shoulder. He checked his Bowie knife and opened his cartridge and cap pouches to make certain that all was in place. Evaline watched his methodical preparation before rising to her feet, her gait no longer as unsteady as previously.

"Are you up for this?" Will asked.

Evaline nodded.

"We won't travel all night. I just want to get us a little further from here. We'll stop and rest soon."

"Okay."

"Follow me. There's something I wanted to show you anyway."

The night sky above them was without blemish, and the stars shone clearly through the surrounding darkness. There was an evening breeze, and it stirred the tops of the hardwoods, sweeping them to and fro as if attempting to clear the black stain from the sky. Will led onward and away from the battlefield in an attempt to avoid all contact, and it was not too long before he entered a smaller clearing without evidence of the scars of battle. He saw no campfires and heard no voices or any other disturbances in their vicinity. Looking up at the night sky, he saw a clear view northward.

"Come here," he whispered to Evaline.

"What's wrong?"

"Nothing. Come up here beside me. This is what I wanted to show you."

Evaline obeyed and stood just to the right of the Confederate. Will extended his arm toward the northern sky and began to trace a pattern there.

"See that shape? It's right where I'm pointing. It looks like a spoon or a dipper."

Evaline continued to study the sky, following Will's finger toward the abstract design.

"I think so."

"See right there? There's the handle. If you follow it on down, you can see the ladle part."

"I see it!" squealed Evaline, as the image seemed to jump out at her.

"Good. Now, do you see the two stars that make up the front of the ladle?"

"Yes."

"Good. In your mind draw a straight line down from them. Do you see that star the line points to?"

"Right der?" Evaline asked, pointing with her finger.

"That's the one. That's the Northern Star, or Polaris if you want to get scientific. The thing about that star is that it never changes. It never moves. The sun, moon, planets and other stars all move in the sky, but that one never does. It's constant, and it always points north. You can use that star to keep your bearings and make sure you're going in the right direction. If you can find the dipper, you can find the star."

"Why don't it move?"

"Remember, I'm just a country schoolteacher, but I believe it has to do with the fact that the top of the earth points directly at that star as it spins. That's why it looks like it stays in one spot."

"I's not so sho' I understands all dat."

"Don't worry. Neither do I."

"So dat's what da song says: 'Follow da drinkin' gourd.'"

"That's right. Follow the drinking gourd."

Evaline remained silent as she studied the distant twinkling point of light.

"Will, why's you tellin' me all dis?"

Will inhaled deeply and slowly exhaled before answering.

"I want you to know where you're going. I don't want you to lose your way if something happens to me. "

"Will, ain't nothin' gonna happen to you."

"Evaline, you don't know that. After what you've seen over the past few days, you know that anything can happen. I'm not trying to frighten you. We all have a purpose, and I want to make sure that I've done all that I could to keep you safe. I want you to make it out of here regardless of whether I do."

Evaline nodded as she contemplated what the Confederate was telling her. She had known him for such a short period of time, and yet she already trusted him implicitly. Of all the humans she had encountered, he seemed selflessly to place her needs above his own, and she could not help feeling the chilling sensation of anxiety as she thought of an ill fate befalling Will. Without speaking, Will resumed their trek, Evaline falling in silently behind him.

*****

The pair continued through the darkness until Will felt more comfortable with their surroundings and felt that he had put some distance between them and the main battle lines. He then found a clear area underneath a maple, and the two rested there until dawn. Will awoke to the sounds of birds singing in harmony with the distant rattle of musketry and the intermittent boom of cannon. The sun was already above the horizon, and a fog clung tenaciously to the surrounding countryside, swirling gently as memories in the mind of a homesick soldier. Will sat up and found Evaline still sleeping nearby. There was no need to wake her, and so Will leaned up against the maple and reached for his haversack. Reaching inside, his hand found the damaged Bible first, but he released it and selected his own copy, the one that had been with him since he left home. Withdrawing his hand, he caressed the front cover as if dusting a treasured heirloom. No bullet hole marred its front, yet Will knew that the book in his hands had saved his life no less dramatically. He opened the book and began to read as the sun continued to rise. A stirring behind him drew Will's attention away from his reading and he turned to see Evaline sitting up. She stretched and rubbed the sleep from her eyes.

"Good morning, Evaline."

"Good mornin'. I oversleep again?"

"Don't worry, I'll take it easy on you. Pneumonia would have killed a lot of guys in the army. You're made out of good stuff. You at least deserve your rest."

"I appreciates it."

"You're welcome."

Evaline's gaze fell upon the open book in Will's hands.

"What you readin'?"

"The Bible."

"Which part?"

"One of my favorite parts in Matthew."

"Will you read it to me?"

Her request reminded him of the requests of his children and students, and he remembered on many occasions looking down into the glassy, expectant eyes of a child as he extended a book in his outstretched hands for Will to read.

"Of course."

His gaze returned to the words in front of him, and his finger traced the verses until it stopped where he had been reading.

"Are not two sparrows sold for a farthing? And one of them shall not fall to the ground without your Father.

But the very hairs of your head are all numbered.

Fear ye not therefore, ye are of more value than many sparrows."

Will stopped reading almost as if to let the words surround both of them. He had lost count of the number of times that he had repeated that verse over and over to himself in the darkest nights of camp or in the deafening roar of battle. It had washed over him time and again as he sat in the eerie silence before his lost Whitfield stole the life from some distant target. He closed his eyes to its music nightly; he opened his eyes to its reassurance every morning.

"I like dat one too," Evaline spoke softly.

"Here," Will directed as he reached for his haversack once more. "Have some of the hardtack before we go."

"All right."

Will read no more, almost as if he could not bear it, and Evaline respected his silence. He did not appear melancholy, but seemed lost in the affairs of a far off place.

"So, where we goes from here?" Evaline asked, having finished her monotonous breakfast.

"Straight on," Will stated as he pointed due north. "I think that most of the fighting has shifted away from us at the moment, and hopefully it will stay that way. This area is still crawling with soldiers, though, and we've still got to be careful. I hope to make for somewhere near Fredericksburg and get you across the Rappahannock River there. Almost all of the fighting these days is south of that river, so you should be out of danger from both armies north of it."

"How far is dat?"

Will shrugged his shoulders.

"I'm not exactly sure, but no more than day or so if we can travel without interference."

Evaline nodded her head without responding verbally, but her expression fell so as to catch Will's attention. She looked at the ground and stirred the leaves with her finger for a moment before asking the question which she had long desired to ask.

"Will, what you gonna do when we gets to da river?"

Will thought of a hundred ways he could answer, all of which evaded the truth that Evaline desired.

"I can't go with you," he stated plainly but with great compassion. Evaline continued to look at the ground as she nodded in understanding.

"I figured dat," Evaline responded. "You gots your own to get back to. It ain't like you Moses or somethin'."

Will laughed.

"Let's just hope it doesn't take us forty years to get to the Promised Land."

"Amen."

"You ready?"

"Let's go."

*****

The countryside passed silently before them as they resumed their journey. As before, Will avoided the open road and crossed the forests and fields of northern Virginia while maintaining a northerly course. He explained the sun's course across the sky to Evaline and how she could use it to keep her direction during the day. She seemed much more familiar with that method than using the stars, but she, nonetheless, continuously looked up at the blue sky as a new curiosity accompanied her expanding knowledge. Will observed her and smiled at the progress of his newest student.

No gunfire reached Will's ears, yet the countryside had a barren and deserted feel to it. The area that they were crossing had seen almost continual conflict since the war's onset. Even what remained unscathed had an empty feel to it as if life had never existed, and even the trees and foliage were mere facsimiles reflecting what had been. It retained a superficial look of beauty and serenity, but Will feared that, much like himself, something in the land had been lost that would never again be set right.

They crossed a creek about midday, and Will made sure that no contamination was upstream before allowing Evaline to drink from it. He was amazed at her endurance, especially after having been so ill. As she drank, Will filled the canteens and sat back upon the bank, staring off into the woods on the far side as he listened to the sounds of the rushing, shallow water over the stones. It was Evaline's voice that brought him back from the place where his mind had journeyed.

"We's dem, ain't we Will?"

Will's expression must have revealed his confusion, for Evaline

77

quickly began to explain her statement.

"Da sparrows, I mean. Jus' like in da Bible."

Will's mind searched desperately for a connection, but found none.

"I'm not sure I understand."

Evaline looked away as if embarrassed.

"Oh, it ain't nothin'."

"No, go ahead. I want to hear."

Evaline took a deep breath before continuing.

"I mean look at us, Will. We sparrows. Ain't nobody pay us much attention when we where we supposed to be, and we hardly gets noticed even when we gone. We only useful if somebody wants somethin' out o' us. We ain't got no money. We ain't famous. And Lord knows I ain't smart enough or pretty enough to get much o' nothing'. And it ain't like somebody gonna pick you out of a crowd, either. You said yoself dat you jus' a country teacher. And here we is, out in da middle o' nowhere with folks fightin' all round us and ain't nobody even paid us no attention."

Evaline's voice wavered slightly with her last statement as if she was holding back more emotion than was superficially apparent.

"We's worthless, Will."

The profoundness of the discourse and the depth of Evaline's emotion silenced the Confederate completely, and he sat staring at the human being in front of him. How could she have known? Did she have eyes with which to look into his very soul? Her words, however simplistic, could not have rung more true if they had been plucked from his own heart. Evaline wiped the tears from her eyes before continuing.

"Will, you think it's true? You think He see all dem sparrows?"

Will nodded his head in sincere affirmation.

"Yes, Evaline, He sees us."

"Do He really care?"

"Enough to die for sparrows like us."

"Even when we falls to the ground?"

"Perhaps then the most."

*****

The afternoon wore on as the pair continued north across the deserted fields and forests. Will stopped as he spotted a split-rail fence in the distance and the simple farmhouse beyond. He watched for some time, but no movement or activity was apparent.

"We're running low on food," Will stated as he motioned toward the house. "I say we go take a look."

"I don't know about all dat," Evaline responded. "You knows what happened the last time we got all curious and went in a house."

"I remember. But there might be some food."

"I's all for eatin'. I jus' ain't too much on dyin'."

"Well said. Now, let's go. "

Will slid the Enfield from his shoulder and held it at the ready, but he still saw no movement as the house grew larger. He took the white handkerchief from his pocket and tied it on to the tip of his ramrod, but still no one appeared to answer. Approaching the front steps, Will called out with no response. The windows were all barred by wooden shutters, and Will gave a quick push to the front door but found it secure. Followed closely by Evaline, he walked the perimeter of the house without incident. A separate kitchen stood off to one side, and Will pushed the door open to find it empty. He placed his hand near the stove and, finding no warmth, touched the cold iron. The ashes inside were old and stale, but hanging from the rafters was what was left of a slab of smoked beef.

"Must have left in a hurry," Will mumbled as he drew his Bowie and cut into what was left of the slab. "At least we'll eat better tonight. This meat is still good."

Having cut what he could, Will explored the rest of the kitchen but found it barren except for an almost empty sack of cornmeal. Inside was probably enough meal to feed the two of them once. Nevertheless, Will was so tired of hardtack that he welcomed any respite no matter how brief. Will took a few of the Confederate bills from his haversack and placed them on top of the stove using a small piece of firewood as a paperweight.

As the pair walked back into the bright light, Will took one of the strips of beef and handed it to Evaline, who readily accepted it. As she did so, Will was struck suddenly by the tattered nature of Evaline's dress. Its condition had been poor from the beginning, but the strenuous journey had deteriorated its already tenuous condition. The hem was shredded, and the fabric was ripped at the neckline, causing it to fall over her shoulder. The only new item that she owned was the Federal Brogans on her feet, and even those did not fit properly. Almost as if in answer to Evaline's need, a flapping over her left shoulder caught Will's attention. Behind her was a clothesline with several items of clothing rippling gently in the afternoon breeze.

"Wait here for just a minute and rest," Will began. "I'm going over there. You can still see me. I'll be back in a second."

Evaline obeyed without questioning, the smoked beef tasting better than anything she could remember. As Will approached the line, he could see that most of the clothes were masculine, but that was of no great concern, for those would be more rugged than would be a dress. Several linen shirts and a few trousers were present, all of differing sizes. Glancing back at Evaline, Will selected the smallest shirt and trousers from the line. The line itself was a small caliber rope, and it was tied between two trees, the excess cascading down the trunks. Will stepped over and, drawing his Bowie, sliced a length of rope from the excess and tossed it across his shoulder. He then clipped a few more of the Confederate bills to the line before returning to Evaline. He stood in front of her and held out the new clothes.

"These are for you," he said with a smile.

Evaline studied the items of clothing for a moment before responding.

"Thank you, Will, but dem's men's clothes."

"I know. It'll work out."

"I ain't never worn no pants before."

"That's hard to believe. As strong-willed as you are, there's no doubt that you wore the pants in the family."

"Ooh, now listen at you, Will Seymour," Evaline mumbled as she took the clothes. "You ought to be ashamed o' yoself. Goin' and gettin' all sassy. Speakin' of britches, I thinks you gettin' too big for yours."

"Just change into the clothes."

Evaline stared at Will for a moment.

"You jus' gonna stand there and watch?"

"Well, no," Will stammered. "I'm just..."

"Why? Ain't good enough for you?"

Will returned her stare and realized instantly that Evaline was teasing him and enjoying herself as she did so.

"You knows what dey say," Evaline continued. "'Once you goes black, you never comes back.'"

"Listen, would you kindly go around the corner and change?"

Evaline had already turned her back to the crimson-faced

gentleman and was laughing out loud as she went.

"Lord, please forgive me for teasin' the Confederate, but I sho' nuff couldn't help myself!"

She disappeared behind the corner of the house, but it was not long before she returned, pulling the pants legs up to keep the excess length from dragging the ground. The shirt fit fairly well with the sleeves being only slightly too long.

"Time for a little tailoring," said Will, as he drew the Bowie and approached Evaline.

"Now you watch yo'self with that big thang," Evaline instructed as she saw the large blade. "You do know dat I was jus' jokin' a minute ago."

Will laughed in response.

"Never tease a Confederate. Come here and we'll have you fixed up in a second."

Will knelt down and gathered up the loose fabric of the pants and, with surgical precision, used the razor edge of the knife to slice away the excess. He left the hem a little long and rolled them up to protect the frayed cuffs. He then sat back and inspected his work with a look of satisfaction.

"What do you think?"

Evaline looked down at the neatly trimmed and rolled cuffs.

"You does good work. I likes 'em."

"Your shoes all right?"

"Yep, dey okay. Big, but okay. What's da rope for?"

"A belt. Loop it around the waist of your pants and tie it in the front."

"I got it."

Evaline paused for a moment as she examined her new clothes and enjoyed the sensation of a full stomach.

"Will, I saw dat you done paid for all these here clothes and for da food. I appreciates it, but I gots no way to pay you back."

Will smiled in response.

"If you give expecting something in return, then you aren't giving for the right reason. I gave you those things because you needed them, and I wanted you to have them. You owe me nothing."

Evaline nodded. She then stretched out her arms and inhaled deeply before letting her arms drop to her side. She looked about her at the peaceful scene as the wind played a melody through the oak leaves.

81

"Today was a good day, Will. I almost forgot I's a slave."

Will nodded in agreement.

"That's because you aren't. And, yes, it is a good day."

Both seemed reluctant to leave, almost as if lingering would somehow preserve the sense of peace and safety which clung tenaciously like a morning mist before the rising sun. But, try as they might, they could not hold on to the moment, and time drove inextricably forward. Will peered back over his shoulder at the way north.

"Are you ready?"

"Lead da way."

*****

The sun continued its westward descent as the pair moved on. Evaline no longer walked behind Will but assumed a position at his side, and Will made no effort to correct her, for he preferred the companionship. His position in the army afforded enough loneliness among his own comrades, but being separated from them made the solitude almost unbearable. As he walked, he occasionally glanced over at the young woman next to him. How much she had changed in his eyes in such a short amount of time. Or perhaps it was not her that had changed at all. Perhaps the fog that had veiled his vision for so long had been lifted, and he saw with a depth that he never imagined. Perhaps the woman at the feet of the Jewish carpenter was finally a living, breathing human. But could he do it? When the time came, could he make the sacrifice that he knew would be necessary for her to live? Would he have the strength? And would he ever see home again?

*****

"Will?"

"Yes?"

"When all dis is over, I means, when you gets me where I needs to be, is you gonna go back and fight again?"

"Yes."

"Why?"

"I can't leave my home and family unprotected."

"'Cause that would be wrong."

"That's right. I owe that to them above all else."

Evaline meditated on Will's words for a moment before

responding.

"You's in a hard spot, Will."

"How do you mean?"

"Well, you's out here helpin' me because it's the right thing to do, even tho' yo own don't want you doin' it. And you can't not fight because you protectin' all dat you love."

Will nodded.

"You think what da other side is doin' is wrong?"

"There's plenty of blame to go around. In war there always is. I'll put it to you this way. If a child of yours was misbehaving, would you want to correct it yourself, or have some stranger from the outside come and start to inflict bodily harm on him until he came to his senses?"

Evaline thought for a moment.

"He's my youngun'. I'd want to handle it."

"You'd want to prevent them from hurting him, right?"

"Sho' would."

"Even though he was doing something wrong?"

"Dat's right. My youngun', my problem."

"I couldn't have said it better myself."

"Dat's way too complicated."

Will laughed.

"And that's only scratching the surface."

"Like I said, I's glad I's not in yo' shoes."

*****

The land stretched away before them as they continued northward. Late in the day, Will saw light shining ahead through the thick brush of the Virginia wilderness. As they approached, Will could make out a large field in front of them. As he stepped out of the shelter of the forest, Will could tell immediately that the field had not been tended in some time, for the crop it had produced was wild and disorderly. An old barn stood in the distance across the field. Will remained motionless and listened for a moment as the breeze played among the briars and grass.

"You hear somethin'?"

"No, but sometimes that worries me most of all."

"Will, you sees dem wild blackberry bushes out der?"

"Yes."

"Dey's blackberries on 'em."

"You're right. It's just that it's so open. We should probably just go around the edges rather than cut straight across."

"We ain't had much food. It won't take but jus' a second."

Uneasiness was heavy upon Will's mind, but perhaps he was just being overcautious. Evaline's request was a small one and the only one that she had offered since they had been together, and the veteran found great difficulty in refusing it.

"Okay, Evaline. But, let's be quick."

"I will. I's a fast worker. What's I gonna use to put 'em in?"

"Here," Will stated as he removed and offered his slouch hat. "That'll work as good as anything."

Evaline, as giddy as a schoolchild, immediately turned and made straight for the middle of the field where the thickest growth of blackberries were. Will followed behind keeping his Enfield at the ready.

"They's good!" Evaline called as she sampled one of the berries. Will looked about him and, finding a healthy plant, plucked one of the berries. The taste reminded him of summer back home where he had picked blackberries until his fingers were sore and purple. He loved blackberry picking, although the fear of finding a rattlesnake among the thickets was constantly on his mind. Will scanned the field's periphery once more but, seeing no change, shouldered his rifle and continued across the field.

"Meet you on the other side when you're done," Will instructed Evaline as he passed the preoccupied young lady. She acknowledged him with a nod of her head.

The open expanse of the field was comforting once Will was accustomed to it, and he soon forgot his previous anxieties. He continued his stroll across the field, numbering each step as he enjoyed the breeze on his face. How capable the world was of producing such beauty and suffering simultaneously. Similarly, how capable his fellow man of committing such acts of kindness and cruelty. How could it be that bitter and sweet water flowed from the same spring? Hypocrite, Will thought. Look at yourself. A teacher and a sharpshooter. A Christian and, by silent consent, a supporter of slavery. Physician, heal thyself.

Will was nearly under the cover of the forest on the opposite side of the field when movement on his left caught his attention. He stopped where he was and stared intently as his eyes adjusted to the distance. At first, he saw nothing, but as his vision sharpened he

84

made out the figure of a single mounted Confederate cavalryman just outside the tree line. His first response was relief, but the sensation was short-lived as he realized the focus of the cavalryman's attention. Evaline, oblivious to all about her, was still busily picking blackberries. A lone Negro in a deserted countryside was not a usual finding, and fear suddenly gripped Will's mind. The cavalryman remained motionless as he studied his prey, the flicking of his horse's tail providing the only movement.

The tranquil scene shattered instantly as the cavalryman and his horse suddenly surged forward and charged up the middle of the field directly for Evaline. The movement was so swift that man and animal seemed to blur as one in a fury of motion. Will stood spellbound, unable to process the scene unfolding in front of him. Only the flash of cold steel and the reflection of the afternoon sun from the sword's blade as it left its scabbard shocked him back to reality.

"No," Will mumbled, his voice rising in pitch and intensity as he realized the cavalryman's intentions. "No!"

Will charged back out into the field waving his arms wildly above his head and screaming with all his might. The cavalryman, either by choice or ignorance, did not heed his warnings and bolted straight toward the young woman, closing the distance incredibly fast. Evaline, suffering the loss of hearing from Will's earlier shot, did not hear the approaching hoof beats but continued on with her task, singing an old hymn as she did so.

"Evaline!" Will screamed. "Evaline!"

Looking up from her work, Evaline saw Will running across the field toward her. At first, her face expressed a puzzled look at the frantic motions of the sharpshooter, but her expression soon changed to sheer terror as she saw the cavalryman bearing down on her. Will saw the blackberries fall to the ground as Evaline dropped them and ran through the grass toward the distant forest. But there was nowhere to run.

The distance had to be one hundred and fifty yards at the minimum, and Will knew that he would never reach Evaline in time. The horse and the sword were already almost upon her, and if he delayed any longer there would be no decision to make at all. Will dropped to his knees as the Enfield rotated around his shoulder. As it came up to rest against his cheek, Will slapped the hammer to full cock. He was now slightly behind the horse and rider as they moved from right to left, Evaline only a few paces ahead and running away from him. Her terrified screams wafted across the open spaces. The barrel of the Enfield tracked the rider with relentless precision as Will's heart rate slowed, and the weapon once more became an extension of his own body. The dream of the misfire flashed only briefly across his mind as he held his breath and pulled the trigger.

But the dream was only that as the Enfield bellowed fire and smoke and sent the deadly projectile hurtling across the expanse. A puff of white smoke erupted from the back of the cavalryman's jacket and reappeared at the front as the rider's arms flailed wildly skyward. His body then went limp and lurched forward in the saddle. The sword dropped to the ground as the rider slumped over the right side of the saddle and slipped off the side of the horse. One of his spurs caught in the stirrup. The horse, unaware of the fate of its rider, continued to drag the body across the field. Evaline, completely spent, stumbled and fell among the tall grass where she lay gasping, fully expecting cold steel to usher her into the presence of her Maker.

Even before the smoke cleared, Will was on his feet and sprinting toward Evaline, constantly throwing glances over his shoulder to the tree line from which the cavalryman had emerged. He reached her position and found her face down in the grass, panting for air.

"Evaline! Are you hurt?" he asked as he pulled her to a sitting position. He saw no injuries. He began to pull her to her feet.

"Come on, Evaline, we've got to hurry," Will urged in a voice more panicked than she had heard before. "We can't stay here! We've got to go!"

"Will, I…"

"It's all right."

"No, Will. I dropped all da berries."

Evaline's voice cracked and her lips trembled.

"It's all right, child," Will stated in the same voice that he used with his children. "But you've got to get up now. Other men heard the shot, and they'll be coming! Quickly, Evaline!"

Summoning all of her strength, Evaline pushed herself up and leaned on Will as the two began to make for the horse.

"Come on, Evaline! To the horse!"

The horse had come to a halt after the urging from its deceased master stopped. He now stood about fifty yards away, his tail flicking in the evening air with the twisted boot protruding ominously from the right stirrup.

"Will," Evaline gasped. "Will, what happened?"

"No time! Keep going!"

The horse seemed to grow farther away as the two struggled across the field. The forest line behind him remained tranquil, but Will knew that would never last. If the other Confederate cavalrymen, which he knew were nearby, saw them before they were able to escape, they would both be as good as dead, and gone would be all hope of either of them going home.

The pair finally reached the horse, and Will ran on ahead. The animal showed no anxiety, and Will quickly flipped the dead man's leg from the stirrup before mounting the animal. His shot placement had been perfect. He could not bring himself to look at the man's face.

"Here, quickly!" Will called to Evaline. She obeyed and moved to the side of the horse. "Put your foot there. Now, climb up and get behind me!"

Grasping her hands, Will helped Evaline climb behind him, her fatigue and fear showing in the trembling of her arms.

"Put your arms around me and lock your hands! Hold on tight! Don't let go!"

Will kicked his heels into the horse's flanks, and the animal bolted toward the forest straight ahead. The horse was not accustomed to the weight of two riders, but Will was merciless and drove the animal ahead, leaving the dead Confederate concealed by the tall grass.

"Will?" Evaline's voice came weakly over Will's shoulder.

"Not now, Evaline."

"Dat man's dead, ain't he?"

"Evaline, I said not now!"

The tree line loomed before them, but Will did not slow his mount. He selected the best opening between two trees and aimed his horse for that gap. Just before entering, he turned to look over his shoulder and saw no one. He knew they would come. Then, the forest swallowed them.

Will knew that he would never outrun the other cavalry with his horse carrying two. His only hope was to hide and for them to pass by. Night was coming soon, and that would help matters, as would the fact that the surrounding forest was thick Virginia wilderness. Nonetheless, Will pushed onward through the brush. As the light began to fail, he spotted a large fallen tree which spanned an almost imperceptible low spot in the ground. For most of its trunk, it contacted the forest floor, except where the soil fell away in one area and left a tiny niche. Will immediately reigned in the horse.

"Get off here," Will commanded as he reached around to help Evaline dismount. He followed suit and made sure that his haversack and rifle were secure, the Colt revolver still tucked securely into his belt. With those essential items, Will struck the horse firmly on the flanks, and Evaline watched in muted horror as the only tool for their escape charged off into the forest.

"To that tree, quickly!" Will commanded as he motioned with his hand. Wading through the thick underbrush, the pair struggled to the tree and Will leaned his Enfield against the trunk. Grabbing a cartridge from his belt, he reloaded the rifle in one fluid motion without speaking.

"I go first," he explained without Evaline having any idea what he was talking about. "When I'm under, you lie down. Then, I'll pull you under with me."

Evaline nodded.

"Understand?"

Evaline nodded again. Will lay immediately on the ground and scooped out the indention in the ground only slightly as to increase the space underneath the trunk. Standing up once more, he looked back the way they had come and saw no obvious trail through the underbrush. Satisfied that he had done all that he could under the circumstances, he lay back down and slid lengthwise under the log, his Enfield in front of him.

"Now you," Will motioned to Evaline. Still not fully aware of what was expected of her, Evaline imitated Will and lay down lengthwise beside the tree trunk. Will then reached out and grasped her around her waist and pulled her close to him, concealing both of them underneath the tree.

"It's the only way they can't find us," Will explained in a whispered voice. "We can't outrun them."

"It's all right."

"It'll be over soon."

"I know."

"It won't be very comfortable here."

"I can take it."

Silence followed and soon the only noise was the birds and the barking of squirrels, but even these sounds ceased as the sun fell behind the western horizon.

"Will?"

"Yes?"

"We couldn't keep da horse?"

"It's too easy to track."

"Oh."

"We have to be quiet now."

"All right."

*****

The footsteps approaching slowly through the dense underbrush came as Will knew that they would. He could only detect one distinct set, but he knew that there were others. Even in the dark, the steps followed their escape through the woods almost perfectly, and the anxiety that weighed down upon Will was almost unbearable as it seemed to draw the very air from his lungs. Will had felt fear in almost every imaginable way, but this time the fear was different. The soldiers coming for him were not the enemy bluecoats, but the men that he had fought alongside. He was truly a man with no country and a perfect hypocrite. One molded from the dust for all others to be modeled from.

Amazing. Amazing how in that black, murky place all became suddenly clear. The heartbeat which fluttered so near his own became his only focus, and the cares that so pervaded his thoughts daily seemed to fade into a hazy distance. His grip on her tightened, but the young woman seemed perfectly at ease. She was asleep; asleep with nothing but a gray-clad South Georgia schoolteacher to protect her. No shelter but the rotting remains of an oak. And yet the God of Creation paused to take notice.

Will strained his ears, and the footfalls through the leaves proceeded without interruption. He drew the pistol from his belt and replaced his arm around Evaline. What would he do if they were found? Could he fire at the sudden appearance of a face at the opening in front of him? Would his courage fail?

"Forgive me," his thoughts screamed as he thought of his wife. "Forgive me for taking such a foolish risk. The cost of doing right is high, my dear. But the cost of forsaking it is my soul itself. Oh, and there is so little of it left to give."

When his thoughts returned to the present, the footsteps were no

89

longer close. As he listened intently, he could hear them proceeding onward through the forest, following the path of the horse. Will exhaled slowly and let the pistol fall. The familiar words of the Bard flashed suddenly across his mind.

"Oh, cursed spite that ever I was born to set it right."

Chapter VI

Sunrise came and went, but Will still did not stir from his hiding place. Evaline had also awakened, but a whispered word from the Confederate kept her still. Finally, about midmorning, Will decided to chance a look at the outside world, as no unusual sounds had reached his ears since the footsteps the previous evening. After explaining his intentions to Evaline and leaving her hidden, Will pulled himself from underneath the backside of the log and peeked cautiously above its upper rim. No soldiers awaited his appearance. Similarly, the thick woods showed no signs of anything unusual, but Will remained where he was for a few minutes, nonetheless. He then stood up and stretched his aching joints and muscles. There was still no sign of movement, and Will realized that it was time to take a chance.

"Come on out," he whispered to Evaline. "I don't see anybody around."

"You sho' about dat?" Evaline asked as she crawled, with Will's assistance, from underneath the log.

"No," Will responded. "Let's go."

"All I's sayin' is dat if you wants ta get ta know me betta, dey sho' is a whole lot betta ways o' doin it than shovin' a lady 'neath some log."

"You're just trying to distract me."

"I is? Oh, and I jus' thought I's trying to make you turn all red again."

"Same difference. Now, come on."

The pair made stealthy progress through the forest, the tangled web of underbrush causing them to choose their path carefully. Will knew the general direction in which they were traveling, but his greater concern was to stay out of the way of any would-be pursuers. For that reason, Will strayed from his original course, at least until he was out of the forest. He also knew that the thick underbrush would work just as well to hide them as it would to conceal their attackers.

About an hour or so after beginning their journey, movement caught Will's attention, and he motioned for Evaline to drop to the ground. As he observed the flickering of motion among the tangled underbrush, he was relieved to discover that the movement was produced by a large animal. At first, he could not determine what the animal was. But moving to a location with a better view, he could see the full tail and mane of a horse. Closer observation revealed that it belonged to the slain Confederate cavalryman.

"What is it?" whispered Evaline, unable to contain her curiosity any longer.

"Horse," replied Will.

"*Our* horse?"

"Looks like it."

"We gonna get it?"

"No."

"Why not?"

Will cautiously and slowly moved back to Evaline, his finger pressed to his lips as he moved.

"Think about it," whispered Will as he reached her side. "Those soldiers had no problem tracking that horse through the woods in the middle of the night. Also, horses aren't cheap, so they're not just going to leave him in the woods for the next person to pick up. I have no doubt that they found the horse, but missed us. They put it out there because they think we'll be so desperate as to grab it the minute we see it."

"We is desperate."

"Maybe so, but it's a trap all the same. They're watching that horse. We're not going anywhere near it."

"I understands, Will."

"Follow me."

Will turned around and retraced his earlier path. When he felt that he was a safe distance away, he stopped and listened but heard no pursuers. He turned west and avoided the vicinity of the horse by swinging out in an arc-shaped route. He scrutinized the surrounding forests for any evidence of a trail, but he found not so much as a leaf overturned. In fact, the area looked as if it had not been visited by humans in a lifetime.

The pair stopped in the early afternoon. Will produced some of the smoked beef, and the pair ate in silence. Evaline's brow remained furrowed throughout the meal, and her uncharacteristic silence caught Will's attention. He respected her silence but remained understandably curious. However, Evaline's voice soon returned and she spared him the effort of investigating.

"Will?"

"Yes?"

"I know you done told me not to talk about it, but what happened back at da field jus' won't let me be."

"Fair enough," Will stated humbly, knowing what her question would be.

"Dat man on da horse. He was one o' yo' own, wasn't he?"

Will nodded.

"He was gonna kill me?"

Will nodded again, his eyes on the ground.

"And you shot him."

"Yes."

"Because o' me."

"Yes."

A long silence followed as if neither knew what to say. To Will, it seemed almost as if Evaline found it impossible to believe that her life would be worth protecting. Even more, the fact that Will would have chosen her life over one of his own seemed incomprehensible.

"You didn't have to do dat," Evaline spoke in a hushed tone, as if she knew intuitively that Will regretted the decision.

"Didn't I?" Will's forceful response startled Evaline. "What I did yesterday was what had to be done. I do not apologize for it, nor will I beg anyone's forgiveness. I do not judge men by the colors they wear but by the intentions of the individual who wears them. He would not have stopped. He could not have been reasoned with. He could not have been bought. It was either I kill him, or you die. I killed him and I do not regret it."

Will's voice rose in intensity as his discourse progressed, and Evaline seemed to shrink in front of him as a fragile flower under the scorching sun. Yet his voice betrayed him, as it belied the conflict that raged within him. Nonetheless, he pointed his finger at Evaline as he made his final point.

"And I will have no reservations about doing the same to anyone who touches you. Do you understand me?"

"All right, Will. It's all right."

Will's breathing slowed as he dropped his hand and stared off into the distance. He closed his eyes momentarily as he regained his composure. Evaline saw him quickly wipe his cheek with his sleeve before he turned back to her, his voice and composure having been reestablished.

"You didn't do anything wrong. We all have our demons. Let's just move on."

"Okay, Will."

*****

The day passed without a word, but amazingly Evaline no longer felt uncomfortable. She respected Will's silence out of her awareness that she could not possibly understand what he was going through. He was right. They both had their demons, but his were much darker. By mid afternoon, though, his head had lifted, and he studied the terrain in front of him. Nothing had changed, and the thick forest offered little in the way of a variety of scenery.

"You gots any idea 'bout where we's at?"

"Well, we're still in the middle of the wilderness. We're still on the right path to Fredericksburg; I just think we're a little farther away than I thought. Plus we've gotten delayed a little. When we get out of all this, it'll be a lot easier to tell exactly where we're at."

"Don't worry. I ain't in no hurry."

"I know. I just want to get you to someplace safe."

"You thinks dey is such a place?"

"Yes, but not here."

Thunder rolled in the distance. Even through the trees, Will could see the threatening clouds stretching up to the heavens.

"Looks like we in for it."

"Maybe so."

"You thinks they's a house or barn or somethin'around here? You knows what happened when I gots caught in da rain last time."

Will nodded.

"Let's keep going. Maybe we can find something."

"A log ain't gonna do dis time."

"You're not going to let me live that down are you?"

"Sho' ain't."

*****

Will pushed the brush away as the fading light illuminated the cabin in front of him. The sunset and increasing clouds left little but a gray afterglow, but Will could still see in that dim light that the cabin had been abandoned for quite some time. It was a simple one room log cabin with a separate kitchen behind and slightly to the west. Its roof appeared intact, but the building was in a general state of disrepair. A simple brick and stone chimney climbed the side of the cabin facing Will and pointed eternally toward the menacing sky. Virginia creeper scaled unmolested and wrapped around the upper portion of the chimney. A single, boarded window interrupted the horizontal pattern of logs and stared out into the forest like some hollow, sightless eye. It was certainly not perfect, but it was shelter. Will turned to Evaline.

"Stay hidden here until I check it out. It looks deserted enough, but I need to make sure."

"Okay."

"It won't take long."

Will silently rose from among the brush and approached the house. There was no movement, otherwise. The window did not open, and there were no creaking boards to announce the coming of an investigator. The Confederate passed around the rear of the cabin first and then made his way around the far side to the front. He first checked the separate kitchen building but found it desolate. He then turned and made his way to the front of the house. The front porch was simple and led up to a board door that stood slightly ajar. The planks groaned as he placed his full weight upon them. He extended the rifle in front of him and used the muzzle to widen the aperture. The door creaked on its wooden hinges but opened only to reveal a barren interior. Will changed his position to better see inside, but his gaze was greeted only by emptiness. He gingerly stepped inside. A single shaft of gray light filtered through the barred window on his left to illuminate the rest of the empty room. A single stone fireplace was directly in front of him, but there was no evidence of a recent fire. The roof appeared intact, and Will saw no evidence of water stains to indicate any leaks. Otherwise, the room was completely unremarkable. Will turned and exited the cabin. Walking to the far left of the porch, Will saw Evaline and motioned for her to come. She obeyed and soon joined him on the porch.

"It's not the best, but it will do. No one's here. I'm going to look around for a lamp or at least something for a little light. You can see if there's one inside. I'll check the outside kitchen."

Will turned to leave but stopped suddenly as if he'd forgotten something.

"Here."

He took the Colt pistol from his belt and handed it to Evaline, who accepted the weapon with some trepidation.

"Do you know how to use that?"

"No."

"The first thing that you do is pull the hammer all the way back until it stops. Like this."

Will took the weapon back momentarily as he demonstrated the function.

"When you hear that click, the hammer is where it needs to be. Then point this at your target and pull the trigger. It'll kick some so hold it tight."

"You sho' you wants me ta have dis?"

Will nodded.

"I'm sure. And don't be afraid to use it. If anyone but me comes around, you hold this on him until we know he can be trusted. Unfortunately, mankind rarely responds to kind words or reason. You show them that you have the power to do them harm and that you're not afraid to do so, then they'll listen. It shouldn't have to be that way, but it is. Wishing that it was different won't change reality."

Will released the hammer gently and let it come to rest on the empty cylinder. He then handed the weapon back to Evaline.

"I'll be back in a minute."

Evaline looked about the cabin for a moment, the uneasiness apparent in her expression.

"Can I go with you?"

Will paused momentarily, but realized immediately why she was asking.

"Sure. Come with me."

The two crossed the yard swiftly and Will pushed the creaking door open enough for them both to go inside. Dust from the long stagnant room danced gently in the gray air. Will quickly scrutinized the walls and soon found an oil lamp hanging from a corroded nail. He gently lifted the lamp and found the wick and glass intact. Sloshing the base gently, he could hear the muffled sloshing of a remnant of oil. Turning his gaze to the floor, Will's eyes fell upon a neat stack of firewood nestled close to the belly of the iron stove. The wood had been protected from the elements, and a sharp kick from Will revealed that it was yet seasoned and sturdy.

"Here, hold this," Will requested as he handed the lamp to Evaline. "On second thought, put the lamp down and load some of this wood on me."

Evaline did as she was told, and Will stood next to the stack of wood, his arms bent at the elbow and projected straight out in front of him. The young woman then picked up several pieces of wood and laid them across his arms. She continued stacking until Will signaled that she had loaded enough.

"This should do. Let's go back."

Evaline grabbed the lamp and pushed the door all the way open so that Will could exit more easily. The pair then covered the distance to the house and entered the front door. Will dropped the wood close to the fireplace and began busying himself with starting the fire. Soon, a warm orange glow filled the room and cast dancing shadows upon the wall. The fireplace and chimney were cheaply built, and Will noticed the loosening of the mortar between the stones, but it certainly was more than adequate for the needs at hand. The thunder boomed again in the distance.

"Ever notice how a fire always makes you feel better?"

"I reckon. Guess it depends on whether you workin' over it or not."

Will chuckled but did not respond to the wisdom of Evaline's statement.

"You ever wish you was jus' back teachin' again?" Evaline's question came without warning.

"All the time. I guess anyone wishes for better days during ones like these."

"You liked teachin'?"

Will nodded his head.

"Very much. You know, it is kind of funny how I used to think how hard I had it teaching all of those children. The fact is, I had no idea how blessed I was. I just couldn't see it. I guess it's part of human nature never to appreciate something fully until it vanishes."

"You think you'll ever teach again?"

"I may not ever make it back, Evaline."

"Will, don't be talkin' like dat."

"I'm not trying to be pessimistic. Even without the war, the Lord never promised me tomorrow. We're just told to make the best out of the time we're given."

"You think da Lord wants you in dis war?"

Will looked at Evaline with a compassionate expression and shrugged his shoulders.

"I'm here for a reason."

Evaline remained silent for a moment.

"Is I?"

The faintest whisper of a smile broke Will's stoic countenance.

"There are no such things as accidental humans."

Evaline returned the smile.

"Can we go over dem letters again?"

"Sure. Let me get my book."

*****

Will's lesson soon exhausted his pupil, and it was not long before she had fallen asleep, her head supported by his bedroll. Nevertheless, Will was amazed at how quickly she appreciated the language and its construction. She reminded him of a thirsty soul that had finally been given water. Will thumbed through the McGuffey Reader, unable to sleep. He wasn't sure of the exact cause of his insomnia, but he felt that perhaps Evaline's questions had struck more of a chord than he was at first willing to admit. His words had been true, yet it had been so long since he had felt purpose. Soon, however, even the concerns of his current situation could not keep him awake, and he dozed off as he reclined against the wall.

*****

The light that appeared during his slumber was like none that he had ever seen, yet it did not burn nor was it painful to behold. Warm and comforting it was, and it seemed to surround and support him and lift the heavy weights from his shoulders. As he basked in the warm rays, Will noticed that the light began to fade until it had reached the intensity of daylight, yet had lost none of its comfort. As his eyes adjusted, he was aware of others about him, all seeming to enjoy the tranquility about them. None were soldiers, but men and women from every race. The surroundings were familiar, not unlike the mountains of central Virginia, with all the brilliant colors of fall radiating from the slopes. Approaching the group was a single individual, a Man of average height, who walked at a pace indicating singleness of purpose. As he neared the group, Will immediately recognized him as the Man from the dream after he had first met Evaline. Even with that recognition, Will felt no apprehension and realized that the comfort he was feeling was all a product of this Man's presence. The entire group turned to face Him as He came to stand in front. He looked out over the group with an expression of satisfaction, but His countenance soon fell, as a gray

98

and ominous light arose behind Him. The hazy light continued to darken as wafts of smoke, tinted by the orange color of flames, rose toward the sky. The Man then stepped slowly to the side and revealed the scene behind Him. In the distance, in the middle of the field, was a huddled figure who lay sobbing quietly. Near her, imbedded in the earth, was a pole to which a chain was attached. The other end of the chain bound the woman's hands and prevented any escape. Behind her and closing in at an alarming rate, were tongues of orange flame which erupted from the grass and consumed all in their path. With a realization that approached panic, Will recognized the woman. It was Evaline.

"Who will go for Me?" the Man asked, a look of profound compassion on His face. "Whom shall I send?"

Great murmurs arose from the crowd as the flames grew ever nearer. All recognized the danger, yet the intensity of the inferno in front of them caused them to shrink back from the task before them, the cost too high to consider. Only Will remained where he was, the horror of what was happening to his friend consuming all else. He then turned to the Man in front of him, his eyes full of determination, his spirit bent on what had to be done.

"Me," his voice sounded clearly in the face of the roaring flames. "I am here. Send me."

The Carpenter gazed at Will before responding.

"Will you go for Me?"

"Through the very flames themselves."

The kind Man nodded.

"Indeed, you will go through the flames. But don't be afraid. You will never be alone, for I will always be with you."

*****

Before Will could respond or act, the light faded altogether, and his eyes fluttered open in the darkness of the cabin. He was still leaning against the wall. As he looked over to his side, Evaline was still asleep on his bedroll. He laid his head back against the wall, his heart rate still elevated from the scene in his dream. He quickly realized that the events had only been a production of his fatigued mind, yet he also knew within himself that the answer he had given was just as authentic as if the events had been factual.

He closed his eyes once more, although he could tell little difference from the darkness in the cabin. He tried to think of pleasant thoughts and home, even though he knew the dangers inherent in dwelling on things that he might never see again. He was remembering the details of his small classroom when he suddenly heard the snapping of a twig from the left side of the house. Every fiber suddenly became completely awake, and he strained every nerve to listen for another sound. Then, he heard a similar sound from the opposite side of the house. A hundred possibilities flashed across his mind, but he knew instinctively that the sources were ominous. Will reached out and grasped the stock of the Enfield and pulled it to him. The fire in the hearth was dead and cold, and he had turned out the lantern a long time ago. Slowly and silently, he raised himself up onto his feet and moved toward Evaline. He again heard a twig snap, closer this time. He placed his hand on her shoulder. Seeing her eyes flutter open, he placed his hand gently across her mouth and shook his head slowly from side to side. He then motioned for her to stand up, but to do so slowly and quietly. There were multiple signs of movement outside. Knowing that there would be no escape through the front door, Will pulled Evaline to the rear of the cabin and the opening of the fireplace. Will could see the fear in Evaline's eyes, but he reassured her with his expression that all would be well, unwilling to reveal his own uncertainty.

Will heard a different snapping sound unlike the one made by moving feet. The cracks were sharper, closer together and seemed to grow in number. As he listened closely, they seemed to be coming from all sides simultaneously. Will could also see that a flickering orange glow accompanied the new sounds, filtering in through the gaps in the boards and accompanied by the acrid smell of smoke. The cabin was burning.

"Come on out, boy!" the voice boomed from outside and shocked both of the cabin's occupants. "We know you're in there, and we know what you did. You gonna pay for what you did to Ben. Only a coward would shoot a man in the back like that! You're surrounded and either way you're gonna die, so I suggest you come out and face it like a man!"

Evaline's terrified expression burned into Will's mind, but he warned her again to say nothing. There was no escape through the windows and door as they were all undoubtedly being watched. The floor was solid and any attempt to break through would be heard, and they still might not be able to escape through the flames from underneath the house.

"You said You would always be with me," Will prayed silently as he frantically looked for an escape. "Help me to see what can't be seen."

Will remembered the fireplace. There were no windows or obvious escape route on that side of the house, and the mortar between the bricks had been dry and fragile. The orange glow barely illuminated the rear of the fireplace as Will drew his Bowie and scraped frantically at the mortar. The sharp blade gouged a deep trench in the chalky material, and it was not long before he was able to push the knife through and out the other side. After similarly loosening the other edges, Will used the knife as a lever to pull the brick in toward himself, leaving a gaping hole in the back of the fireplace. Smoke was beginning to fill the cabin.

"You ain't got much time!" a different voice taunted from outside. "You best come on out and get it over with!"

Will peeked out through the hole and, much to his relief, saw no one in the rear of the cabin. Reaching his hand through the opening, he grasped the next brick down and easily pulled it loose from its support. Working feverishly, Will pulled more and more of the bricks loose, Evaline coming to help in the cramped space. Once the opening was large enough to squeeze through, Will looked out once more and saw that the way was still clear. He turned to Evaline.

"Me first. Follow quickly! There's little time!"

Will then turned abruptly and, putting his lengthy Enfield through first, pulled himself through and into the back yard. He readied his rifle as Evaline followed close behind him. A form silhouetted against the flames burst around the corner and leveled a weapon at the pair, but Will's response was swift and the blast from the Enfield knocked the man off his feet.

"Run, Evaline! Run!"

Will immediately flattened himself in the shadows against the back corner of the house as Evaline dashed toward the woods. He instinctively reached for the Colt but remembered that he had given it to Evaline. Another shadow quickly rounded the corner, and Will knocked him unconscious with the butt of his rifle. The muzzle of a carbine then appeared around the corner, but Will grabbed the weapon and pulled it and its owner around the edge of the house. Simultaneously, another figure rounded the opposite corner of the house. Will pointed the carbine's muzzle in the direction of the oncoming threat and pulled the trigger with his thumb, in spite of the resistance of the weapon's owner. Amid the cloud of white smoke, Will saw the man fall, and he quickly snapped the weapon up to connect with the face of its owner.

The man who followed was massive, and his fist was so swift that Will did not notice until he reeled from its impact. The darkness, stabbed here and there by the ominous orange glow, was spinning. The blows from his assailant were relentless, and he soon found himself upon the ground. Will struggled to rise, but found it impossible, as a swift kick from his attacker thudded against his ribcage and drove all the air from his lungs. Will heard the unmistakable sound of a cocking hammer, and as he turned his head, he saw the familiar silhouette of a LeMat revolver aimed at his head.

"Picked a fight with the wrong person, boy," came the gruff voice that had first startled them in the cabin. "You ought to be ashamed to wear that uniform."

"What I've done…what I'm doing is better than all I've done before. My uniform doesn't define me. I define it."

"Lofty words from a coward. You're not worth a court martial, and I'm not sure I'm willing to wait for the firing squad. In fact, I've just about had enough of you…"

The boom that followed surprised both the men as did the burst of dust from the front of the uniform of the cavalryman. He took a few backwards steps but did not drop his weapon. He looked down in shock at his uniform and then his gaze lifted to look behind Will. A look of rage crossed the man's face as the distinct sound of a hammer cocking reached Will's ears.

"You stupid n…"

The second boom knocked the man off his feet and he fell with a thud upon his back. He quivered and trembled for a moment until a last rush of air escaped through his clenched teeth, and then all was still. Will wheeled around to see the unmistakable form of Evaline standing directly behind him, the Colt pistol held firmly in a two-handed grip. Will struggled to his feet.

"Quickly, Evaline. There may be more."

Will touched her arm, and her gaze slowly shifted to him as she gradually lowered the pistol and handed it to the Confederate.

"Here, Will."

"You hang on to that for now."

"I don't want it no more."

"No, but you need it."

Evaline didn't move.

"Trust me," Will whispered.

Evaline nodded. Will turned and lifted his Enfield from the dust and shouldered the weapon. He then moved to the large man lying motionless on the ground. Swiftly, he kneeled down and unwrapped the dead fingers from the LeMat revolver. Turning the cylinder to check the charges, Will then shoved the weapon into his belt. He then turned his attention to the carbine lying closer to the house. He lifted the weapon and immediately recognized it as a captured Spencer carbine. With no time to examine it further, he then stood and placed the weapon over his other shoulder. The two unconscious soldiers still remained motionless. Will knew that none had seen his face, and without their leader, they would be unlikely to continue the pursuit. He was a soldier, but never a cold-blooded killer. After procuring a few of the haversacks, the pair disappeared into the woods.

*****

Will pushed onward until almost dawn before stopping to rest. Evaline offered no resistance as she, too, wanted to put as much distance as possible between them and the cabin. When his instincts reassured him that they were safe, Will found a comfortable area and placed his bedroll upon the ground. Evaline, in spite of utter exhaustion, remained restless and did not fall asleep. She rolled continuously, and Will could hear her inhale and exhale deep, anxious breaths. Will remained silent, observing her struggle with great compassion. Finally, Evaline sat up and stared up into blackness before speaking, a tremor evident in her voice.

"Is it always dis way, Will?"

"You mean killing?"

Evaline nodded.

"The first time was awful. It will get better."

"I don't want it to get no better. Dat man ain't never gonna get up. He ain't never gonna breathe again. And all dat is 'cause of me."

"Evaline, you're no murderer."

"Den how come I feels like one?"

"Because you're a good person. You still understand the value of a life."

"Will, you's a good man. How come it comes so easy to you?"

Will remained silent, the depth of her question striking at the very nature of a fallen mankind.

"Because your heart gets hard."

Evaline thought for a moment.

"Even yours?"

"Even mine."

Evaline's voice carried even more emotion than previously.

"I don't never want mine to gets like dat."

"Nor do I."

Will remained silent for a moment as his mind groped for some way to comfort his friend, knowing within that God himself could only provide such comfort.

"I have two things to thank you for, Evaline. Probably even more than that, but these two are the most obvious. First of all, thank you for saving my life. If you had not done what you did, I would not be here talking with you now. Secondly, I want to thank you for reminding me what I was like before the war. Because of you, I am not the man I was becoming."

Evaline continued to listen.

"Do you remember the story of Esther?"

"From da Bible?"

Will nodded.

"She was placed where she was for a reason. You are here for a reason. You have a purpose. Don't let anyone ever tell you anything differently. Don't let anyone ever try to take from you what God alone has given you."

Evaline's trembling subsided.

"In the morning, when the sun rises, you'll feel better. God's grace arrives with the sunlight, and there is no less of it the following morning. He'll still be here."

"With us sparrows?"

Will smiled.

"Yes, with the sparrows."

Evaline contemplated Will's words as she peered out into the darkness, now no longer as

impenetrable as it had been. She then laid her head back on the bedroll and drifted off to sleep.

*****

As soon as the sunlight drove away enough of the darkness to assure visibility, Will set to examining his new acquisitions. Evaline remained asleep nearby, and he did not disturb her slumber. Removing the LeMat revolver from his belt, he found that all nine chambers were loaded and that the shorter shotgun-type barrel underneath the primary one was also charged. Will had seen the LeMat revolver before but had never fired one. Will pulled the hammer back to full cock and noticed that the nine-shot cylinder revolved around the central shotgun barrel. He then noticed that a small lever was present on the LeMat's hammer and could be placed in either an upper or a lower position. If in the upper position, the revolver fired the nine shot cylinder; while if in the lower position, the gun would fire the shotgun barrel. Will found leaving the hammer in the lower position to be a bit unnerving, and he quickly moved the hammer to the upper position and placed the revolver on the ground nearby.

Will found the Spencer to be a much more intriguing weapon. He had heard of the new Union repeating rifle but knew little else about it. The carbine length was much shorter than he was used to, and he found it lighter as well. Inspecting the end of the stock, Will noticed a metallic ring. Pulling this out revealed a hollow, metallic tube with a spring inside. As he removed the tube fully, six self-contained bullets fell out. He placed the rifle down for a moment and inspected one of the shells. The lead bullet and powder charge were contained in one metallic case. No more just being able to load the powder and bullet down the barrel to achieve, at most, three shots per minute as was the case with the Enfield. This rifle could shoot much faster. Will raised the rifle to his shoulder and inspected the sights before replacing the bullets in the stock and reinserting the metal magazine.

Placing the rifle in his lap once again, Will moved the trigger guard forward and noticed how a single bullet was pulled forward from the magazine and, as the trigger guard was moved rearward, placed into the chamber. Once the hammer was cocked, the rifle was ready to fire. Working the trigger guard forward and backward once again, Will noticed how the old bullet was extracted and ejected while being replaced by a new one from the magazine.

"So that's how you work," Will whispered as his mind fathomed the intricate workings of the rifle's mechanism. Although nothing would ever replace his respect for his beloved Enfield, he was certainly thankful for the extra firepower that the Spencer would offer.

As had become his custom, Will was soon gathering his meager possessions, securing his weapons, and making sure that all of Evaline's needs were met. Will felt a great urgency about the entire journey, although he would have been the first to admit that there were no specific deadlines. Each moment that the pair spent together seemed to have a life of its own, but the recent experience at the cabin had emphasized how important it was for Evaline to be away from the front lines. Will knew that the sooner she reached territory beyond the war zone and resumed her journey to Canada, the better it would be for Evaline.

By midmorning, the pair was once again making their way north through the Virginia frontier. Evaline frequently asked Will's opinion about where they were and about how much farther it was to the river. Part of the Confederate believed that her frequent questions stemmed directly from her desire for freedom and escape from the horrors to which she had been exposed since she had made Will's acquaintance. However, there was another part of the soldier that felt perhaps her longing for freedom was overshadowed by the dread of their separation. The Rappahannock was Will's high water mark, and he could pass no farther. After crossing that landmark, she would once again be without his constant guidance and companionship, and loneliness would hold her in its dark grasp. For that reason, she both welcomed the coming of the river and loathed it too.

In early afternoon, the pair stopped briefly and ate a meager lunch, for Will continued to conserve what little food they had. The weather was quite pleasant, and it was sometimes difficult to resume the journey after they stopped to rest. After they finished their provisions, a distant whistling wafted through the trees, and Evaline listened intently to the shrill sound.

"What's dat?"

"Train whistle," Will responded without much thought.

"Oh, so dat's what dat is."

"You've never heard one before?"

"Yeah, but not dis close. Where I was in Lynchburg wasn't nowhere near da tracks. I ain't never *seen* one though."

"Really, you've never seen a train?"

"Nope. Have you ridden on one?"

Will laughed as he responded.

"You could say that. I was with the 31st Georgia before I was with the 3rd Georgia. We marched with General Jackson, and he was fond of using the trains to 'leap frog' his troops to make us able to cover distances more quickly. He would take the last regiment in line, place them on the train, and carry them to the front of the column. He would keep repeating this over and over so that all of the units would get some rest but, at the same time, we would keep moving."

"It sho' would be nice to take a ride now."

"I agree. The only problem with that is that it would be so easy for someone to capture us. I also suspect that these trains are going to Fredericksburg or some other city, places we want to avoid. The fewer people we encounter the better."

"I knows all dat," Evaline responded. "But dey ain't no harm in wishin'."

"No, I guess not."

"You think dat we could at least go and see it?"

Will shrugged his shoulders.

"I don't see why not. We have to go that way anyway."

"Is we ready?"

"I think so. Let's move on."

The train whistle drew closer as Will and Evaline moved in the direction of the track. Then the lumbering noise diminished and faded into the distance once it passed. The pair was not close enough to see the train, but Will knew that with any luck another would be scheduled to pass soon. Trains were a lifeline to the armies but were becoming scarcer as the war devastated increasing amounts of territory in Northern Virginia. Will suspected that most of the trains in this area would be carrying supplies to the Confederates, but he also knew that he would have to exercise caution to avoid being spotted by any guards who might be on the train.

Evaline's excitement at the opportunity to see a train brought a smile to Will's face, as it reminded him of a child waiting for a candy cane and an orange on Christmas morning. It was amazing to see how important the mundane things of life were to her. She had been absolutely correct when she explained to Will that humans do not miss things of which they have no knowledge. Now that she had been exposed, however, she desired to know more and found great fascination in experiences that most would have taken for granted. How much richer life would be, Will thought, if humans could only see the value of the experiences in life that are often deemed trivial.

The distance to the rail bed was not far, and soon Will and

Evaline stepped out into an open area that was in stark contrast to the tangled undergrowth behind them. The railway cut a swath through the forest and extended in both directions as far as the eye could see. The red earth, upturned during the making of the railway, coated the sides of the rail bed. There was no sign of the earlier locomotive and, for the moment, all was quiet.

"You thinks dat another train gonna come by soon?"

"Probably. Nothing works exactly on time in the Confederacy, but with the close fighting, these trains are going to try to get as many supplies to the troops as possible. I suspect that there will be one coming and going pretty frequently."

"I know dat we needs to be on our way. It's okay if we can't stay to watch."

"We've got a little time to spare," Will responded. "We'll wait here for a bit and see what happens."

The two travelers sat down at the edge of the forest underneath the shade of the overhanging foliage. The breeze through the tops of the trees provided the only sound.

"When we see a train coming, we'll hide in the edge of the woods so that no one sees us," Will instructed. "It's pretty impressive to see one go by. They're so big that the ground shakes beneath you."

Evaline nodded her head in acknowledgment while she continued to watch the track. Will's keen vision searched the forest across from them but saw nothing out of the ordinary. Then, movement off to his left beyond Evaline flashed across his peripheral vision. Turning his head, he saw no source for the disturbance except for the random movement of leaves in the breeze. Still, he found himself unable to dismiss the disruption and was unable to stop scrutinizing the area of movement. Minutes passed, and nothing appeared amiss until Will caught a brief, but distinct glimpse of a horse's head about one hundred yards to his left. Will immediately touched Evaline on the arm and motioned for her to remain silent as she followed him. Evaline knew that all was not well but trusted Will's judgment and complied with his instructions. Once inside the forest, Will leaned closer to Evaline's good ear and whispered.

"There are some men on horseback coming at us from the left. I haven't seen them, but I suspect that they are approaching from the right, too, to try to catch us in the middle."

"Who is dey?"

"I'm not exactly sure, but I suspect that these are more of our friends from the cabin. I didn't think that they would follow after what happened during their last visit, but I underestimated them."

"What we gonna do?"

Just as Evaline asked the question, Will heard the distant but distinct sound of a train whistle. As the sound wafted through the forest, a daring plan of escape accompanied it, and Will suddenly realized his only option.

"You told me earlier that you wanted to ride a train," Will began. "You may very well get your chance."

Evaline's expression disclosed her underlying anxiety.

"I ain't so sho' about da way dat sounds."

"Trust me," Will began. "There is no other way out. We can't outrun their horses. If we can get on that train, then we can level the field some, and I may be able to hold them off."

Evaline was terrified, but she could never deny that the Confederate had rescued her from impossible situations before.

"Okay, Will. What do I needs to do?"

"I want you to stay low here just inside the forest edge. Don't move, and stay hidden. I'm going to create a distraction and throw them off guard while I move toward the oncoming train. As it passes, I'll jump on board. When the train passes, you'll run to me, and I'll pull you into the train. Then, we'll have a chance to make it out of here."

Evaline nodded.

"Are you okay? Do you know what to do?"

"Yes, but I don't like you runnin' off like dis again."

"I know, but I'll be back before you know it. I'm not going to leave you. I'll see you on the train."

Will then turned and, keeping a low profile, advanced with his Spencer at the ready and his Enfield across his back. Evaline drew the Colt pistol and found a hiding place just inside the line of trees. The train whistle drew closer.

Will could hear the horses coming through the forest and was surprised that the troopers had not dismounted. In spite of the loss that he had inflicted upon them, he still sensed that they had little respect for him and were awaiting their chance to ride him down like an animal. Will closed the distance as much as he possibly could and then assumed a crouching position among the underbrush. He cocked the hammer on his Spencer and placed the weapon against his shoulder. Although he saw no sign of movement, Will could hear the unmistakable sounds of the animals approaching through the forest. A horse's head became visible, followed by a view of its rider who, with pistol drawn, scrutinized the forest ahead. The distance was short. Will quickly aligned his sights and, after breathing a prayer, pulled the trigger.

Will was on his feet sprinting toward the tracks long before the echo of his shot had died away into the forest. His surprise attack had its intended effect; the other horsemen were too shocked to react immediately, and the dense underbrush did not allow a clear shot at the escaping marksman. Will heard a cry behind him, followed by several shots, but the bullets were all wide and passed through the underbrush. Glancing ahead, Will could see the locomotive rushing down the tracks, smoke billowing from the stack. Pulled along by the locomotive were several supply cars, each closed by a large door. There was no sign of any guards, nor was there any evidence that the train carried troops. The door on the fifth car back was slightly ajar, apparently loosened by its rambling journey. As the locomotive passed, Will sprinted across the short open distance to the rail bed. Every passing second an irreplaceable treasure for him, Will grabbed the side of the car and swung himself up and into the vehicle, two more bullets thudding against the side of the car as he did so. As Will swung his Enfield around, the rifle bellowed smoke and fire out the open door to unhorse the lead rider who had galloped ahead to warn the conductor of this unwanted passenger. Switching to the Spencer, Will unleashed a hail of bullets at the trailing horsemen and caused them temporarily to keep their distance. Glancing ahead, Will saw Evaline just inside the tree line. The train was closing the distance rapidly. Will knew that he had only one chance, and that his timing had to be perfect. He placed the Spencer on the floor beside him and took the LeMat revolver from his belt. Crouching by the door, Will watched Evaline's position and counted in his head to make his diversion at the appropriate time. At precisely the right moment, Will screamed through the open door.

"Now, Evaline! Run!"

At that exact moment, Will leaned out of the open door and pointed his weapon rearward as Evaline began her sprint to the train. Will was greeted immediately by a horseman who had pulled to within a few feet of the open door, but the blast from the LeMat blew him back over his horse. Swiftly, Will fired off several more shots at the other horsemen as he provided covering fire for Evaline.

Through his peripheral vision, Will saw Evaline reach the train just as he squeezed off his last shot. Swinging about in one smooth motion, Will grabbed her under her arms and, with a rolling motion, lifted her through the open door and into the car. In the back right corner of the car were several sacks of corn meal, and Will flung them into a makeshift barrier before pushing Evaline behind its protection.

"Stay down, you hear me? Stay down behind these no matter what happens!"

Will then turned sharply to see a face appear at the door as the rider fired his pistol into the gloom. Will rolled to the side as the bullet slammed into the meal sacks in front of Evaline. The Confederate returned fire, but the rider had already pulled back behind the door. Returning the LeMat to his belt, Will quickly reloaded his Enfield. In spite of Will's warning, Evaline peered over the top of the barrier in front of her and watched the soldier's skillful movements. The reloading of his weapon seemed to consist of one continuous motion, as one movement flowed into the next. He then leaned forward and out the door before taking a rapid, but precise shot. He then returned to the inside of the car to repeat the reloading process as bullets continued to pound the outside of the car.

In spite of their numerical superiority, the riders were suffering greatly at the hands of the marksman as he was picking them off one by one. The conductor, apparently unable to hear the shots over the noise of the engine, moved the train at full steam, and none of the riders were able to get close enough to alert him. Will continued his relentless offensive until none of the horsemen remained, and he breathed an audible sigh of relief. Sitting back a little from the edge of the door, he continued to monitor the outside for any sign of trouble. Evaline again peered over the top of her barricade and asked if she could move, but Will signaled that she should stay where she was. A sound came from above Will's head and his eyes immediately investigated the roof. The sound reoccurred, and Will was positive that he heard the sound of boots on the wood overhead. Will cocked the Enfield and continued to study the roof.

There was a sudden blur of movement at the top of the door, followed by a dull metallic clank as a round object was thrown into the center of the car. Will followed the trajectory and realized, to his horror, that the object was an explosive shell with a lit fuse sputtering white smoke into the stagnant air. Will was well aware of the devastation that such an explosion could create, as he had seen soldiers hurl the lighted cannonballs into enemy positions. An explosion of that magnitude in the confined space of the car would kill or incapacitate everyone inside. With herculean speed, Will reached out, grasped the shell, and in one motion flung the deadly object out the open door. No sooner had it passed into the open than the shell exploded, sending a blinding flash of light, shrapnel, and acrid smoke back into the car. The shock slammed into Will and knocked him onto his back. Before he could rise, a lone figure silhouetted against the outside light, swung down from the top of the car through the open door and landed on his feet inside the vehicle. His attack was swift and vicious, and it seemed to Will as if his opponent had been storing all of his malice to unleash at just such a time. Will resisted valiantly, but his adversary was much less weary, and soon Will found himself incapacitated with his arm twisted painfully behind his back. Evaline's terrified expression was visible just above her barrier.

"She's next," muttered the malicious voice in his ear. The sensation of a multitude of Georgia summers washed over Will, and he remembered the utter fatigue that the toil of working the fields had brought. He had pushed himself beyond all limits in those times, and that same strength unexpectedly flowed through him once more as it filled his vessels and penetrated to the very muscles and sinews themselves. Without warning, Will's free hand shot back over his shoulder and connected with his opponent's face. The grip on his arm was suddenly released, and Will continued his assault with his elbow. Shoving the man backwards, Will drew the LeMat from his belt as he fell utterly exhausted to his knees. Flipping the hammer selector to fire the shotgun barrel, Will took aim.

"I've just about had enough of you."

The recoil from the pistol shoved Will onto his back and blew his opponent completely out of the car through the open door. Will dropped the pistol with a moan and rolled over onto his stomach where he gulped air in great drawing gasps. His face was on the floor, the dust stirred with each expiration. Evaline sprang from her hiding place and kneeled at his side, her hand on his back.

"Will, Will, is you okay?"

"Evaline," came the raspy response. "I am so tired."

"I know you is, Will," came the compassionate response. "I know you is."

The pair suddenly heard the squeal of the brakes as the explosion of the bomb had finally captured the attention of the conductor. Will was utterly spent but struggled to his feet as he felt the train begin to slow. Evaline steadied him, and the Confederate studied his young companion for a moment.

"I am so sorry."

The Confederate's voice was trembling.

"My goodness, Will, whatever for?"

Evaline brushed the tear from her cheek and Will, remembering his previous words to his friend, smiled compassionately. The slow passage of the scenery through the open door then brought his thoughts back to the present.

"The train is stopping. When it gets to a safer speed, we'll jump off and disappear. I'll go first and make sure that none of our friends are still around."

Will moved unsteadily toward the door and hopped out onto the bank of the rail bed. Gazing about his surroundings, he saw no evidence of another person. He then motioned for Evaline to follow. Helping her jump to the ground, the two quickly disappeared into the forest long before the great hulk of the train lumbered to a stop.

Chapter VII

Will and Evaline pushed through the forest as far as their weary bodies would allow before they collapsed in utter exhaustion onto the leafy forest floor. There, the pair remained until nightfall, having neither the desire nor the strength to push on. In spite of his exhaustion, Will awoke before dawn and sat in the darkness contemplating all that had occurred. He turned for a moment and looked in a northerly direction. How far had they come, and just how far was he from his goal? Where was the Rappahannock? Even as his practical side asked these questions in earnest, he could not help but sense an accompanying unease as he thought about parting with Evaline. There remained no debate about the necessity of his remaining behind. He could not lead her all the way. His duty and heart lay with his home state, and he was perfectly willing to give his life upon that altar.

Yet there was more. As he observed the sleeping figure, he realized that parting with her would be like losing one of his own, as taking a child that had slept upon his shoulder and cuddled beneath his protective arm and leaving her in a vast wilderness while wolves circled all about. And then he would simply turn his back and leave her, the whimpers of fear burning into what was left of his humanity. She had awakened in him something that he feared was long dead. And yet when the old Will, that child not yet completely banished, came bursting to the surface, the compassion that accompanied threatened to overwhelm him. He had long suppressed any hint of nostalgia, compassion, and kindness in an attempt to deal with what was occurring all about him. Then, suddenly, the floodgates would open and all the faces, sights, sounds, and agonies would rush upon him and sweep him far away from duty and honor and irresistibly back to his home beneath a canopy of pines. Like a child seeking shelter in the arms of his mother. Will felt the warmth trickle down his cheek, but did not hinder it. He closed his eyes, but the process once started was irreversible, and the Confederate felt himself fall deeper still into that place of swirling colors and music of heavenly places.

*****

Evaline's eyes fluttered open, and yet a peaceful sense caused her to remain where she was and stare up at the leafy covering above.

Only the sounds of the forest greeted her, and she gently turned her head to find Will nearby, his back toward her with only the side of his face visible. He remained perfectly still, his gaze fixed somewhere in the distance, lost both in time and place. Suddenly, something glistened upon his cheek and ran like a river from its source. Still, he did not move, and no change of expression accompanied the appearance of the tear. Why? Why did he weep? For her? For his comrades lying dead in the forest? For his family? For Georgia? Her thoughts were filled with explanations, and yet above all came the sudden clear realization that he wept for them all. And for what was to come.

*****

The pair spent the morning eating breakfast composed of smoked beef and a little cornbread that they found in the haversacks. Only a short time after resuming their journey, Will spotted a wild pear tree, and the two enjoyed several pieces of fruit before stuffing as many as they could into the haversacks. As they continued, they occasionally heard voices, but none were of military origin, and Will was able to skillfully avoid any contact. The land was otherwise barren and devastated, yet hope still remained beneath its scarred surface, awaiting the spring of peace to burst once again into full bloom.

*****

"What did you do in Lynchburg?"

"What?"

"What was your duty? I mean, did you work inside or outside?"

"Mercy no, I ain't no inside slave. I's too clumsy for dat. I's a field hand."

"How did you do it? I mean day after day?"

"You know, Will, it ain't dat hard to do somethin' if it's all you know. If you don't know dey ain't nothin' better, den you ain't got nothin' to hope for."

"True. You know that's why it's dangerous to let slaves learn to read. You would learn and teach others about freedom. It has nothing to do with your capability."

"I see dat now. But, see I didn't know what I was missin' until you showed me."

"You've only scratched the surface."

115

"Yeah, but ain't no turnin' back now."

"I've opened up a can of worms, haven't I?"

"Sho' has."

"Or Pandora's box."

"What?"

"Never mind."

"You sho' you know where you's goin'?"

Will stopped for a moment to inspect the terrain about him. He then turned his gaze to the sky as if looking for Polaris among the blue overhead.

"I didn't think the river would be this far. But then again, we've gotten thrown off the trail with our little encounters. Don't worry, we're still going north."

"Will Seymour, if you ain't careful, you's gonna keep goin' north till you ends up in Abe Lincoln's lap."

"I'm not *that* lost."

"Sho' you ain't."

Will took a deep breath and continued onward.

"Now, what about you? I done tol' you all about me. You always been a sharpshooter?"

"No, not at first. Like I mentioned earlier, I joined the army with the Thirty-First Georgia from Decatur County. Later on, our commanders saw the need for soldiers who could shoot long distances and hit their targets consistently. They held tests to see which men would qualify, and I was one of them. I've been there ever since."

"How you do it?"

"You mean hit things far away?"

"Yeah. I mean specially when dey movin' like dat horseman was."

Will thought for a moment.

"That's hard to explain. I mean practice is definitely part of it, but it's more than that. I don't know if this will make any sense to you at all, but I can *feel* when I'm going to hit something. Sometimes I rely more on the way the gun feels on my shoulder than my other senses."

"Kinda like somebody who can play an instrument real good. Dey can play by ear. It jus' feels right."

"Exactly. I just wish I was playing the banjo."

"I bet you do."

*****

The remainder of the day passed without incident, and although Will looked frequently over his shoulder, he saw no evidence of pursuit. Around sunset, the pair crossed a pristine creek, and Will refilled the canteens. Stopping within a stone's throw from the northern bank, Will decided to camp for the night and restart fresh in the morning. Although he had no direct evidence, he felt like they would reach the Rappahannock the next day, and that would be as far as he could go. He had already risked much more than was prudent, and Providence itself was all that had ensured his success thus far. The pair ate the last of the cornbread and some pears before Will produced a candle that he had acquired at the last house. Soon, the small orange glow was illuminating a warm and flickering circle beneath the canopy overhead.

"You think you'll be fine without a fire tonight?"

"Yeah. It ain't cold at all."

"Okay."

"Will, can I ask you somethin'?"

"Sure."

"I don't mean to pry into yo' business, but I noticed back at the first house we was in that you had some paper in yo' Bible. It looks like you been hangin' on to it fo' some time."

Will nodded in response.

"Is it from yo' wife?"

"No," came the singular response. Will's pause almost made Evaline abandon her line of questioning, but he soon spoke again.

"Would you like to see it?"

"Will, honest, I ain't askin' so you'd let me see it. But, I will tell you I's curious."

"I don't mind."

Will removed the haversack from his shoulder and upon opening it, slowly removed the yellowed paper. Then, holding it gingerly, he passed it to Evaline. He then moved the candle to provide adequate light for her.

"You sho' you want me to look at dis?"

"It's okay. I wouldn't let you see it if I didn't want you to."

Feeling somewhat guilty for having asked, Evaline nonetheless opened the folded piece of weathered paper. She expected the flickering candle light to reveal a letter which she would not have been able to read, and her viewing would have been no great

117

sacrifice to Will. However, instead of the elegant markings of a formal letter, Evaline was greeted by a drawing of such simplicity that it could only have been produced by a child. In the center of the paper stood a soldier, drawn in stick proportions but with undeniable characteristics. He was fully dressed in his gray uniform, several large buttons displayed prominently upon his jacket. His slouch hat was slightly off center, and his rifle lacked several essential features such as a trigger and hammer. The expression upon the soldier's face, however, was one of contentment in spite of these inadequacies. Behind the soldier was a simple square schoolhouse with multiple children, drawn in similar stick fashion, playing in the background. Underneath the soldier, written in large, bold letters with a confidence and pride rarely found in adults was the phonetic word, "DADDE." Evaline stared at the combination of letters, attempting to remember the sounds that were associated with each one. The meaning of the single inscription rushed upon her as she blended the sounds together as best she could.

"Daddy?" Evaline asked, her brow wrinkled.

Will nodded in response.

Amid the hush of the moment, all became flawlessly clear as Evaline's mind conjured an image of Will leaving home, his children clinging desperately to his uniform as duty called him away. They all begged him to stay, to sit with them once more by the fire, and read them the stories of old. "Hold our hands," they pleaded, "and touch our faces before the cold wind blows. Stay with us," their faces cried, "and let the shadow that lurks to extinguish your very existence remain in the distance. Run away." This was not goodbye. This was forever. Yet even as they cried, his youngest slipped a folded piece of paper into his pocket, a drawing created with the utmost care and inscribed with the one word that had always meant the world entire. Daddy.

Through all that followed, the paper had persevered. Through intolerable cold, burning heat, nightmares of the battlefield, and persistent hunger, it had remained to remind him of what could never die. It had heard the whistling of the bullets, the shriek of the shells, and the agony of the wounded. Yet within its borders was Georgia. His Georgia. Within its fibers wafted the soft wind as it passed through the evergreens, and its aroma was a handful of brown earth upturned by the blade of a plow. Childhood images and sensations from the drawing had pulled the Confederate irresistibly away from what he had become and back to what he had always been. Within its crumpled edges remained the single preserving element of his humanity, the final surviving component of the structure that held back the relentless tide that threatened to wash away all that he was. It was all that stood between him and the abyss until Evaline came.

With a hushed sigh, Evaline gently folded the paper exactly as it had been and, holding it reverently in her hands, handed it back to Will. The Confederate showed no sign of embarrassment or regret as he received the page and looked into Evaline's face with an expression that could never have been put to words.

"I understands," she stated softly. "Now, I understands."

Will nodded and then opened the haversack to replace the precious item back between the pages of his Bible. Then, he blew the candle out.

*****

Will was fast asleep when the approaching footsteps disrupted his slumber. He quickly grabbed his Enfield and crawled to where Evaline was sleeping, but found that the young woman was already awake, the Colt pistol in her hand. He pressed his finger firmly over his lips, and Evaline nodded in understanding. Will then helped her to her feet, and the pair moved to the opposite side of an oak to await the coming invader. Will's eyes had adjusted to the darkness and, with the help of an early moon, he was able to discern the blackness in front of him. Silently, he readied the Enfield and aimed it in the direction of the footsteps. As the Confederate settled into position, he listened closely and was able to discern only one pair of footsteps coming directly toward them. The footsteps were confident, as one who knew his way around the forests well, but not particularly stealthy as one would expect if produced by a dubious source. As he continued to monitor directly ahead, Will detected the shadowy movement of a single person walking calmly through the wilderness. The Confederate remained completely still, hoping that the intruder would pass them by undetected, but the sudden sound of the invader tripping over Will's bedroll ended that hope. The shadow quickly rose to his knees.

"Who's there?" called a voice that lacked military gruffness.

"Stay where you are, keep your mouth closed, and you may live to find out. There are two of us here and we've both got our guns on you. You twitch, and we fire."

Swiftly and silently, Will lowered his rifle and retrieved his flint and steel from his haversack. Within a moment, he had kindled a small flame in the leaves and relit the candle. The small flame, however, did not extend far enough for Will to see their new visitor.

"You sit with your hands up in the air, understand?"

"Yes."

"Are you armed?"

"No."

"Is anyone else with you?"

"No."

"Are you lying to me?"

"No."

"You'll be the first to go if you are. Don't move."

Will then turned to Evaline.

"Walk with me and keep your gun on him," he whispered and directed with his hands. "If he moves a muscle, you shoot. Understand?"

Evaline nodded. Will then moved forward cautiously, the Enfield trained steadily on the position of the newcomer. Evaline walked just to Will's left and carried the revolver in one hand and the candle in the other. The tiny circle of light that extended out from the candle crept forward until it illuminated the man sitting on the forest floor, Will's bedroll just behind him. Sitting there in front of them, unshaken and confident, was a middle-aged black man. Neither Will nor Evaline had expected to see a black man, as he spoke as an educated man and had no detectible accent. He was dressed well, but in clothing suitable for the outdoors. He observed his Confederate captor with a look of disdain, but he could not hide his surprise on seeing Evaline behind the pistol.

"What is your name?" Will asked.

"Edward Jackson."

"What are you doing here?"

"I was just about to ask her the same thing."

"You didn't answer my question."

There was no reply.

"You're going to tell me what I want to know one way or the other. I don't mean you any harm, but I will find out if that intention is mutual. Why are you here?"

Edward's gaze shifted to Evaline.

120

"Has he hurt you?"

"No," replied Evaline. The pistol did not change position. "You best answer his questions."

"Are you a runaway?" Will asked. "Is that it?"

"Absolutely not. I'm a free man."

"Then why are you here?"

There was still no answer. Will exhaled audibly.

"You may not answer my questions, but I assure you that you're not going anywhere until I'm sure that you mean us no harm."

"Looks to me as if you're the only one here who means any of us harm."

"You so sure about that?"

"Absolutely," Edward replied coldly.

"Then stand up," Will instructed.

Edward did not immediately comply, but once again trained his gaze on the young woman, his expression seeming to attempt to evoke a response from her that was not readily forthcoming. The Colt did not waver.

"What has he done to you? Why are you doing this?"

Evaline cocked the hammer on the pistol.

"I done tol' you dat you better do what he says."

Keeping his penetrating gaze fixed on Evaline, Edward rose slowly to his feet and stood motionless, his proud features dimmed not in the least by his circumstances. Will did not drop his weapon until he had moved behind Edward and secured his hands with a section of rope. The Confederate then shouldered his weapon and searched his captive thoroughly for any weapons. Satisfied that Edward was unarmed, Will motioned for him to sit once more as the soldier moved to his front. Will, his Enfield across his lap, then sat on the ground in front of his captive and met his gaze head on, searching deeply into the personality and intentions of the man before him. He then turned to Evaline.

"Would you mind making us a little fire while I keep our guest company? Just a little one will be fine."

Evaline seemed unwilling to drop her weapon.

"It's fine. I'll keep a close eye on him."

Evaline, reassured by Will's words, slowly dropped the Colt after carefully releasing the hammer. She then placed the candle by Will's side and set about piling a small stack of wood. Edward's gaze followed Evaline's every move, but Will did not release his

121

penetrating gaze from Edward.

"Are you hungry?" the Confederate asked.

"No."

"You're not carrying any supplies."

There was no response.

"We don't have much, but we'll share what we've got."

Edward shook his head.

"Are you some sort of spy?" Will asked.

"A black man stands out like a sore thumb. We don't make very good spies."

"True, but a free black man running around in the Virginia wilderness in the middle of the night is not usual fare either. You wouldn't be doing whatever it is that you're doing if it could be done in daylight."

"The same argument could be said of you. You haven't said anything about why you're out here with her."

"You didn't ask."

"I wasn't the one holding the gun."

"Fair enough. You tell me why you're here and what you're up to, and I'll tell you our story."

Edward shook his head again.

"Very well, then, how does this sound? I'll tell *you* why you're here, and then I'll tell you about us."

Will's statement caught Edward off guard, and anxiety momentarily flashed across his face. Curiosity, however, emerged as the dominant emotion.

"You know why I'm here?"

"I've got a pretty good idea."

The Confederate's expression, as evidenced by the steadily growing fire, was confident, and Edward found it very difficult to determine if he actually knew the answer, or if his statement was merely part of some more elaborate plot to discover the truth. However, the Confederate soon dispelled all doubt as he revealed his answer.

"You're involved with helping the runaways."

Edward's expression did not belie his underlying shock at the soldier's response.

"Really? And just how did you reach that conclusion?"

"Several things, really, but I also trust my instincts. Many of us in the South know the basics about how escaped slaves are directed from one safe house to the next all the way to Canada. It takes an educated person like yourself to keep that organized. You also said earlier that blacks stand out like sore thumbs, but that's certainly not true on plantations. It wouldn't surprise me at all if you couldn't infiltrate some of them in the area and recruit some of the slaves to join you."

"You've got this all figured out, haven't you?"

"Well, maybe not all of it, but certainly feel free to set the record straight. You also seem pretty annoyed that Evaline, my companion, didn't jump in to join you when you showed up."

"People can be made to believe anything, even if it's not true."

"Oh, I can assure you that Evaline hasn't been made to believe anything. She's come to her own conclusions."

"You mean *your* conclusions."

"No. Hers."

"Well, now it's my turn to read your mind."

"Go ahead."

"I would suspect that you're a deserter, and that along the way you've come across a young woman of your liking, possibly a runaway, that you're taking with you for the services she can provide."

Will sensed that Edward was only trying to anger him, and he responded with a simple answer.

"Perhaps you should ask her."

Edward's gaze shifted from the unyielding Confederate to the young woman who, having finished her task, was seated nearby observing the spirited discourse. His expression, while wordless, still proposed the obvious question.

"He ain't no deserter. And I sho' 'nuff ain't what you sayin' I is."

Edward had to admit to himself that Evaline's response did not hold the air of an oppressed subject, but rather the confidence of one completely comfortable in speaking her mind. She no longer cowered under authority as did most slaves. Instead, she stood as defiantly as a soldier behind a stone wall, the steadfastness of her gaze as devastating as any volley. Something had happened; something that Edward had not yet encountered.

Forgive me," Edward asked with sincerity as he ignored the Confederate and gazed at Evaline. "I did not mean to offend."

Evaline nodded but generally seemed unimpressed by the gesture. Edward then turned to Will.

"Are you going to leave me tied up like this?"

"For now. Unless you can give me some reason to trust you."

Edward remained silent.

"Then you remain bound," Will explained. "Your freedom depends on you and your intentions. You'll have to forgive me, but I cannot afford the luxury of giving you the benefit of the doubt."

Will reached around his back and produced another length of rope.

"Stretch your legs out and keep your feet together."

Edward did not comply.

"I won't be tied up like some animal."

"You may not be an animal, but you're dangerous until proven otherwise. The choice remains entirely up to you. Until then, I'll do whatever it takes to protect us. Now, stretch out your legs."

Edward returned the steely gaze of the soldier only momentarily before slowly stretching one of his legs forward, digging his heel into the forest floor as he did so. At first, he appeared to follow suit with the other leg, when suddenly the extremity flew forward and struck Will a glancing blow across his right shoulder as the Confederate turned to avoid the attack. Edward swiftly attempted to rise to his feet as Will was momentarily caught off guard, but the advantage was short-lived as the Confederate regained his balance and lunged forward. Edward, his hands still tied securely behind his back, endured the full force of the blow and fell backward. In an instant, Will had him pinned, and the ominous sound of the Bowie being drawn from its sheath filled the air. All struggling stopped immediately as Edward stared up at the cold steel hovering above him, the light from the small fire glowing coldly from its blade.

"What's the matter with you?" Will snarled, his previous calm demeanor having been replaced by something much more menacing. "I told you we meant you no harm!"

Edward's gaze shifted from the razor-edged blade to Will's face. So much emotion remained buried behind the rugged features, and Edward seemed determined to test his mettle to the fullest.

"Go ahead," Edward grunted under the strain. "Go ahead, if you've got the guts!"

Will, much more insightful than his adversary gave him credit for, immediately changed his expression from one of rage to one of pure annoyance.

"If I needed to kill you, I'd have already done it."

124

With those words, Will stood swiftly and, grasping Edward's right ankle, dragged him to a nearby oak of small, but sufficient diameter. He then pulled Edward's left ankle around the opposite side of the tree. With unparalleled swiftness, Will tied Edward's feet together on the far side of the tree. His hands still bound, Edward found himself completely immobilized.

"Now, stay!" Will barked as he rose to his feet and pointed his Bowie at Edward before sheathing it.

"You're going to just leave me here?"

"Not by yourself."

"You can't stay awake forever."

"You'd be surprised."

Will, having tired of the conversation, walked back to the fire and ignored Edward's continued attempts to bully him.

"Are you all right?" Will asked Evaline.

"Yeah. But what we gonna do about him?"

"Not sure exactly," Will mumbled as he shot a quick glance over his shoulder. "My gut tells me that he's in with freeing the slaves, but he could be a spy. The first is more likely. In either case he doesn't trust me, and he's not about to tell me anything. Until I know for sure, I'm not letting him out of my sight tonight."

"Can I talk to him?"

Will hesitated for a moment.

"Sure. I just wouldn't tell him too many details."

Evaline nodded in acknowledgment as she moved away from the fire. Oddly, she felt no fear as she approached the bound visitor. Edward watched her move toward him almost as if he intended to change her disposition by the sheer force of his gaze. Evaline kept her distance from him in spite of his bonds. Before assuming a seated position, she returned his gaze confidently.

"You know, things'll go a lot betta for you if you do what he says."

"Is he sending you over here to do his work for him?"

"He ain't sent me. I come on my own."

"Then why are you with him if you're not here to do whatever it is that he wants you to do?"

"Will don't trust you, and I don't neither, so I ain't gonna tell you all the details, but you could say that Will done helped me more in a few days than a lot of other people dat I's known a long time."

"Helping you or himself?"

"Oh, he ain't got nothin' out o' this deal. I can tell you dat."

"You sure about that? How do you know?"

Evaline inhaled deeply.

"Listen, is you really tryin' to help da slaves, or is you jus' spying for da Yankees? Cause if you's a spy, maybe I should jus' go ahead and shoot you where you is."

"You couldn't shoot anyone even if you wanted."

"You think?"

Edward hesitated momentarily, almost as if he sensed something in Evaline's response that caught him off guard. He had assumed that he understood all that there was to know of the woman before him, but he began to sense that she possessed a profoundly different personality than what he expected. He quickly regained his composure.

"If I'm a spy for the Yankees, why should you shoot me? You should want to join me."

Evaline laughed quietly.

"What country you been livin' in? Dem men in blue ain't hardly got any more love for us coloreds than da men in gray. I ain't exactly excited about becomin' massa Lincoln's slave."

Evaline's insight was impressive as Edward knew himself that the only safety for runaways lay in making the long and dangerous journey to Canada. The general belief of most Americans, North and South, was that the Negro race was inferior and that the best solution was to deport them back from whence they came or maintain them in their current status. True, there were those who saw through the thick and shaded curtain that lay across most people's hearts, but these remained in the minority.

"Who told you all of that?" Edward asked. "Him?"

"He ain't told me nothing' that I hadn't seen with my own eyes."

"Then just what *has* he done for you?"

Evaline paused for a moment, understanding the implication buried in Edward's tone of voice.

"He's my friend," Evaline responded calmly. "And he ain't laid a hand on me."

Evaline then rose to her feet and turned her back on her shocked prisoner. Having taken a few steps toward the fire, she stopped suddenly and turned to face Edward once more.

"You know, you sho' is a piece of work. You goes around gettin' all upset when people looks at us and judges us because we black before dey even knows us. And den you gonna sit der and say all kinds o' bad stuff about Will jus' 'cause he's white. Dat don't make no sense."

Evaline then turned once again and returned to the fire. Will, seeing her return, picked up the Spencer and moved to sit a short distance from Edward. He sat confidently with his legs stretched out in front of him, crossed at the ankles. He laid the Spencer gently across his knees and stared directly at Edward, who initially returned his gaze.

"And just what are you doing?" growled Edward.

"Showing you that I can go without sleep."

"And later teach me the error of my ways?"

"No. If I know anything about Evaline, she's already done that."

"And how do you know?"

"Because that's what she did for me."

*****

The night crept by slowly, but Will kept his promise and never ceased his constant vigilance over his prisoner. Edward dosed in and out of an uneasy sleep, fearful of the intentions of the nearby Confederate. Dawn found both Edward and Evaline asleep while Will continued to study the mechanism of his Spencer. The dilemma of what to do with Edward was foremost on his mind as he studied the rifle, but no attractive solution was immediately apparent. Will could not leave him bound, yet he did not trust him enough to set him free. The only viable solution was one that Will did find particularly palatable. Yet, if he could get Evaline across the Rappahannock, then all of his travails would pale in comparison.

The early morning rays drove the gloom from the forest floor, and a gentle breeze began to rustle the leaves over Will's head. The last wisps of smoke from the dying embers wafted across Will and reminded him of hundreds of other mornings where he had awakened to the smell of wood smoke. Edward was the first to stir, but upon stretching he was reminded of his bonds and quickly looked at his feet to find them still tied firmly around the tree. Peering over to his right, he was greeted by the unending vigilance of the Confederate. In the flickering gloom of the previous night, Edward had been unable to see his captor plainly, and he found himself surprised at the man staring back at him. Will, although his features had been deeply etched by the horrors of war, still held an expression of intelligence that could never be washed completely away. In spite of the kindness that filtered through the rough exterior, Will's blue eyes were incredibly discerning and seemed to pierce all that would attempt to shield the truth. He was tall and lean, yet dignified. The weathered gray coat he wore like the robe of a king, and his weapon he wielded like a scepter. He was not the man Edward had expected.

"Good morning, sunshine," Will greeted with a smile.

Edward did not respond immediately.

"You must not be a morning person," Will taunted. "If you'll behave, I'll untie you from that tree."

"Very well."

"Very well meaning that you're going to behave?"

"Yes."

"Very well, then."

Will rose from his seated position and moved over to where Edward's feet were tied. With his weapon at the ready, Will knelt down and nimbly untied his hands and feet before placing the ropes in his haversack. He then looked directly at Edward, all signs of joking laid aside.

"I'm giving you the benefit of the doubt here. I'm giving you a chance to prove yourself, even if you don't deserve it. But, let me tell you something, and I want this to be clear. If you at any time endanger us or even appear to be, I'll shoot you without hesitation and leave your carcass for the animals to deal with. And don't think you can run. I can hit you from distances you can't imagine. You understand?"

There was no denying that Will meant exactly what he said, as his previous expression was replaced by a steely coldness, and Edward marveled that both personalities could exist in one human being.

"You're taking me with you?"

"I don't trust you at all, but I'm no murderer. I also think it's unwise simply to release you here to go about whatever it is that you were up to. You'll have to forgive me if I assume that you're up to no good. You've certainly given me no evidence to the contrary."

"You don't understand, I have to..."

"Have to what?" Will interrupted. "Is there something you want to tell me?"

Edward fell silent and cast his eyes down to the ground,

unwilling to look at the soldier before him.

"Very well, then. You'll be joining us until you see fit to let us in on whatever your occupation is. I'm leaving your hands bound, and you'll walk in front of me at all times. We don't have much to eat, but, as I told you before, we'll share what we've got. As soon as I feel we've put enough distance behind us, we'll turn you loose."

Will grabbed one of the few remaining pears and handed it to Edward who, after momentarily studying the fruit, accepted it and began to eat. Evaline then passed a canteen to him, and he drank from it before passing it back. Will then stood, his Enfield slung across his back and the Spencer at the ready.

"Time to move on. Edward, you get in front of me."

Edward still eyed the Southerner with a suspicious glance, but he also realized that he had little choice in the matter, and so he reluctantly obeyed. Will kept his distance behind Edward to avoid any sudden attack, should his new companion tire of his present condition. Evaline joined them, and the trio set off through the forest.

"Now, this is one unusual sight," Will mumbled to himself. "A Confederate, a runaway slave, and a freeman running off through the woods together."

The wilderness seemed to have no end. It consisted of never-ending stretches of tangled trees and underbrush piled on top of each other and then twisted into some impenetrable fabric. Birds weaved in and out of the thick scrub and cocked their heads to the side as if in amazement at the identity of those who had invaded their domain. The traveling had been tedious before, but now with the addition of Edward, the pace was agonizingly slow. Will pushed onward, fueled not only by the desire to assist Evaline, but by the equally intense yearning to be rid of his cumbersome prisoner. He continued to agonize over his direction, sensing somehow that he should have already reached the river. In addition, he felt a sense of embarrassment in his previous confidence that he could successfully navigate a foreign terrain. Yet, he also knew that his previous conclusions had been both accurate and logical. Edward probably knew the terrain better than any in the group, but Will was not about to reveal his anxieties to his prisoner.

As the sun began its slow descent toward the western horizon, Will called his column to a halt again as he studied the terrain once more. Will's expression did not go unnoticed by Edward, and he studied the Confederate for a moment before speaking.

"You strike me as a man who needs direction," Edward began.

"Not in the way you might imagine."

"I'm not talking from a philosophical standpoint. I mean from a navigation standpoint."

"I'm fine."

"No, you're not."

Will didn't respond, but having studied his surroundings sufficiently, he motioned for Edward to resume his forward motion.

"I think I can help."

"Even if you could, why should I trust you? It's not like you've exactly been open and honest with me."

Edward inhaled deeply and studied Evaline's expression before responding.

"You were right earlier," Edward began without removing his gaze from Evaline. "I am what you would call a conductor on the Underground Railroad. It is my job to guide the runaways to the next safe house across the Rappahannock."

Edward stopped momentarily.

"You know you could shoot me right here for what I'm telling you."

Will nodded.

"I know, but I told you I meant you no harm, and I mean to show you that I'm a man of my word."

"Are you going to tell me your *real* story now?"

"I already did."

Evaline nodded in agreement as Edward realized that Will had been telling him the truth. An unfathomable one, but the truth nonetheless.

"Very well," Edward continued. "Then let me impress you with a little observation of my own. My assessment of you earlier was poor, so allow me to redeem myself."

"Go ahead."

"You're not merely a regular foot soldier. You're one of the sharpshooters."

"Fair enough. And just how did you come to that conclusion?"

"You told me earlier that you could hit me at unbelievable distances if I tried to escape. I did not perceive that as an idle threat."

"That was wise."

"And I can take you at your word that you are not leading us into some sort of trap, but you are honestly trying to get her across the Rappahannock?"

"Listen," Evaline piped in. "You can bet dat if Will here was tryin' to get me into some kind o' trap, he sho' 'nuff has given up plenty o' chances to do it. We's been surrounded by more soldiers dan you could shake a stick at."

Edward's eyes, in spite of Evaline's reassurance, still moved nervously between her and the Confederate. Never before had he seen such an unlikely combination of allies, but something deep within, although he was loathe to admit it, reminded him that he had never seen two people more devoted to the well-being of the other.

"All right, then," Edward began. "I can help you. If you're really doing what you say you are for the reasons that you say, then you should let Evaline come with me. I know this country far better than you, and I have made this journey many times. I also know the safe houses and the safest route for her to take. Situations like this are exactly the ones that I can deal with."

"This area is a little different than the other times that you've passed through. The armies are much closer, and we've already had unfortunate encounters with them. You'll have to forgive me if I'm not willing to let go of my responsibility so quickly. The distance between here and the Rappahannock may not be too far as the crow flies, but I can promise you that we haven't seen the last of the soldiers. I could use your help navigating, and you need my protection."

"Your presence really isn't necessary. We can avoid the Confederates, and I really have nothing to fear from the northern troops."

"Is that so? Then why not turn her over to the first Union picket that you come across? And remind me, exactly why are safe houses necessary all the way across the North to Canada if there is such widespread support for the Negro above the Mason-Dixon?"

Edward did not respond, but Evaline instead.

"I ain't about to leave Will. You can help us if you wants to, but whatever we's gonna do, we's gonna do with him."

Edward seemed annoyed at Evaline's unwillingness to leave her gray-clad companion behind, and he cast a condemning glance at Will.

"All this trouble for an inferior?" Edward asked sarcastically.

"She's not an inferior," the Confederate responded. "She's my friend."

*****

Will slept poorly that night as his thoughts were occupied by Evaline's future. He did not trust Edward, although he had no specific reason to doubt the authenticity of his claims. Yet it was more than just his new companion that caused him to feel anxious. He could not tell exactly what it was that produced his doubts, and that fact was probably what troubled him the most. He looked over at Evaline sleeping soundly on his bedroll. Somehow, invisible though the threat might be, she was still in great danger, and Will despised the shadowy nature of what was undeniably lumbering through the forest toward them.

*****

Daybreak found all three of the companions still in the same places as they had been before sundown, and, as usual, Will was the first to awaken fully. He sat for a moment, listening to the chorus of songbirds announcing the arrival of another day. Soon, Edward and Evaline were both awake, and the small group sat looking at each other as if they expected the other to begin the inevitable discussion. Edward finally broke the silence.

"We're almost through the worst part of the wilderness. I think our first priority is to get food and supplies. Not too far from here is a road that runs east and west. Only a little way down that road is a safe house, and we should be able to get what we need there. From that point on, we make straight for the Rappahannock. I know the ford there very well. You just have to make sure you know where it is; otherwise, you'll run right into the Confederate troops there. Fredericksburg has always got something going on around it."

"You trust these safe houses?"

"I have had several contacts with them. We can trust them. They're good people."

Will nodded in response.

"Are we ready?" Edward asked.

"Let's go," Will responded. "Same way as before. Edward, you lead the way. I may have loosed your hands, but I give you the same warning that I gave you when you were still tied up. You lead us straight and true, you hear? If for no other reason than for her sake."

Edward nodded.

"You ready?" Will asked as he turned toward Evaline.

"I's ready."

"Then let's go."

*****

As the trio traveled, the thickets did seem to thin as Edward had predicted, and movement among the underbrush became less of a chore. The sun penetrated the branches with greater ease, and as Will viewed the terrain ahead, he could begin to appreciate what seemed to be a clearing. Catching Edward's attention, Will pointed to the lighter area ahead.

"That's the road I was talking about earlier," Edward responded in a hushed tone. "It's not infrequent that there are travelers along it, so we need to be as quiet as possible. We'll travel alongside it in the woods until we reach the house, and then we'll cross."

"How far up ahead is it?"

"Two hundred yards at the most."

Edward then turned once again and resumed his previous course. Something in the pit of Will's stomach remained unsettled; yet for some reason, the unease was not directed at Edward. Will's grasp on the Spencer tightened as his head moved slowly from side to side observing his flanks.

Just as he had promised, Edward turned west about fifty yards from the road and began to follow its course. Looking through the underbrush, Will could see the cut of the dirt road as it scored through the forest, but he saw no traffic upon it, military or civilian. He continued to inspect behind every tree trunk and obstruction, fully expecting at some point to uncover an ambush waiting for them. Evaline seemed perfectly at ease, and Will thought it best to keep his anxieties to himself, as informing the young woman about them would serve no good purpose.

After traveling for perhaps a mile or so along the road, Edward stopped suddenly and pulled his small group together. He continued to speak in a whisper as if expecting someone to overhear.

"The safe house is not far from here. We need to cross the road and then make our way there."

Will looked at Evaline, who seemed to be showing no signs of distress.

"You still holding up all right?"

"I's fine."

"Then let's move on. Just one thing. When we cross the road, I want to lead the way."

Edward's brow wrinkled for a moment.

"Why is that?"

"I want to be the first to check out the other side. I want you two to stay here on this side until I give you the signal that everything is safe. I trust my instincts."

Will could see in Edward's expression that he did not trust his intentions and that he remained doubtful of his true purpose.

"Just give me this request. I'll never be out of your sight. Everything here is not as it should be, that's all I can tell you."

"You seen somethin,' Will?"

"No, but I always expect to."

Edward sighed heavily as he contemplated Will's request.

"Fine, but never out of my sight."

"Fair enough."

Will slid the Enfield from his shoulder, quickly assessed its status, and slung the carbine across his neck before moving toward the road. He felt as some false prophet speaking to the others of that which he had no evidence. Yet the deep sense of uneasiness would not leave him, and he could not allow them to proceed until he had made sure that nothing was amiss.

As he approached the road, the forest began to clear, revealing the usual open state of Virginia forests. Upon reaching the tree line at the road's edge, Will knelt down and closed his eyes. He listened intently but heard nothing except the gentle rustling of the breeze in the tops of the hardwoods. Opening his eyes, he studied the ruts of the dirt road but saw no evidence of any recent traffic. As far as he could see to his left and right, he saw no movement. Standing up, he stepped out into the road amidst a sense of vulnerability that he had not felt in quite some time. He heard only the sound of the loose dirt under his shoes as he crossed the road and arrived at the other side. He turned around and studied his surroundings once more, but nothing had changed. Looking back through the forest, he saw Evaline and Edward hiding among the trunks, Edward's piercing gaze never leaving the Confederate even at a distance. Will waved them forward, feeling almost as a commanding officer ordering his men into the face of the enemy.

As the pair approached Will, he observed them making their way among the trees and suddenly felt great compassion. Lost souls, weaving in and out of life's moments, searching for a peace that would only come when this world had passed away completely. And how few would find that peace, for the road and gate were so small, eclipsed by the noise of the broad and wide road upon which the world about them traveled. Perhaps he was not so different from them after all, for the world about him swirled also in an inferno of violence that threatened to sweep his humanity from the narrow path. Had it not been for the unseen hand in front of him, gentle yet firm, he would have been completely lost long ago. And so he was to them.

As soon as Edward's feet touched the road's dirt surface, Will heard the thunder of the hoof beats off to his left, and the ominous sensation that had smoldered in his innermost self burst into full flame.

"Get back!" Will yelled, but the horsemen were already turning the corner and bearing down on Will. Edward and Evaline scurried back into the forest, but they had already been spotted by the approaching force. Will stepped out to the middle of the road and raised his hands up as a signal to stop.

"Wait, wait! They're mine!" he called, but the horde pressed ever forward.

"Deserter!" came the cry, followed by a shot and a puff of white smoke. The bullet sang an ominous tune as it passed his ear and hammered into a trunk behind him. Instinctively, Will raised the Enfield and, with the pull of the trigger, unhorsed the lead rider. He could no longer see Evaline and Edward, and he dove quickly back across the road to follow them. The men were already pouring into the woods in pursuit.

"Get back to the wilderness!" Will screamed as took up a position behind a maple and swapped the Enfield for his Spencer. Cocking the hammer, he felled yet another rider just as he was passing into the underbrush. A bullet tore at the bark above his head, and Will quickly dispatched the shooter with a round that sent dust flying from the front of his coat.

"Cry havoc!" Will grunted through clenched teeth as he felled another horseman, the bark from the maple raining about him. He darted swiftly from behind the maple for another shot, but his attackers had realized the futility of a frontal assault against the Confederate and were all scampering to his flanks to flush him.

However, just as Will was ready to squeeze off a shot at the lead horse, all of the remaining riders turned suddenly and disappeared into the dense forest beyond. Will remained motionless, the Spencer still bonded firmly to his shoulder. Sensing no movement, Will burst forward in pursuit.

The noise of the horses crashing through the underbrush was unmistakable, and the shouting of commands as the men hunted Will's companions tore at his soul. Gunshots rang out, followed closely by the screams of a woman and then silence. Two more shots rang out further to Will's left. A horse flashed briefly between two distant trunks, but there was no opportunity for a shot. Will continued running, ambivalent to the underbrush tearing at him as he forged ahead. The hoof beats grew fainter, even as Will ran at top speed. He soon had to stop altogether, and he leaned forward on his knees, sucking in as much of the forest air as possible.

Falling to his knees, Will closed his eyes and listened intently, partly to listen for any sound of the enemy, and partly to shut out the shroud of agony that suddenly descended over him.

There was sudden movement off to his left. His eyes quickly moved in that direction and, seeing nothing, he swiftly flattened himself against a nearby hickory. The movement was intermittent, the rustling of the leaves starting and stopping as someone moved cautiously through the forest. Will eased the Spencer to the ground and pulled the LeMat from his belt. When the footsteps were just behind the hickory, Will whirled around and struck the intruder squarely in the chest, knocking him flat on his back. The sound of a cocking hammer was followed swiftly by the thrusting of the weapon into the intruder's face, and it was only the sound of a familiar voice that halted Will from pulling the trigger.

"Will!"

Peering into the face of his captive, Will recognized Edward, his face bloodied from a small gash carved by a grazing bullet into the left side of his forehead.

"Will, don't! I didn't have anything to do with this! It was the Home Guard."

Will, having regained his composure, pointed the LeMat away and slowly released the hammer. He knew that Edward was correct, as the Home Guards would have no love for runaways, or for one perceived as a deserter.

"I know. I'm sorry. I thought you were one of them."

Will looked about frantically.

"Where is Evaline?"

Edward responded only with a slow shaking of his head. Will's eyes closed and his head dropped as if in shame.

"What are we going to do?"

Will inhaled deeply and slowly lifted his head toward the sky without opening his eyes. As he exhaled slowly, he lowered his face and opened his eyes, the determination showing through his icy stare.

"We're going to find her, and you're coming with me."

Chapter VIII

Without delay, Will quickly recovered his Enfield and in one seamless motion reloaded the weapon. The Confederate was much too modest to take pride in his work, but on this occasion he did, if only for a moment, inspect the carnage that his marksmanship had incurred. The bodies lay strewn across the forest floor with their horses standing nearby in silent vigil. Still firmly in the grip of one of the men was a Spencer identical to the one that he had acquired earlier. Finding two of these weapons in such a short period of time was more than mere coincidence, and Will quickly emptied the new weapon of its remaining cartridges to replace the ones he had spent defending himself. Placing the extra shells in his pocket, he stood and looked once more at the fallen about him. Try as he might, he was unable to conjure up any semblance of compassion for those so willing to extinguish lives that they knew nothing about. There remained no excuse for such ignorance. Never, even in his war-hardened state, would he dream of attacking another without just provocation. But upon defending himself in such a predicament, he had always promised that his opponent would pay a heavy price for his lack of discernment.

Realizing that he was wasting time, Will quickly turned and picked up another Enfield from the forest floor. He then grasped the reigns of two of the horses, secured the new rifles, and began to lead the mounts back to Edward who leaned heavily against a nearby tree. Will could tell in a glance that the man was completely spent, both emotionally and physically. Nevertheless, he brought one of the horses to Edward and handed him the reins.

"First fire-fight?"

Edward nodded.

"It'll pass. I'm going to need for you to dig deep now. You think you can do it? For her?"

"I can do it."

"Good. Then let's ride. We're going to need the horses for the time being to catch them. It shouldn't be too hard to track them. We've just got to be careful because they can hear us coming."

"Honestly, do you think we have any chance of finding her?"

"Yes. And I'm always honest."

The two men then mounted the animals, and Will took the lead as he plunged back deeper into the wilderness. However, Will soon turned his mount to face Edward once more.

"Here, you carry the Spencer."

Edward nodded, taking the weapon and slinging it across his shoulder. Will remained motionless for a moment longer, his gaze never leaving Edward as if to reinforce the trust that the Confederate was now placing in him by allowing him to ride armed and to his rear. The soldier then nodded slowly as he turned his mount.

"Don't lose it. These weapons are our lifeblood."

*****

The snapped branches and upturned earth made the task of tracking the Home Guard easier than Will had expected. Even the heavy brush of the wilderness was unable to mask the signature of the horses, as the large animals had pushed with some speed ahead of the pursuing Confederate. Even with an armed freeman riding just behind him, Will's mind was still occupied only by Evaline's fate. He could only assume that the stiff resistance that the group had met at Will's hands had forced them to head cross-country to an area of safety or reinforcement. However, a clever leader would not find it difficult to set an ambush in the thick underbrush where they could easily rid themselves of their pursuers. Yet, Will's instinct sensed panic in the air. Not the panic of a captured slave, but of an inexperienced leader retreating in fear from the face of an apparently superior enemy. Will remembered General Jackson's admonishment never to back down from pursuing the enemy, and he swore to himself that he would push on until the job was done.

"If You'll give me the strength," Will whispered under his breath. "I'll never back down."

*****

The sun was Will's ally, and yet it seemed to move more swiftly than ever across the sky toward its rendezvous with the western horizon. Time was running out, for Will knew that if night fell before he found Evaline, he would likely never find her. Edward, too, was aware of this fact and watched the falling sun with growing apprehension. Will stopped momentarily as if to enjoy the fleeting rays, but he closed his eyes and shut out all distractions as he listened intently to the world about him. Faintly and intermittently, he heard the whisper of distant voices. Will's hand instantly extended backward at Edward to signal him to stop. Turning around in the saddle, Will's hand moved to his lips and then motioned for Edward to dismount. Silently, the two men slid off of their mounts and tied the horses to a nearby tree. Will remained silent but worked feverishly to untie the Enfields from his horse's flank. He then handed one of the rifles to Edward while placing the butt of the rifle on the ground. Nimbly, his fingers reached into his cartridge box, and in only a matter of seconds, the rifle was loaded. Will then exchanged the loaded rifle for the one Edward was holding and repeated the process.

"I don't know how many of them are left," Will whispered as he rammed the charge down the barrel. "You stay close behind me at all times. Do not say a word. When I call for them, I'll need you to hand the rifles to me precisely when I ask for them. You cannot delay. Do you understand?"

Will's tone was not that of a master to a servant, but instead of one ally to another. Will knew he could not rescue Evaline alone, and he would need Edward's help if they were ever to see her again.

"I can do it," Edward responded.

"Then follow me."

Leaving the horses behind, Will turned left and began to undertake a circular path around the location where he guessed the voices were coming. He stopped frequently, if only briefly, to listen. He still could not make out any words, but the tone of the voices was one of frustration, mixed with a sense of urgency. Feeling his own sense of growing urgency, Will plunged ahead through the forest looking back only briefly to ensure that Edward was keeping pace. The darker interior of the forest began to give way to rays of light that filtered in from straight ahead as a clearing became apparent. Will flattened himself out against the back of a tree, motioning for Edward to do the same. Holding the Enfield against his chest, he could hear the voices once again only a short distance ahead in the clearing. Peering carefully around the edge of the tree, he searched quickly for any movement nearby. Seeing none, he motioned for Edward to follow and raced to just inside the tree line before coming to rest on his knees with his left shoulder against a hickory trunk.

Lifting his head above a fallen trunk directly in his path, Will peered out into the clearing. About fifty yards and slightly to his left was a barn which had fallen into some disrepair, as many of the boards along the sides were missing, and gaps were apparent at random intervals in the roof. There was no livestock visible, and Will guessed that the structure had not been used in some time. Altogether, it was a tranquil landscape except for the activity taking place just inside the barn. To his horror, Will saw that three men had quickly thrown a length of rope up and over one of the remaining rafters and fashioned a noose at one end. The noose was now wrapped tightly around Evaline's neck, and the young woman was standing precariously, hands tied behind her back, on an old wooden stool. She had obviously been handled roughly, as the clothes that Will had given earlier fell about her form in a tangled and shapeless mass.

Just as Will's mind was attempting to assimilate all that was occurring, he saw one of the men step forward and give a swift kick to the stool that was the only barrier between Evaline and certain death. The stool did not completely give way at first, but the man's second kick followed swiftly behind the first.

In an instant, the Enfield was up and rested across the log in front of Will. It was too late to prevent the loss of support from beneath Evaline, and instead of targeting her attackers, the Confederate took aim at the tiny cord that extended up into the rafters. The rifle felt right against his shoulder, a trusted and dependable friend when all else was frail and fleeting. It was more than a cold, inanimate object of steel and wood, for it seemed to beat in accord with his own pulse, the rhythm of the two in perfect harmony as the thin front blade settled on top of the rope. Will squeezed the trigger.

The projectile exploded from the barrel and raced across the open space before slicing the cord neatly in two just as the stool crumbled beneath Evaline. Instead of feeling a sudden jerk as her full weight fell upon the anchored rope, she collapsed onto the dirt floor with the cord hanging harmlessly around her neck.

"Now!" screamed Will as his open hand extended back to Edward. True to his word, Edward quickly tossed the ready rifle into Will's waiting palm. The hand closed instinctively around the stock as the Confederate swung the weapon around until it rested upon the trunk ahead of him. One of the men in the barn had drawn a pistol and aimed the weapon directly at Evaline. Will's second shot knocked the man off his feet and sent the pistol flying harmlessly through the air. A round from the Spencer found its mark as the second man attempted to drag Evaline out of the open doorway to finish the deed out of sight of Will's deadly fire. The third man took flight, but Will was already on his feet and running out into the open field. He threw the Spencer up to his shoulder and squeezed off a shot that clipped the fleeing man on his right arm. He then fell on the dusty floor of the barn and did not rise.

Will chambered another round in the Spencer as he charged across the field and through the open doorway. Swiftly, he knelt at the young woman's side and loosened the rope around her neck before slipping it over her head and tossing it away. Even before he could finish the task, Evaline had wrapped her arms around his neck.

"Will," the young woman breathed into his shoulder. "I knowed you'd come. I's prayin' and I knowed even when they put dat rope around my neck dat you'd come for me."

A momentary pause followed before Will was able to gather himself enough to speak.

"I'm so sorry, child, that it took me so long. I got here as fast as I could."

The two remained motionless as Will held the young woman as one of his own. At that moment, Edward entered the barn and marveled at what he saw before him. It violated every natural law that he had ever been taught. He knew previously without any shadow of doubt that the Confederates cared nothing for his race. Yet doubt began to enter into what had been a certainty only a few moments before, as there was nothing artificial or forced in the scene before him. Movement suddenly distracted Edward as the young man lying in the dust began to move. The change had not gone unnoticed by Will, and the Confederate quickly handed the Spencer to his companion.

"If he tries to escape, shoot him."

Edward nodded and moved closer to the young man, keeping the carbine trained on him at all times. Will then turned his attention back to Evaline.

"Are you all right?"

"I's okay."

"Excuse me, then, while I handle some business."

Evaline's expression held a measure of concern as she did not fully understand Will's intentions toward the young man. The Confederate rose to his feet and paced calmly to stand in front of the terrified man lying in the dust. He was young, not yet out of his teens, with blonde hair and striking blue eyes. Will's mind immediately conjured up a hundred other similar faces that he had taught through the years, but the lesson he was about to teach this particular student was completely different than any he had ever taught in South Georgia. The young man tried to meet Will's steely gaze in an attempt to show his bravery, but Will could easily sense his inner trepidations.

"It's my judgment that you've fallen in with the wrong crowd," Will began.

"I'd say it's more you that's hangin' out with the wrong folks."

"And why, would you say, is that the case? No one in my group opened fire on you without cause."

"You're a deserter."

"Am I now? You're mistaken, and it would have been a good idea to make sure of your facts before passing judgment on others and deciding to hand out the death penalty with such impunity."

"You would have made the same judgment if you had been in our shoes and seen you come out of the woods with them," replied the young man.

"For someone who just met me, you seem to know an awful lot about what goes on in my head. Your assumptions disturb me."

Without hesitation, Will unsheathed the intimidating Bowie and approached the young man whose eyes grew suddenly wide in fear. However, instead of using the blade for a more ominous purpose, Will knelt down and lifted the wounded right arm. With surprising speed, Will sliced the bloodied sleeve open to reveal a wound that carved deeply into the overlying skin but had spared the muscles underneath.

"How many men have you killed, son?"

There was no reply.

"Then let me tell you something," Will continued as he tended the wound. "It's not too late to stop believing the lies that they're telling you. They say that there's a difference in God's sight between killing for your country or self-defense as opposed to killing for your own purposes, and I guess that's so. But I'll tell you this. There's very little difference in here."

Will's finger pointed ominously toward the boy's heart.

"You can try to cover it up with whatever you want. Hate, anger-- you name it. You can even try to tell yourself that you enjoy it, and it's just the natural order of things. None of that matters. When you finally reach the point that the killing no longer bothers you, that the enemy is no longer even human, then you've reached a point when

143

you yourself are no longer human. You're an animal."

Will finished tending the wound and sheathed the Bowie.

"So I tell you once more; you've fallen in with the wrong crowd. You have no need to fear me. God himself will hold you responsible."

Will then stood up.

"The wound on your arm is going to be fine. Keep it clean. I don't care what the doctors say, a little soap and water never hurt anything. The way I see it, that wound is the least of your problems. You'd better get home and rethink what you're doing. Now get out of here before you run into someone with less patience than I."

The boy hesitated for a moment as he stared up at Will and Edward. Then, still unsure of his captor's intentions, he slowly rose from the dust and made his way slowly out the rear of the barn, casting several nervous glances across his shoulder as he did so. Will and Edward watched him disappear into the distance, each with a different opinion as to what his fate would be.

"He's never going to change," Edward stated with conviction. "You should have finished him when you had the chance rather than scraping him on the arm."

"Who said I was trying to scrape him on the arm?" Will replied in a dark tone.

*****

The journey back to the horses was a silent one, almost as if the gravity of the circumstances that had just passed were beyond the capability of words to describe. Perhaps most of all, Will was grateful to have Evaline back in his company, as he was certain that he could not have borne the loss of someone for whom he felt so responsible. Failure had been avoided only by a hair's breadth, and Will could only breathe a silent prayer of thanks that his nerve had not failed him. Try as he might, however, the image of the stool collapsing and the horrible image of Evaline hanging at the end of an intact rope would not leave his mind. The horses remained tied exactly where the men had left them. Will loosed his horse and had Evaline mount up for the return journey after securing the unloaded Enfields to its flank. He had already reloaded his own weapon prior to leaving the barn. Looking about him at the surrounding woods, he momentarily gave the appearance of someone looking for something he had lost, but the moment passed, and Will began to lead his companions back along the trail that they had followed earlier.

"You ain't gonna ride, Will?" Evaline asked as she watched the Confederate lead the pair on foot.

"No, not right now," Will responded with an exhausted smile. "I think I'll walk for a little."

"You thinks better when you walks? Is dat it?"

Will laughed to himself as he watched the ground in front of his feet.

"Something like that."

*****

There was no opportunity to cover the distance back to the road before nightfall, and so the trio began to set up for another night in the woods. There was no fire, as Will still felt very uneasy about his surroundings, although his exterior did not reveal his inner concerns. Edward also felt uneasy and sensed that at any moment the Home Guard would ambush them once more. In the fading light, he watched the movements of the Confederate, and although he was at first reluctant to admit it, he felt a comfort in his presence that he had not felt in quite some time. His own occupation was dangerous, and capture while helping escaped slaves meant almost certain death. Yet the loneliness of his profession was perhaps more difficult to endure than the threat of death itself. Dying alone was the worst fate Edward could imagine. Yet the loneliness he felt seemed to pale in comparison to that borne by the gray-clad man nearby.

Edward had heard stories of the sharpshooters, and none were particularly flattering. They were supposedly a rugged and heartless group of warriors who took a sort of sadistic pride in their handiwork. In addition to picking targets of elevated rank, they were also known to have selected their distant targets by something as trivial as what the other soldier was wearing. If shoes were needed, then an appropriately sized target was chosen. The same was done for any type of clothing or item that was needed. They worked alone or in small groups as opposed to the larger infantry units, and the stealth of their attacks was sometimes just as deadly as the bullets themselves. They were an entirely different class of soldier, waging war on the mind as well as the body.

Yet as Edward observed the Confederate marksman, he saw none of these baser elements. In his mind he tried to apply them to him

145

regardless, but the stereotype would not adhere. He was a simple, yet educated man. His manner of speaking, although decorated by a heavy Southern accent, somehow seemed out of place in one possessing such marksmanship. There was no doubt that he cared for Evaline and was perfectly willing to sacrifice all that he had for her survival.

Edward rose from where he was seated and moved next to Will, sitting beside him. Will did not openly acknowledge his presence but continued to stare at the ground near his feet, where he traced a tangle of lines with a long hickory stick.

"Some day, huh?" Edward broke the silence.

Will nodded before responding.

"Yes. Some day. Better than most, but worse than some. How is your head?"

"It's fine. Only a scratch."

"You did well at the barn. You kept up your end of the bargain."

Edward was silent momentarily as he stifled his amazement that this man who single-handedly saved Evaline would ever consider thanking him for merely handing him the rifles.

"You're welcome, but I really didn't do anything."

"Of course you did. You had my back. You did well."

"Well, thank you."

"Tell me something."

"Okay."

"These people that you spoke of, the ones that we were trying to reach before the Home Guard got in our way. How well do you know them? Are they trustworthy?"

"I would place my life in their hands without a thought. I have known them for many years."

"And if they are a part of the Underground Railroad, exactly how will they feel about a Confederate showing up on their front steps?"

Prior to the question, Edward had not given the scenario much thought, although it had crossed his mind earlier that this particular situation might give him an opportunity to rid himself of his Southern companion. However, after realizing who Will truly was these thoughts had vanished, and Edward could see that Will had a legitimate concern.

"They are good Christian folks, Will. I don't mean like those that act good on Sunday only to live like the Devil the rest of the week. I mean that they get it, Will. All of it. You'll be treated with respect.

146

Just give me a chance to explain things when we get there because, like you said, I seriously doubt that they have ever seen the likes of you strolling up to their house."

Will nodded in response, satisfied at least that he had expressed his concerns to Edward. Tomorrow would be a new day, and he would face its challenges as he always had…one at a time.

*****

In spite of the near catastrophe at the hands of the Home Guard, Will slept well. Perhaps it was simply out of sheer exhaustion, but that night his slumbering mind remained clear of the usual torments often suffered by a soldier such as he. He awakened shortly before dawn with a renewed sense of strength and purpose as he went about his usual routine of checking the readiness of his weapons. Even though from his human viewpoint he could not see the future, he remained keenly aware, nonetheless, that events were falling out as they should. He was not merely adrift and rudderless upon the ocean of chance. He was alive for a reason and had found Evaline for that same reason.

As Will methodically reloaded the Spencer, he stopped for a moment and turned his eyes toward the sky. Above him was a majestic canopy of hickory, poplar, ash, and oak, and a gentle morning breeze was rustling the green canopy in a chorus honoring the sunrise. Will closed his eyes and listened even more intently. How different the wind of South Georgia sounded in the long-needled pines of home. It was almost a whisper, and yet buried within that softest of choirs was the sound of his name. Will listened again to the rustling of the Virginia forest but heard only the randomness of the inanimate. With a heaviness in his heart, Will slipped the last cartridge into the Spencer.

*****

Evaline and Edward were up not long after sunrise and began gathering their few belongings. There was very little food left, but Will insisted that the pair eat what was left, as he explained to them that he both thought and fought better on an empty stomach. After all, hunger pains were his constant companion in the Army of Northern Virginia, and he would hardly know how to conduct himself if that were not the case.

"I'll lead us back to the road, but once we're there, you take

147

over," Will explained as Edward stood to his feet. "I hope your friends are in a generous mood. We could sure use some supplies. Not that anybody really has that much to share these days."

"I'm sure they'll do what they can," Edward replied.

"As will we all," the Confederate responded as he turned his attention to Evaline. "You ready?"

Evaline responded with a smile and nodded her head in agreement. The events of the previous day still clung to her thoughts and cast a dark cloud over her emotions. She was eternally grateful to be alive, but her narrow escape constantly flashed through her mind. Leaving the scene of the incident as far behind her as possible was a welcome thought.

*****

The gray coat of the Confederate weaved skillfully among the trunks of the hardwoods as he lead his companions back the road from which their ordeal had begun. Will avoided the scene of the earlier battle and led them back by a slightly different route. Upon reaching the road, Will motioned for the pair to stop, and he stood gazing silently at the earthen highway for some time.

"We're going to try this again," he stated with the slightest hint of a smile. "Stay here while I have a look around."

Will slid the Enfield from his shoulder and readied the weapon by cocking the hammer. Stepping to the edge of the road, he swiftly scanned the area and crossed to the other side. As he entered the woods on the far side, he stopped and listened intently but heard no disturbances. He then turned and walked back to the road's edge and motioned for the two to join him. Emerging from the woods like hunted game, Evaline and Edward swiftly crossed the road and rode their horses past Will into the safety of the forest beyond. Will remained motionless and tuned his senses to focus on the slightest abnormality. Sensing none, Will lowered the hammer on the Enfield and turned to join his companions.

*****

As the trio journeyed into the forest beyond, Edward took the lead, and Will fell to the rear behind Evaline. The density and tangled nature of the forest began to abate, and the sparse undergrowth made traveling easier. As Will moved on, he felt unsettled, but it had nothing to do with an unseen enemy or

Edward's leadership. He had learned, through his travails as a soldier, to allow duty to overcome fear and to perform his duties flawlessly in the face of almost certain destruction. Facing Edward's acquaintances, however, was a task of a different nature altogether. He dreaded the encounter and were it not for Evaline, he would have turned and avoided it altogether. They would never understand him, never accept him. He would never convince them of his love of his home and how slavery was never the issue that caused him and his brothers to fight so tenaciously against such overwhelming odds. They would see only his gray covering, and all would be settled. The judgment would be passed instantly with no hope of appeal or plea. They would never hear the sound of his name through the long-needled pines of home.

*****

It was late in the afternoon when the group began to approach the farmhouse. The house sat in a small clearing with its rear facing the forest. It was a modest house, kept clean and tidy with a whitewashed fence surrounding all sides but the front. The forest sloped up gently as it approached the rear of the house, and Edward approached it confidently but cautiously as the trio emerged from the woods. There was a single gate in the center of the rear fence, and Edward stopped just before reaching it. Turning to Will, Edward dismounted and motioned for Evaline to move toward the gate.

"Stay here while I go and let them know that you are here. Don't worry. The fact that you are with us will be enough to convince them that you mean no harm. You have been kind to us, and the favor will be repaid."

"Very well," Will replied. "I'll wait for you to tell me when to come on."

Edward nodded and then turned back to Evaline. He unlatched the gate and the pair walked through it together, leaving the gray soldier to accept his fate. Evaline looked back at her friend with a hint of guilt at leaving him behind, but a nod from Will let her know that all was well. Unknown to the Confederate was the fact that Evaline's greatest concern was not that he was in danger, but the fear that he would be gone when she returned and that she would never see him again.

*****

Will waited for what seemed like an eternity, but he had expected no less. He could only imagine the discussion concerning his presence that was taking place in the house, and he was certain that several pairs of eyes were intermittently peering out the rear windows to size up what sort of man he might be. For that reason, Will made sure that he remained in plain view in spite of the fact that it went against all of his training. Nearby, Will found a straight hickory branch and, after retrieving it, sat down on the ground next to the inside gate and began to whittle grooves into one end to keep his mind occupied.

He was almost finished carving the grooves for the handle when the back door silently opened, and Edward walked out and began to make his way toward Will. It was dusk, and the long shadows and afterglow of sunset had given way to the murky gray of twilight. Will rose to his feet and gathered his few things about him. A part of him fully expected to be dismissed completely as an unwelcome intruder. After all, sending him away was a simple solution and would require none of the usual unpleasant methods of getting rid of unwanted visitors. However, Will did not sense that approach from Edward as he came to stand in front of him.

"Are you ready?" Edward asked.

"For what?" Will asked half jokingly.

"To come in. They have finally agreed to let you stay."

"How is Evaline?"

Edward held his response momentarily, still amazed that Will's first concern was the young woman.

"She is fine and being well cared for. I'm sorry about your wait. It took me a little longer than I thought it would."

"I told you that it wasn't going to be easy. People don't change their opinions very easily."

"Tell me about it," Edward replied. "So, are you ready to come in?"

Will nodded in response, and Edward then turned to lead the Confederate through the back door and to the warm glow beckoning from beyond.

Chapter IX

Will followed closely behind Edward as he walked up the back steps and through the rear door. He instinctively reached up to remove his hat upon entering the dwelling, but was quickly reminded that the article had been lost when Evaline was picking blackberries. He did remember to slip the Enfield and Spencer from his shoulder and leave them on the small porch. Passing through the rear entrance, Will immediately saw the warm glow of a fireplace from across the room. The room was well-furnished by Will's standards and most of the furniture was professionally made and not hewn roughly from common lumber. In the middle of the room was a rectangular table draped neatly with a white embroidered tablecloth and set with four porcelain place settings. Across the table sat Evaline, smiling broadly at the return of her friend. As Will entered the room, Evaline stood to her feet.

"See, dat's him! Dat's Will dat I been tellin' you about."

Will's attention was then drawn to his right where Evaline's comments were directed. There, standing silently to scrutinize the gray invader, was a middle aged couple. Evident from their facial expressions was the fact that the Confederate was present only against their better judgment. In spite of their unwelcoming expressions, Will smiled a thin smile and bowed his head in greeting.

"Good evening," Will began in hopes of avoiding an awkward silence. "Thank you for letting me come in. I promise I won't..."

"No appreciation is necessary," interrupted the gentleman in a flat tone. "It was the Christian thing to do."

Will nodded, accepting the distrust that was aimed at him.

"As I'm sure that you've been told, my name is William Mark Seymour and..."

Will hesitated as a thousand different ways to proceed crossed his mind simultaneously. There was so much of which he could speak, and many of the topics would have been close to his heart. He thought of telling them about where he was from, or perhaps even the reason that he and his brothers struggled on against the odds set against them. He even thought about hinting at the good deeds that he had done for his fellow man, but in the end he thought better of continuing along those lines and instead settled on a simple, but profound statement.

"...Evaline is my friend."

With those words, spoken with such sincerity, the atmosphere in the room suddenly changed, and it was no longer the Confederate who was on the defensive. The couple shifted uneasily as they appeared to search for some way to respond to this implausible situation. Evaline too seemed to await anxiously their response, as the fate of her friend seemed to depend on the statements that followed. Will, once again noting the four place settings on the table, understood his position and had no desire to humiliate his new acquaintances under their own roof.

"I want to thank you for letting me come in for a moment to see that Evaline is well cared for. If you all have a barn or some similar place that you don't mind me using, then I'll stay there tonight. I've lived so long out in the open that I'm not sure I can sleep indoors anymore."

Evaline, beginning to understand what was taking place, was the first to respond.

"Dey ain't no need in dat, Will. You can stay in here with da rest of us."

"It's fine, Evaline. Don't worry, I'm not going anywhere. I'll still be here in the morning."

Will then smiled and nodded respectfully to the couple before turning to Edward.

"I'll meet up with you in the morning."

Edward nodded in understanding and without hesitation put forth his hand to shake Will's. As the soldier turned to exit, he hesitated and faced his hostess once more.

"Ma'am, if I might trouble you by making one request."

Will motioned for her to step closer as if he were about to tell her something of great importance. She hesitated initially, but after giving her husband a sheepish glance, she moved next to the Confederate.

"If I might trouble you for a needle and a piece of thread I would be greatly obliged," Will requested in a whisper. "You see, we haven't had the easiest of journeys and Evaline is missing the two top buttons on her shirt which, I'm afraid, makes it difficult for her to protect her modesty. If you could provide her with some decent covering in the meantime, I would be glad to mend what I can."

"You can sew?" the hostess asked flatly.

"Ma'am, I can do many things I never dreamed possible."

"You don't have any extra buttons."

"Don't worry about that. I can make do with what I have."

She studied the Confederate momentarily and strangely did not sense any deceit. Before she could respond, her husband stepped forward to save her from the awkward situation.

"Follow me. I'll show you where you can stay."

Will hesitated a moment longer, but his hostess made no sign of movement. Realizing that his request was being denied, he nodded his head courteously and turned to follow the husband. Without speaking another word, the Confederate slipped through the door and was gone.

"Dey wasn't no cause for dat," Evaline stated with an icy chill that lingered long after her words had fallen from the air.

"What do you mean?" the hostess replied as if to deny any understanding of what had just occurred.

"You knows exactly what I mean. You jus' brings him in here and den sends him right back out without even givin' him yo names. Not to mention dat you don't even offer him no food or nothin'."

"Evaline, there are many dangerous things in this world, and we are only doing our best to protect you from what we can."

"From him? You thinks dat's what I need protectin' from?"

"Like I said, I don't expect for you to understand everything, but I do ask that you trust us."

"Why should I? Didn't you jus' hear what he said?"

"Trust me, most of that was just for show."

"You thinks so? I knows of several dead people wearin' gray coats within jus' a few miles o' here dat would say different."

"I've seen many of his kind come and go."

"I thought dat too, but trust me, you ain't never seen no one like him before."

"And why is it that you believe I should feel the same about him as you do?"

"'Cause you still breathin'."

*****

Before leaving the back porch, Will scooped up the Enfield and the Spencer by their straps and hoisted them over his shoulder. He then followed the man down the steps and around the right side of the house. Will's gaze never left the silent man as he studied his host at only an arm's length to his front. He seemed to have little concern for the soldier following behind him, and his eyes seemed directed at the ground as if he expected some unforeseen danger to spring from the earth itself. His was a tall man with broad shoulders, but the arms hung in a limp, almost defeated position at his sides, and he loped along as though carrying a great weight. The dark shape of the barn loomed up ahead, and Will knew that his time was brief. As the older man lifted the wooden crossbar to open the door, Will stepped to his side and assisted by pushing up on the end of the slab. The man then stretched out his hand, and with a steady arm rubbed his calloused hands over the door face before giving it a steady push. With a creaking groan the door swung open to reveal a palpable darkness.

"Seeing as to what you're used to, I suspect you won't be needing much."

Will nodded instinctively in the darkness. He then entered the barn and turned to face his host.

"You would be correct."

"There's a couple of lanterns over there. I suspect you got ways to light one."

"Yes, sir. I do."

"Then that's about it, I suppose."

"Yes, sir. You have been more than kind. This will be just fine. I will see you in the morning."

There was a long pause as the older man stopped and studied the Confederate in the blackness, as if he saw something in the absence of light that he did not perceive in its presence.

"Will you now?"

Will nodded instinctively once again.

"Yes, sir. I have to finish what I've started."

The older man did not move.

"So you do."

With those words he lingered a second longer, his stalwart frame silhouetted against the gray background for an instant before he turned and made his way back to the house by the way in which he came. As soon as he had departed, Will felt blindly for the lantern in the direction his host had indicated earlier. Luckily, his hand soon pressed against the cold tin and glass of the lamp. Removing his haversack, Will found his flint and steel and made a small fire in a handful of hay before lighting the lamp. He then snuffed out the hay with his foot and lifted the lantern for a better look at his surroundings. The barn was small and fairly typical with no distinguishing characteristics. Simple in its design, it was a square building with a small loft that stretched across the rear of the barn. Yet, as Will studied the structure, he could see that in spite of its simplicity, the carpenter had taken time to round corners and make certain that all of the joints dovetailed exactly. There were a scant number of tools hung neatly along the right wall but no livestock present, although the scent of farm animals hung heavily in the air. Looking back for a second glance, Will saw the other lantern and wasted no time in lighting it. Hanging the two lanterns on two separate posts to more evenly distribute the light, Will then sat beneath one of the lights and began to check his weapons methodically, his mind continuing to ruminate over the many questions that vexed him as he did so.

The environment in which he found himself was completely foreign, and he felt most unwelcome. He had heard much about those who opposed slavery but never imagined that he would become so engrained in the process of assisting a slave. Yet, Will also understood better than any that he was exactly where he was supposed to be. In spite of his sense of inadequacy, he knew that God alone had ordained his steps to bring him into contact with Evaline exactly when he did. For whatever reason, there was something that he could offer that no one else could.

As Will sat lost in deep thought, his attention was suddenly captured by a small flickering light that appeared near the house and began to make its way toward the barn. Will continued to watch its progress through the open barn door. As the light approached, he could not see its owner until the light from the lanterns in the barn illuminated the face of the woman from the house. In her hand she carried yet another lantern, but draped over her left arm was Evaline's shirt. She stood in the door opening almost as if she expected a harsh greeting from a discontented and shunned soldier, but Will remained where he was and smiled in greeting.

"Does your husband know you're out here talking to some strange man in the barn?"

The amber glow from the lanterns minimized the blush upon the woman's cheek, but she smiled in response, thankful for a reprieve in the heavy, uncomfortable atmosphere.

"Let's just say that my husband is a man of few words, and I often find it necessary to supplement his paucity of speech so we are not misunderstood."

"I can relate. Try wearing a gray uniform sometime and you will almost certainly be misunderstood."

The Confederate's host maintained her composure as she shifted her weight.

"I want to apologize for earlier as we extended none of the usual pleasantries to you that we would have to any other guest. As Evaline just reminded me, we did not even tell you our names."

"No offense was taken, ma'am," Will responded. "I don't blame anyone for being cautious in these times."

"In any case, my husband is John, and my name is Carolyn. Here, I thought you might want these."

Carolyn stepped forward and handed Evaline's shirt to Will along with a needle, two buttons and a length of thread.

"I could have taken care of that for you, but I surmised by the way you asked earlier that you are the type of man who prefers to fix problems himself."

Will nodded in appreciation.

"If only some problems were as easily solved with needle and thread," Will mused audibly. Carolyn's eyes temporarily departed from the soldier and searched about the barn as if looking for something hidden in the shadows before finally settling back upon the seated Confederate.

"Evaline has told me much of what has happened to you on your journey here."

"She is quite the story-teller."

"Yes, but I see now that she does not exaggerate."

Will looked up at Caroline as he detected a distinct change in her voice. He realized, with acute clarity, that he was witnessing a change in the older woman's opinion of him and that if he did not return the gesture her trust could vanish easily. Somehow, Evaline's account of their journey had shoved aside all preconceived notions and had brought clarity to the vision of a woman who had previously only seen the contemporary issues as black and white, right and wrong. And so his chance lay before him, and the Confederate, not without some trepidation, lay aside the hardened covering that had shielded him for so long and let humanity surface once more.

"I do not know what the future holds," Will responded quietly, as a father musing over the uncertain destiny of his child. "There is so much that I cannot protect her from."

Carolyn nodded in agreement as she paused to contemplate her answer. Suddenly, her lips curled into a smile as a thought came to her mind.

"Evaline has told me that you are a teacher, correct?"

"Yes. I used to teach. At least I taught those who would listen."

"Are you familiar with the writings of Charles Dickens? Particularly a work called *A Christmas Carol*?"

Will nodded.

"I received a copy not long before I left for the army. It was an excellent story."

"Indeed it was and is. I suspect that over time it will become one of his most famous works. Speaking of that story, do you remember the three spirits of Christmas?"

Will thought for a moment.

"Yes. Past, present and future, if my memory serves me well."

"Indeed it does. And if you will recall, old Scrooge is not at all afraid of the spirits of the present and past, but neither of them has any compassion on him at all. Yet, the future spirit is an entirely different matter. Its form is dark and shadowy, and its face is hidden by an ebony cloak. It never speaks to him but only points with a haunting finger. It is the future that Scrooge fears, and with all of the terror of the unknown, it is the future that finally grasps his full attention. It is only at the end when Scrooge sees his name upon the tombstone that he begs the spirit to allow him to sponge away the writing with a changed life. Yet, in spite of all of its dark and forbidding nature, it is the only one of the spirits that has compassion on him."

Will remained silent, understanding the parallels that Carolyn was drawing between his journey and the work of fiction.

"We are all terrified of the future because we know it not," Carolyn continued. "No matter our efforts, we cannot penetrate its cloak to see what lies ahead. And yet beside all that fear, we humans so easily forget that it is God himself who pens our story onto the pages of our life book and that He is infinitely good. He knows the future as well as our present and past, and yet with ultimate compassion He leaves a future full of promises that He will keep completely. Fear not, William Seymour. The future for you and Evaline, regardless of the outcome of this war, may yet prove to be the most compassionate of all."

A host of responses flooded the Confederate's mind simultaneously, and he felt completely inadequate to express any of them. Will could not remember the last time that another human being had spoken such words of comfort to him, and he felt infinitely unworthy. Perhaps it was for the better that the woman before him knew nothing of the deeds of which he was capable or that he had already performed in the defense of his homeland. Or perhaps it would matter little to her if she did know. For a fleeting moment Will wished that he had never come here and that he could have remained immersed in the chaos that is war. To see again a glimpse of humanity as it was meant to be was almost unbearable. To think of it, instead, as only a dream of a past life that no longer existed was somehow simpler. And yet here it was, standing before him in a living, breathing form. The war had not completely snuffed it out, and suddenly the hope rose within that there still existed a small corner of his beloved Georgia where his own family waited patiently for him, longing to soothe away the scars of conflict with words such as had just fallen upon his ears. Perhaps Georgia still lived and loved him and would wait for his return.

"It is a dangerous thing to give a man hope," Will responded with a grateful smile and a slow shaking of his head.

"You *are* a dangerous man," Carolyn responded respectfully. "But I believe that your actions show that you are a good man."

Will inhaled deeply and allowed the air to escape slowly. He bowed his head and closed his eyes as he began to speak.

"People will not remember me or my brothers in gray in the years to come. I fear that it is only a matter of time before me and my kind will be no more, and the others will write about us in any manner that they desire, while their own involvement and responsibilities in all of this insanity will politely be put aside for a version of higher truth. Perhaps it is my greatest pain to think that my sons will forget the sacrifices that we have made and will hang their heads in shame at the very mention of our names."

"You fight for the imprisonment of your fellow man," Carolyn stated flatly.

"Do I? The entire world has freed its slaves without so much as firing a shot. Was not the same outcome possible here if that were the sole cause of this horrible bloodshed? I had no desire to fight until the Federals poured into Virginia and began to destroy the homes and farms of my brothers. I own no slaves and profit not one penny from them. You are correct in one thing, though. My sin was that I ignored my fellow man, and I have paid a heavy price for it."

"Then why must you fight on if the price is so heavy?" came the unsympathetic response. Will's gaze shifted off to the distance, and he paused briefly before speaking.

"When I close my eyes, I see the smoke rising from the homes in Fredericksburg and Winchester and flames bursting from their doors and windows. I see the Shenandoah in flames and I hear the bellowing of the farm horses as the Federals shot them to prevent spring planting. I see the women and children begging those people not to burn their homes, to no avail."

Will then turned back to Carolyn.

"I am terrified by the vision of my wife and children left homeless and without food or clothing. I see them destitute, silhouetted against the flames of my home. I starve, fight and die a little more every day only to protect the men about me and to perhaps delay the coming of the flames to my little corner of Georgia."

"I hate slavery and all that it represents," Carolyn responded.

"As you should. But it was not necessary to burn towns and homes to make such a sentiment known. It did not have to be this way."

Carolyn was temporarily taken aback as she was forced to admit that she had never thought about the conflict in such a personal way. A moment passed before she responded.

"I must admit that I have never heard of Confederates burning towns, but neither have I laid eyes upon a more disheveled and filthy group of humanity. But I will grudgingly admit that there is a completely different air that surrounds you and your comrades. I am quite sure that I will leave this world without understanding what it is that makes some of you so different, but it is there nonetheless, and I am perplexed by it."

A host of possible responses flooded Will's mind, but he already sensed that trying further to explain his position would offer no additional advantages. The woman before him had been infinitely kind, and Will felt it best to express his gratitude in the simplest and most sincere way possible.

"Thank you," came the honest response. Carolyn smiled once again and nodded her head in acknowledgment.

"Well, I had best head back up to the house, but I will return shortly with you some food. Again, I must apologize for not offering it earlier."

"No apology is necessary. Army rations leave much to be desired, and an empty stomach is not an unfamiliar thing."

"Even the animals get fed around here, and I suppose, in spite of our differences, you deserve it as much as they," Carolyn stated with a smile as she turned to leave the opening of the barn. Will watched the retreat of the flickering light until it disappeared into the house once more. The Confederate then set to work replacing the buttons on Evaline's shirt. As promised, the light from Carolyn's lantern soon returned, and she brought with her a plate of roast beef, corn bread, and garden peas. She apologized once for the meal's meager portions, but Will felt as if he had been given a taste of home. He thanked her for the meal, and she then turned once more to return to the house. At the base of the steps to the front porch, Carolyn turned and looked back at the barn. Through the still open front door, she could see Will hunched over Evaline's shirt, bathed in the golden light of the two lanterns as he worked diligently to replace the missing buttons. She then extinguished the lantern and ascended the steps to the house.

*****

Carolyn found it very difficult to sleep, and no matter how hard she pursued rest, it remained elusive. After tossing for several minutes to no avail, she sat upon the edge of the bed. She was unable to ascertain the exact cause of her insomnia, but her attention was drawn to the window. She parted the wooden blinds slightly and gazed out in the direction of the barn. The structure was now dark, and Carolyn was certain that their Confederate guest lay inside resting peacefully as contrasted to her predicament. Or perhaps his sleep was not peaceful at all and dwelled heavily upon those horrible things of war that she could not even begin to fathom. As she contemplated, her husband's voice suddenly materialized from the darkness behind her.

"There's something different about him, isn't there?"

Carolyn did not move away from the window or at first give any indication the she heard the question at all.

"Yes," came the simple but profound response.

*****

The rising of the sun the following morning found Carolyn awake, as sleep had come only sparingly. Her husband had already risen and was busily completing the morning chores. As the gray light yielded to more vivid colors, she walked through the front door and out onto the porch. To her surprise, she found Evaline's shirt draped over the back of one of the wooden rocking chairs. She stretched out her hand and retrieved the article of clothing, inspecting the soldier's handiwork as she did so. The replacement buttons had been sewn on with delicate care, and Carolyn found little evidence that the original articles had ever been removed. She glanced quickly toward the barn, but seeing no movement there, she returned inside to the bedroom. There, she focused her attention on the top shelf of the small closet where an almost new, chestnut-colored slouch hat remained in silent testimony to another time. With reverent hands, she removed the hat and touched the brim and leather band as she would the face of a child. Memories of its owner filled her mind. She then sat slowly upon the edge of the bed and closed her eyes as the tears began to flow in silent tribute. When she had regained her composure, she dried her eyes and returned to the front of the house where she saw her husband returning to the house. However, he was not alone, as Will accompanied him, apparently assisting with the chores of the day. Before reaching the house, and just out of earshot, the two men stopped and faced each other, speaking casually as two old acquaintances would after Sunday worship. Carolyn wondered what they spoke about, but then what woman ever knows the thoughts that occupy the hearts of men? She then turned to return Evaline's mended shirt and to finish breakfast.

With breakfast ready, Carolyn called everyone back to the table to which had been added an obvious extra place setting. As Will entered the house with John, his gaze fell upon Evaline, fully dressed and beaming in her mended shirt.

"Don't I know you from somewhere? You look awfully familiar," Will asked playfully.

"I thinks so," Evaline responded. "You looks familiar too. I thinks you da one dat run off with my sister las' year."

Will began to shake his head.

"In fact, I knows dat it's you 'cause she got three chilluns dat looks jus' like you."

Will caught Carolyn's attention.

"She's been like this the whole trip."

"I can only imagine."

*****

For a brief moment, as the group sat together around the table, the war seemed to fade away. No one spoke of the violence so close at hand that threatened to tear their entire world apart. Instead, they all spoke of simpler times, hard work, and peaceful afternoons. Love and laughter were the topics of choice, and all seemed to believe that if they could only grasp the moment for an instant longer, then perhaps they could will flesh and blood to cover the bare bones of the memories themselves. But, as it always does, time refused to be fettered and slipped away. Will thanked John and Carolyn for the food and hospitality and then began to collect his meager things.

"Here, take this with you," Carolyn stated as she handed Will some cornbread, apples and pears in a linen sack. "It's not much, but it should hold you over until you can make your next stop."

"You're not far from Fredericksburg as the crow flies," John began as he focused his attention on Will. "You already know all of this, Edward, but I want both of you to know it. You need to go northeast from here. You're pretty much out of the thick of the wilderness. Your traveling may be a little easier, but you're going to be more exposed as well. Keep your eyes open. Avoid the town itself. It's too dangerous, and you won't need to go there anyway. West of the town you will find a ford across the Rappahannock River. It's marked by two large pieces of rock well above the water with a gap between them. We call them "The Sisters." The river gets very shallow there, and you can cross on foot, but be cautious as the current is swift. Once across, you will need to travel about three miles due north until you reach a rough-hewn wooden house. The front gate is marked by a stone fence, and on the right side of the entrance is a red tin lantern. That is your next waypoint, and you'll find very good folks there. From there you will be give directions to the next house in line and so on from there."

John then shifted his gaze to Evaline and observed her with a compassionate expression before continuing.

"You have a long trip ahead of you, child, but do not lose heart. You will make it, just as others have before you."

Evaline nodded in gratitude, knowing from her past experience that the weight of her journey would not soon lessen.

"In any case," John continued. "You all had better be on your way. These are not safe times, and this is not always a safe place."

Sensing the urgency as well, the three travelers bid their farewells and exited through the front door, opposite the way they had entered from the woods at the rear of the house. Will was the last to leave, but Carolyn caught his arm before he descended the steps. The Confederate turned to face her as she held out the brown slouch hat that she had retrieved from the closet.

"Evaline told me how your hat was lost when she went berry picking. I'm sure that you and that hat had been through a lot together, and every soldier needs a good hat. I'd like for you to have this one."

Will inspected the hat without touching it and saw that it was of good quality, but Carolyn's demeanor caught his attention even more than her gift. Will could tell that her desire to give the gift was sincere, yet he also sensed a hesitation as if it required all of her strength to part with it.

"Whose was it?" Will asked humbly yet insightfully. Carolyn hesitated only a moment, almost as if she knew that the Confederate would see through the thinly-veiled emotions.

"It was my son's."

"The war took him, did it not?"

Carolyn nodded.

"Ma'am, I appreciate this, but I'm not sure…"

"Please," Carolyn interrupted. "Humor an old woman and accept it. Please forgive me, but you remind me so much of him, and I can think of nothing better than if this were safely in your possession"

After hesitating a moment, Will reached out and gently took the hat, sensing that a refusal would hurt Carolyn more than parting with the reminder of her son. He then placed the hat on his head to find that it fit perfectly.

"Very well," Carolyn stated with satisfaction. "You had best be on your way. It is not safe to linger here."

"Thank you, ma'am," Will stated as he touched his finger to the brim of the hat. "For everything. I will take care of what you have treasured so dearly."

Will then turned to descend the steps, but just as his foot set foot upon the Virginia soil he heard Carolyn's voice call his name once more. He turned to see her advance toward him as if she had to tell him something of great importance which she wanted no one else to hear.

"You have judged rightly in assuming that her safety cannot be guaranteed in the hands of the Federals," Carolyn continued in a whisper. "Her treatment with many from both sides will be equally harsh, and as a woman her abuse from the men could be severe. There are many who would care for her, but you cannot assume that that will happen in all cases. Trust no one. She must get to Canada. Do whatever you must to assure it. Promise me that."

"I will do what I must," Will responded sincerely. "I give you my word. If something happens to her, I promise you with all that is in me that it will only be because there will be yet another son of Georgia who will not be returning home."

Will then turned and rejoined Evaline and Edward, who were both mounted and waiting just out of earshot. Carolyn stood and watched them cross the field in front of the house until they disappeared into the distant line of trees. She inhaled deeply and exhaled slowly as John stood by her side.

"Why does it hurt to see them go when I hardly even know them?" Carolyn asked.

"It does not take as long as we sometimes believe to know a person's heart," he replied. "Kindred spirits are birds that are difficult to set free."

He touched her gently on the arm before turning and retrieving his pitchfork to resume his haying. He understood his wife's sentiments but had always found communicating them to be difficult. Besides, those thoughts were deeply personal, perhaps even too personal to speak aloud for fear that they would spring to life of their own accord. The loss of his son had not eased that difficulty, yet he had to agree with his wife. There was indeed something familiar about the visitor in gray, and it was difficult to see him go.

*****

John was still deep in thought when the blue-clad troopers appeared from the woods to his right. Riding four abreast, they were almost upon him before he noticed. John halted where he was and the lead soldier called out in greeting.

"Good morning sir," he called with a large grin.

John placed the prongs of the pitchfork so that the teeth bit into the ground as he leaned on the handle.

"Good morning to you. What can I do for you gentlemen?"

"We have been out riding patrol and were wondering if you have seen anything strange going on in the area?"

"Every day is strange in a war zone," replied John. "But nothing out of the ordinary."

The lead trooper nodded his head.

"We heard a lot of gunfire about two days ago in this direction away from the main battle lines."

"I'm not surprised," John continued unflinchingly. "That is a common experience for us as well."

"It does not frighten you to stay here?"

"This is my home. I belong here."

At that time, Carolyn, having heard the voices, turned the corner of the house and saw her husband standing before the four mounted men.

"John, is everything all right?"

"Yes, Carolyn," John stated while motioning her to stay where she was. "Everything is fine."

"Is this your wife?" the lead trooper questioned.

"Yes."

"Ma'am, we were just asking your husband if you folks have seen anything strange around here."

Carolyn shook her head in response, a sense of dread filling her in the presence of these four strangers. Without trying to arouse suspicion, she carefully glanced over her shoulder in the direction that Will had left, almost hoping to see the Confederate returning. Only empty space greeted her.

"Well, I am certainly relieved that you good folks have remained unmolested by the riff-raff that can be found running around these parts. However, preserving the Union is a taxing business and, unfortunately, our rations do not always supply all of our needs. In those times, we request that the citizens that we are protecting assist us in this area so that we can continue in our duty."

"You are welcome to what we have, but I will tell you that my wife and I are starving as it is. I hate to disappoint you, but we do not have food enough to feed the four of you."

The lead trooper stared at John with piercing eyes before responding, but John did not flinch under the strain.

"Is that what you told the people who just left?"

"What people?"

"Don't insult me. We heard voices in this direction before riding

165

here."

"Neighbors. Nothing more."

"There is no one for miles around. Which way did they ride off? I'm sure they can't have gone that far, and we should be able to catch them and verify your story."

"I mean no disrespect to you or to your cause," John replied. "Our son fought and died with the Second Pennsylvania. I only mean to tell you that we have been looted for this entire war, and there is now nothing left. Look about you. The whole countryside is destitute. Feel free to look for yourselves."

"Oh, we plan to," the lead horseman stated, as he motioned for the other three to dismount. "It is well within my orders to confiscate anything that we find suspicious or useful for that matter."

"For what cause?"

"You Virginians always seem to have a story, but it is very rarely one that I can believe. This war has to be won, and I intend to deprive the enemy of every resource at his disposal. My instinct tells me that you have been assisting the enemy, and I intend to pursue that belief until proven otherwise."

The three men quickly closed the distance between themselves and John, and the largest of the three stood directly in front of him.

"John…" Carolyn began.

"It's all right, Carolyn. Stay where you are."

"What you plan to do with this?" the big man gestured at the pitchfork, his face uncomfortably close to John's.

"You all don't understand," John again tried to explain. "There is nothing disloyal about us."

"I'm sure that you are quite loyal to your government in Richmond," the mounted trooper responded.

With lightning speed, the stalwart man facing John snatched the pitchfork out of his hand and shoved him backwards as Carolyn cried out in shock. John took a few steps backward but was able to regain his balance. One of the other dismounted troopers quickly walked over to Carolyn and grabbed her roughly by the arm.

"You get your hands off of my wife!" John shouted, but no sooner had he done so, the big man's fist sent him reeling to the ground. Carolyn looked again frantically over her shoulder, but there was nothing to see.

"You keep your mouth closed!" the large man bellowed as his

finger pointed directly in John's face.

"You see," the mounted trooper continued. "It only takes such a short time for a person's true hostility to rise to the surface. Now, do you care to change your story?"

"There is no other story to tell!"

Carolyn was then shoved to the ground. The trooper with her then placed his boot on her neck, his spurs dangerously close to her throat.

"I'm sure that there are at least leftovers of whatever you served your other guests this morning," he chided. "We'll just help ourselves to that, and then we'll have a look around and help ourselves to whatever else we want. After all, who's going to stop us?"

Almost as if in response to the interrogatory, a small puff of white smoke appeared along the distant forest line, followed by a lethal whistle as the Minie ball hissed past and struck the trooper holding Carolyn squarely in the chest. Dust flew from the front and back of the jacket as the projectile drove the man onto the ground where he remained motionless. Only then did the report from the Enfield reach their ears. Hardly had the echo died away when a second puff of smoke appeared, and the big man in front of John was spun completely around and landed with a thud upon his face where, with a hiss and groan, the last air escaped from his lungs.

"Cover!" the mounted trooper shouted. "Sharpshooter!"

The mounted trooper swung down from his horse and broke for the rear of the house at full speed while the last dismounted trooper snatched Carolyn up from the ground and dragged her toward the rear as well. John, still dazed, was unable to resist as he struggled to rise from the ground. Just before passing behind the house, Carolyn once again looked back along the forest edge and saw a single rider bearing down upon the house at full gallop.

The hoof beats were soon audible, and John raised his eyes to see Will reign in the animal at the last possible moment and vault off of the horse, his Spencer at the ready. John raised his hand.

"Will, Will! Two of them. In back! They've got Carolyn!"

"I know, John!" Will responded. "I'll get her! You get to cover!"

Will's posture was low, but determined as he rapidly skirted the side of the house and motioned for John not to follow.

With the intrepidity of a lone wolf, Will darted around the far corner of the house. He saw no evidence of the two men, though he could hear the muffled sound of struggling on the far side of the barn where he had spent the night. Pressing the attack, Will bolted across the distance to the barn and flattened his back against its side, his Spencer across his chest. Controlling his breathing, he could still hear muffled sounds coming from the other side.

"Let her go, and I'll let you leave!" Will shouted. "Leave her and we have no quarrel. Choose to continue as you are and you, and I will have business to discuss."

"Brave words from a man who shoots others when they have no chance to defend themselves! Only a coward shoots men from that distance!"

Will sensed that the voice was getting closer as his opponent was speaking and was well aware that the two men would appear from both corners of the barn simultaneously to catch him in a pincer movement. In fact, Will was counting on that fact but knew as well that his timing and aim had to be perfect. He also knew that one of them still held Carolyn captive and likely muffled her voice with his hand over her mouth. Will cocked the Spencer and then called out in a loud voice.

"Carolyn, keep your head down!"

Almost instantly, a cry resounded from Will's left along with the appearance of the trooper holding Carolyn. He threw up his revolver to fire at Will, all the while struggling with Carolyn. Her head was down and Will already had the carbine trained on his opponent when he pulled the trigger and left Carolyn the only person standing. With a smooth motion, Will dropped the carbine to his side and drew the LeMat revolver from his belt with his right hand and trained it on the lead trooper who suddenly appeared from around the right corner. The LeMat bellowed smoke and flame, and the trooper dropped to his knees and then slumped over on his right side.

"Was that distance more to your liking?" Will growled as he returned the LeMat to his belt. Carolyn had fallen to her knees at the corner of the barn and was staring at her hands, mumbling softly.

"Oh, my dear Lord… oh, my dear Lord…"

Will quickly knelt at her side and touched her on the arm.

"It's all right. It's over. Take some deep breaths. The feeling will pass soon."

Looking up to his right, Will saw John, now on his feet, stumbling to his companion's side. He was still unsteady from his earlier blow, but nothing could keep him from Carolyn. Upon reaching her, he knelt and lifted her to her feet and held her closely. Will stepped aside, suddenly feeling much more the cause of the present troubles than the solution. He shouldered the Spencer and cast a nervous glance back toward the distant tree line from which he had come.

"Thank you," John's shaky voice broke the silence. Will turned to him and met his misty gaze.

"I do terrible things," Will responded. "It has become all of which I am capable."

"It is not always an evil thing for God's man to be armed," came John's reply. Will's gaze fell to the earth while the three stood in silence for some time, as the soothing sounds of the Virginia morning returned.

Chapter X

From the cover of the distant forest line, Edward and Evaline waited as they heard the two distant shots ring out from the vicinity of the barn. Neither dared to move or breathe, but something deep within each feared the worst. An eternity seemed to pass before the lone Confederate reappeared, leading one of the Federal's horses across the open field. He returned at a much slower pace, as one who had an eternity to contemplate the world as it had become. He finally entered the woods, halting his horse to look down at the pair without speaking.

"All is well?" Edward asked in a somber tone.

"All is not as it should be, but all is well. John and Carolyn are fine. The others did not fare as well."

Will led the new horse over to where Evaline was standing.

"Will, I's glad dat you got 'em," Evaline added. "Dey deserved it."

"We all deserve it," Will mumbled quietly as he urged his horse slowly forward. He then halted the animal and stared ahead for a moment before turning to face his companions. "We had better get moving before something worse comes this way."

Evaline and Edward looked at each other for a moment before remounting and falling in line behind Will. After leading for a moment, Will halted and moved his horse to the side. "Sorry, I forgot," Will stated as he motioned Edward to the front. "You lead on, Edward. My mind was elsewhere."

With a moment of hesitation, Edward resumed the lead, and Will pointed Evaline forward before falling to the rear.

*****

Evaline glanced back over her shoulder as the small column resumed its forward momentum and observed the quiet Confederate. She found herself wondering what type of man he was before being consumed by the violence of war and whether or not she would even recognize him. Undoubtedly, he pondered the same question, as he tried to sort out what he had been and what he had become. Knowing that disturbing the silence was an intrusion on something intensely personal, Evaline turned and focused her attention on the road ahead.

*****

The day passed quickly and the trio made good time as their mounts passed over the Virginia terrain. Edward knew the path well and had little difficulty in navigating the trail. Early in the afternoon, Edward motioned for Will to ride up next to him, and Will pulled his mount up alongside.

"We should reach the river tomorrow," Edward began. "We just need to keep this heading, and we should connect with the Rappahannock around the area of 'The Sisters.' The terrain shouldn't be too difficult since we've left the Wilderness behind. But there will be a lot more open ground, so we'll have to watch ourselves."

Edward halted his speech as he was interrupted by a distant rumbling of gunfire.

"And we'll have to keep an eye out for old friends, both Blue and Gray."

Will nodded his head.

"It's a shame that mankind is always the most profound danger of all."

"It may be better to try to move at night," Edward continued. "So what I propose is that we go ahead and stop up in the edge of this forest, rest for what is left of daylight, and then proceed on at night. That's the usual operation of our business anyway, but we have been thrown off course by our unusual encounters."

"To say that the past few days have been unusual is an understatement. And this war has been full of the unusual."

Edward raised his eyebrows and nodded in agreement. He then turned to Evaline.

"You feel like stopping and resting for a bit before starting up again at nightfall?"

"Dat's fine with me."

Edward then pointed ahead to a spot just inside the tree line.

"That looks like a good spot."

*****

All three of the travelers welcomed the reprieve and passed the time by eating and talking of simpler times. Will soon found a straight poplar branch and began to whittle as he sat upon a fallen tree, his gray shell jacket spread out on the log next to him. As the afternoon sun began to filter in through the late summer foliage, Edward took a seat next to Will and examined his handiwork.

"Making anything in particular?"

Will stopped his whittling and scrutinized the straight limb, which was now completely bare of its bark.

"Not really," Will replied. "Looks like a spear to me. Sometimes I don't get inspired until after I start carving."

"Carve first and ask questions later?"

"Something like that."

"You know, I never thanked you for all that you have done. Not just for us, but for John and Carolyn as well."

Will smiled in sincere appreciation.

"You are welcome, but it does come with some regret. It is a shame that the impressions I now make upon people usually involve someone's death. There was a time in the not-too-distant past that I would have been remembered for my knowledge of Shakespeare or my teaching technique. Now, those days are over, and I fear never to return."

"Forgive me for saying so, but I believe that you are much too hard on yourself. There are times when difficult things must be done, and I have never seen you do what you do so well unless it was in the defense of another." Edward's gaze then moved to Evaline, who lay resting against Will's bedroll.

"Do you see her? She is a perfect example of what I mean. She would not be here today were it not for you."

"Nor would I be here if it were not for her," Will replied. He then closed his eyes and leaned his head back as if soaking in all of the sensations around him.

"Do you hear those birds, Edward?" Edward listened for a moment as the music from a chorus of songbirds filled his ears.

"Yes."

"I have always wondered why they do not sound as they once did in my younger years."

"Because your innocence is gone."

"I have had my eyes opened, have I not?"

"Indeed you have, as have we all."

Will took a deep breath before continuing.

"Where is your family?"

Edward smiled a broad grin before answering.

"You, my friend, are looking at a self-made man. I, too, was once a slave but had the good fortune of coming under the care of an owner who believed that I had more potential than mere field work. He took it upon himself to teach me to read and write and, shortly

172

before his passing, granted me my freedom. I had long before been separated from my family and had no idea where to start looking for them. I had never married and had no one depending on me, so I suppose that predisposed me to the work I do now. I wanted to give something back, to do for someone else what had been done for me."

"How many times have you made this trip?"

"Countless times."

Edward then inhaled deeply and released the breath slowly.

"May I tell you what I believe? By that I mean what I believe the future holds."

"Of course."

Edward leaned forward and folded his hands together and moved them in unison to provide emphasis for his arguments. "There are very few innocents in this whole war as far as governments are concerned, but I do believe that there are men on both sides whose reasons for fighting are honorable and true. I also believe that the bondage of my people is merely a means to an end in the minds of some on both sides. I must now flee from both halves of this nation, but it is my prayer that a day is coming when I will hide from no one."

Edward then fell silent and the two men sat quietly as the former slave focused his attention on the gray shell jacket lying on the log next to Edward. He then stood and, with a smooth motion, picked the coat up and swung it over his shoulders. He then threaded his arms through the sleeves and stood before Will, his back facing out toward the field just beyond the tree line with the sun illuminating his back. Will stared up in disbelief.

"It fits. At least yours does."

"You don't have to do that. I get your point."

Evaline awoke as the two were conversing and she too, rubbing the sleep from her eyes, stared at Edward in disbelief.

"What is you doing?" she asked as she rose to her feet.

"Making a point," Edward stated as he smoothed out the weathered coat.

"I'd say you is. I can see you followin' ole Marse Robert himself!"

"I can think of many who would be worse examples to follow."

Will could not help but smile at the almost comical scene before him. He was also painfully aware that he had crossed a boundary into some unknown country, the likes of which he had never before seen. Yet, it was familiar. It felt like home.

Will was still basking in the light of that one moment of eternity when a sinister whistle once again broke the tranquility. There was no time to react as the bullet struck Edward in the back and sprayed Will with a fine mist as it exited. Instinctively, Will hurled himself at Evaline and drove her to the ground as Edward slumped forward to the earth. His body hit the ground before the distant shot boomed in Will's ears. Evaline screamed in terror.

"Stay down, Evaline!" Will ordered in an almost panicked voice as he realized what was happening. "For goodness sake, stay down!"

"Edward!" Evaline screamed as she reached out from underneath Will toward her fallen companion. "Edward! Will, Will, what's happened? Let me up! Let me up!"

"Evaline, stay down, I told you!" Will screamed, just as another bullet flew by and struck the trunk of a tree just above Evaline's head. The rifle's report followed a few seconds later. Will quickly grasped Evaline by the shoulders and pulled her deeper into the forest behind a fallen tree. Will then flattened himself on the ground and peered around the end of the massive trunk.

"Will, what is happenin'?"

"Not now, Evaline!"

"Will, I's scared."

"So am I."

"Will, Edward's out der."

"Stay here. I'm going to him."

Will crawled around the end of the tree and plowed through the leaf-covered forest floor toward his friend. Even if he could not see him, Will could have found his way to him by the gurgling sound that wafted to him from the fallen man's position. Crawling a few feet more, Will found himself within arm's length of Edward.

"Edward," Will whispered. "Edward, I'm here. I'm gonna get you out of here."

At first there was no response, but then Will noticed a slight movement of Edward's head as it slowly turned to look at Will. Even with his dark complexion, Will could see life's color draining from it quickly. He struggled for each breath, and the sound of it was almost more than Will could bear. Edward's facial expression was beyond human description, and it burned itself deeply into the Confederate's soul. Unable to turn away, Will felt the full force of the dying man's gaze begging for help when there was none to give. With a final effort, Edward extended his arm and stretched out his hand to Will. The Confederate grasped the hand and pulled himself closer to Edward. With nothing more to offer than the companionship of a friend, Will held the dying man as he would have his own brother until the agonizingly painful breathing slowed and then, with a shudder, stopped altogether.

Will remained where he was in spite of the danger, unable to move. He could hear Evaline calling to him, but he did not answer. A part of him would have been content to stay there and never move again, but an unexplainable desire to press on swept over him, and he finally commanded his arms to move. Gently, and with great respect, Will removed his stained coat from Edward's body and began to crawl back the way he had come. Stopping suddenly, he looked back one last time at the fallen man.

"I'm so sorry," he whispered.

Evaline knew Edward's fate immediately as soon as Will crawled back carrying his gray jacket, but she could not bring herself to accept the obvious.

"He's gone, ain't he, Will?"

The grief in Will's expression could not be hidden.

"There wasn't anything I could do..."

Will's sentence was cut short as a third bullet skimmed across the top of the log and showered the pair with splinters. Evaline screamed in shock and Will immediately grabbed her arm and pulled her deeper into the forest and down a small slope to shield her from the exposed edge of the tree line. Evaline buried her face into Will's chest and grabbed his arms with a vice like grip. Will could feel her shaking as she sobbed.

"What's happenin', Will? Why did dey do dat to Edward?"

"I don't know, child."

"It was done by someone like you, wasn't it?"

Will hesitated for a moment.

"It was done by someone who can do what I do."

"One o' yours?"

"I don't know. If it was, it doesn't make sense to shoot someone wearing gray. It could have been a mistake."

Evaline remained silent for a moment as she controlled her sobs.

"What we gonna do?"

"I'm not sure. He's got us pinned down here. We have to wait until night and then try to find our way out of the other side of the forest."

"Dey ain't nothin' we can do for Edward, is der?"

"No."

"We gots to leave him, don't we?"

"Yes. They will be watching the body closely, and if we go back, we'll be done for."

"We jus' gonna stay here for right now?"

"Yes. We're just going to stay right here and rest until night. Then I'm going to get you out of here."

"Promise?"

"I promise."

*****

The pair remained motionless as the afternoon sun crawled down what remained of the western sky and slipped beneath the horizon. Only when the darkness was palpable did Will dare to move from his position. He had heard the trickling of a small brook nearby, and he silently made his way with Evaline down to its edge. Will sat on a smooth stone, washed his face, and soaked his jacket before beginning to scrub away the stains. The pair remained silent, almost as if the act were a last memorial to Edward. Flipping the jacket over, Will explored the bullet hole and marveled at the shot placement. The sound of the shot had taken about two seconds to reach them, and, from his experience, Will estimated that the shot had been taken from at least six hundred yards away if not more. He placed his finger through the hole and, perhaps it was just his imagination, but the hole seemed slightly smaller than the usual .58 caliber.

"Perhaps a Sharps rifle, .52 caliber," Will whispered, almost inaudibly.

Will finished his work as best he could in the darkness and wrung out the excess water. He then gently took Evaline by the arm and motioned for her to follow him. There was no moon, which Will knew was a blessing, but it made traversing the forest more difficult. Will chose his steps carefully, trying to proceed as silently as possible in the general direction of Fredricksburg. He stopped every few minutes to scrutinize the sounds of the forest and at first heard nothing suspicious. Will stopped short and motioned for Evaline to remain where she was. Training his ear, Will was sure that he heard the hesitating steps of someone approaching. Every few seconds, the steps stopped as if the intruder was inspecting his surroundings. The steps then resumed and drew progressively closer. Will could barely make out a murky shadow as it approached. The Bowie was cold and silent as Will drew it from its sheath and crouched like a tiger before its prey. When the shadow was only a few feet away, Will sprang silently and wrapped his arms around the shadow's neck before shoving him to the ground and placing the cold steel next to his throat. A muffled cry from the young male was stifled, but not before a sense of recognition swept across Will's mind. The young man struggled, but the Confederate was clearly superior and had no difficulty subduing his prey.

"This will go a whole lot better for you if you just hold still, now," Will commanded. "I may not be able to see you very well, but my ears never forget a voice."

Will's free hand then reached down the arm and his fingers found the bandage just where he had placed it.

"Who is it, Will?" Evaline interrupted. "You knows him?"

Will hesitated before answering, almost as if he were debating whether or not to reveal his captive's identity.

"Let's just say we met him earlier in a less than desirable situation."

Will let off just enough pressure to snatch the young man up to a sitting position and, even in the blackness, could make out the young man who had been a member of the Home Guard.

"I suspect that you're still hanging around with the wrong folks."

A gasp rose from Evaline.

"Dat's da boy what tried ta hang me? Da one dat you let go?"

"I'm afraid so, and I'm afraid he hasn't learned his lesson. Now, why don't you be polite and tell Evaline that it's nice to see her again."

The boy was silent. Will pressed the Bowie more firmly against the side of his neck.

"I'll only ask nicely once."

There was only a slight hesitation before the young man spoke.

"It doesn't make any difference. Both of you are as good as dead anyway."

"Now, we don't exactly see it that way," Will replied. "But I think, for the record, that you need to tell us exactly what you mean by that."

"You know exactly what I mean," the young man snarled sarcastically. The back of Will's hand flew swiftly in the dark and struck his captive a stinging blow across the face. He then grabbed a fistful of hair and shoved him back on the ground.

"My patience is running low, boy, and that is not a good thing for you," Will growled as his growing anger hissed between his teeth. "Don't sass me or insult my intelligence. I ask you a question, and you give me an answer, or I'll finish what I started right here and now. I've just lost a friend and, believe me, you do not have the luxury to sit and wait to talk to me at a time that better suits my mood."

Will's grip tightened on the fistful of hair as the young man squirmed beneath him.

"You tell me what you know about this sharpshooter. And don't you dare lie to me and tell me you know nothing. Your very presence in the forest at this time tells me that you're doing his spotting for him by finding out exactly where we are."

The squirming stopped temporarily as the young man sensed the change in Will's tone.

"He's one of Berdan's men. The best I've ever seen. He makes what you can do look like child's play."

Will remembered the hole in the back of his jacket.

"One of Berdan's? A Yankee? What are you doing working with a Yankee?"

"He ain't exactly particular in what or who he shoots at. A rogue sharpshooter is what they call him. He ain't fightin' for no noble cause or anything like that. He just wants to shoot. It doesn't matter to him who he works with. When I left you last time, it was my pleasure to lead him right to you."

"He killed an innocent man."

"Well, he should have ducked if he didn't want to get shot."

Will's fist shot back in the darkness and connected viciously with the young man's face.

"My nose, my nose!" he cried.

"Well, you should have ducked if you didn't want to get hit," Will snarled. He then flipped the young man over on his face and, grabbing his length of rope, tied his hands securely behind his back before tying his ankles.

"Not a sound out of you, you understand? If you so much as squeak, it'll be the last sound you ever make."

Will then sheathed his Bowie and returned to Evaline.

"Try to get some rest," he whispered so as to keep their conversation private. "My instincts tell me that we shouldn't move too much more, especially not with him and his kind wandering the woods. This is all very strange and we've got to keep our wits about us."

"Will, what did he mean, one of Berdan's men?"

"Berdan's men are a regiment of Yankee sharpshooters, supposedly some of the best. We can always pick them out because they wear green uniforms instead of the usual blue."

"Why, Will?...Edward was black..."

"For once that boy is probably telling us the truth. That shooter is not in this war for any noble reason. He's a killer, and it doesn't matter who gets in his way."

Evaline paused for a moment.

"Can you stop 'em, Will?"

A thousand potential responses flooded Will's mind as doubt crept in alongside the night's blackness.

"There's very little that can keep a good South Georgia boy down," he stated as he mustered a smile and placed his hand on her shoulder.

*****

The night crept by and gave Will far too long alone with his thoughts. He would never have told Evaline the cold truth out of fear of terrifying her, yet his instincts told him that she probably knew already. The fact of the matter was that Will had no idea as to how they were going to escape. The shooter had every advantage and had probably scoped out the terrain some time ago as to become adept at trapping his prey. Will knew that he and Evaline were always going to be one step behind, and the consequences of that fact were deadly.

Once the sun was up and the woods once again navigable, Will searched their perimeter but saw no signs of any movement overnight. After giving a moment for Evaline to eat some of their provisions, Will untied the young man's feet and snatched him to a standing position and forced him forward with the Enfield's muzzle in his back.

"Don't stop until I tell you," Will barked. "And only walk where I tell you. I don't want you leading the way."

Will chose a path that led away from a direct path to Fredricksburg, hoping to pass through the forest and exit unseen. Only a short period of time passed before Will could see a light through the trunks ahead, and he stopped their small group and turned to Evaline.

"Do you trust me, Evaline?" he asked in a hushed voice.

A perplexed expression crossed Evaline's face as she contemplated why Will would ask such a question.

"You knows I do, Will."

Will nodded in response.

"Then trust me now. Everything is going to be fine."

He then turned back to his captive.

"This is where we part ways, son," Will began as he untied the young man's hands. "For the second time."

A fearful expression flashed across the youthful features as he expected the Confederate to exact his revenge. To his surprise, the soldier pointed to the way out of the forest.

"You're free to go. I won't stop you. Where we are going, you cannot come."

The young man hesitated as if confused before turning to approach the edge of the forest. Almost halfway there, Will called to him, and he stopped to turn and face the Confederate.

"If you should happen to see your friend, tell him that I'm coming."

Without responding, the young man turned once again and resumed his journey. Will observed him for a moment and then turned to Evaline.

"I said dat I was gonna trust you, but dat don't mean dat I understands you," Evaline stated as she watched the man go. "I don't understand why you let him go again."

"War and murder are two different things. It's not my duty to give him what he deserves. What I must do, I always do in defense."

"So what we gonna do now?"

"Wait."

"I hates waitin'."

"I know. It's the hardest thing to do. Maybe we won't have to wait too long…"

Will's sentence was suddenly interrupted by the sound of a distant rifle shot, and by the time Will had turned back to follow his captive's course, the young man was already on the ground. He had perhaps taken ten steps out of the forest when he had been struck by the bullet. Will watched in astonishment as the young man writhed in the grass, tensed momentarily with arms stretched toward the heavens, and then fell motionless. So caught by surprise was Will that he forgot temporarily about Evaline. Jarred back to his senses, he gently placed his hand on the young lady's arm and pulled her to a kneeling position, even though he knew no one could see them that far into the woods.

"Unbelievable," Will whispered. "He shot his own man."

Will inhaled deeply.

"I will not underestimate you again."

Will then turned to Evaline, who needed no explanation of the events that had just occurred.

"He knowed we was comin' dis way, didn't he?"

Will sat beside Evaline and removed his hat to run his fingers through his hair.

"Somehow, he did."

"We ain't gonna be able to get outta here, is we?"

There was no immediate verbal response from Will, but Evaline could sense a distinct change in his demeanor. The facial muscles rhythmically contracted and relaxed as he clenched his jaw, while both hands were clenched until the knuckles were white. His breathing was heavy but regular, and his entire body seemed to swell with the rage billowing within. She would never have spoken of it openly, but the danger that loomed just outside the tree line was hardly more terrifying than the change that she saw in the man next to her.

"He can't be reasoned with, Evaline," Will began in a deep, ominous tone. "We can't bargain or bribe our way out of this, and nothing will appease him but our deaths. He has done this to others before, and the thrill of it has turned him into an animal whose appetite cannot be satisfied but with greater and greater bloodshed. There will be no going home as long as he lives."

Fear, long suppressed within Evaline, resurged amid the musings of her friend, and the question, born of complete despair, burst from her lungs.

"Den what we gonna do, Will?"

The Confederate responded by replacing his hat and staring straight ahead at the body of the young man lying just outside the shadows of the forest.

"I'm gonna kill him."

The Confederate then took a deep breath and turned to Evaline, the dark mood having been replaced with something much more familiar. He managed a thin smile and rose to his full height.

"Come with me," he invited. "We have work to do."

*****

Work brought distraction to the captive pair as they labored for their very lives. The sun overhead tracked the minutes with the finality of those breathing their last. Evaline, armed with the Bowie, cut three small poplar saplings, each sturdy enough to hold weight and taller than Will. Then, assuming a position on a nearby stone, she removed all of the branches and sharpened the end of one of the sticks while flattening the opposite. She divided the other saplings into four equal lengths and flattened all eight ends. Having finished this task, she joined Will in his search for as many small bullace grape vines, smilax, and young malleable twigs that she could find. Having found a full armload, she brought them back and dropped them to the forest floor near Will, who was already busy weaving the vines and twigs into a spherical mass. Evaline stood for a moment observing the man before her as his fingers nimbly intertwined the flexible pieces of wood. He was completely captivated by his work, and he worked as a man who completely understood that time was short and that the sunlight that illuminated the blue sky overhead might well be the last he would ever enjoy. Evaline's gaze lingered for a moment longer before she returned to her duties.

*****

The sun was low in the western sky when Will and Evaline placed the final touches on their creation. Their labor had produced the form of a man, taller and broader than Will, made entirely of branches and vines which were woven together around the poles that Evaline had prepared earlier. The longer pole with the sharpened end serve as the vertical support, and Will had affixed his spherical creation to the top to serve as a head. The other four poles were attached to the vertical one to serve as arms and legs. The poles were woven so tightly into the mass of branches and vines that they had no difficulty in maintaining their positions. Sticking the sharp end into the ground for stability, Will took a step back and admired his creation. Evaline also inspected the end results as well, turning her head to the side as if to inspect it from a different angle.

"I don't care what you says," she began. "Dey ain't no way dat thing can shoot as good as you."

Will chuckled.

"It doesn't have to."

"Exactly what it supposed to do den?"

"It's supposed to give our friend something else to shoot at."

"I'm not sure I understands all dat."

"That's all right. There's one other thing that I need you to help with. How good are you at braiding?"

Evaline pointed to her closely-cropped curly hair.

"How good you thinks I is?"

"Did you ever braid any of the white children's hair?"

"Sometime."

"Well, I'm sure that you will be a lot better at it than I am."

Will then produced three very long bullace grape vines.

"I'm going to hold these ends and I need you to braid this all the way out to the other end. This won't be as good as a long length of rope, but it'll have to do."

Evaline kneeled down in front of Will and began swiftly but gracefully to braid the three separate vines into a tight cord.

"You've braided more hair than you're letting on."

"No, I told you da truth. I gots dis good braidin' mules' tails."

"Well, your training is sure coming in handy now."

Evaline soon reached the end of the vine and held the braid together while Will tied off each end with smaller vines. The pair then repeated the process with another set of vines and finally tied the two end products together to form one long cord. Having finished, Will sat back and scrutinized the quickly fading light.

"Rest a while," Will began. "There are some things I still have to do, but you've helped me all that you can for now. I could not have done it without you."

Evaline nodded in response.

"If it's all da same, I'll jus' stick around with you."

Will smiled and nodded as he turned his attention to the two Enfields leaning against a nearby tree. As he had done previously following his dream concerning the misfire, he swiftly used his bullet-puller to remove the Minie balls and pour the powder from the barrels. His motions proceeding without hesitation. He then retrieved two cartridges and poured their contents down the barrel before seating a new Minie ball with the ramrod.

"Is you afraid?" Evaline asked, almost as if the true intention of the question was to confirm that she was not alone.

"There could never be courage without it."

Evaline nodded and then lowered her eyes to look at the forest floor.

"Evaline, I need you to listen very carefully. As soon as it is fully dark, I'm going to move up to a position just inside the tree line. You are going to need to go in the opposite direction deeper into the forest. Around sunrise, you are going to hear gunshots, one distant and the other near. If the distant gunshot is the final one you hear and it is not followed by any further close shots, then I want you run as fast as you can out the opposite side of the forest and make for another stand of timber before he has time to adjust. Then, follow the instructions that John gave you."

Evaline's gaze did not rise from the forest floor, but she slowly began to shake her head.

"I ain't half as strong as you thinks I is."

The Confederate grasped the rifles and shouldered them over each side before stopping to look at the frightened young woman in front of him.

"I think that perhaps you are right. You're much stronger than I could ever imagine."

Chapter XI

Darkness had once again fallen and enveloped the countryside in a thick velvety covering when Will cautiously approached the tree line with his inanimate companion. Evaline was safe within the deep recesses of the forest, and although he knew that it was in her best interest for her to be as far away from him as possible, Will missed the companionship, nonetheless.

There was no moon to penetrate the overcast heavens, and Will was grateful, for he knew that his opponent would be as blind as he. Moving to the forest edge, Will located four thirty pound stones he had selected during daylight. He then, with utmost caution in spite of the darkness, gingerly stepped beyond the trees into the field beyond. A few feet beyond the tree line, in a space that would be completely vulnerable in daylight, Will dug a narrow one foot deep hole with his Bowie. Into this hole, he then placed the lower end of the supporting pole of his wooden companion and was relieved that the mannequin stood in place with no assistance. Returning to the forest, he retrieved the four stones and surrounded the pole to provide extra support. He then lifted the decoy carefully from the hole and laid it parallel to the ground so that the bottom of the mannequin's pole rested just inside the forward edge of the hole. Again, using his Bowie, he cut a short but stout branch from a nearby beech tree, sharpened one end after carving a groove for his rope to pass through, and firmly drove it into the ground directly in front of the group of stones. He then tied his homemade rope about halfway up the decoy, looped it around the groove in the beech pole, and then returned to the forest edge. With a quick snap of his wrist, the tension on the rope tightened and pulled his creation to a standing position with the lower end of the pole dropping squarely in the hole.

"Excellent," mumbled Will into the darkness. Just inside the forest edge, about six feet to the left of the decoy, Will had noticed a fallen poplar tree that provided an excellent bench rest, and Will began carving a groove in the trunk to provide extra stability for the Enfield. About eight feet further to the left was a V-shaped dogwood tree that afforded another excellent gun rest, and Will leaned the second Enfield against that tree. He then returned to the decoy and placed his gray jacket and hat upon it before placing it back into its previous position. He then returned to the forest and stood staring out into the vast blackness of the field as one would stare after a loved one who has left and is never to return.

*****

The night was little less than agonizing for the young soldier. Many times had he slept the night before a battle but never had the outcome of the conflict rested solely upon his shoulders. Perhaps the boy had been right. Perhaps he was outclassed, and the best he could offer would be nothing against such a foe. Perhaps all had been in vain and all of the obstacles he had overcome had served to place him in this lonely spot to spend a few final hours enjoying what there was left of what life had to offer. Will's exhausted mind tried to focus on something positive, but he was still struggling to do so when sleep overtook him.

*****

The blackness fell from his eyes as the Confederate awakened in his dream and found himself back home in a stand of tall southern pines. The sun was warm upon his shoulders, and a gentle breeze hummed through the long needles. The scent of turpentine and jasmine filled the air. Aware that he was not alone, Will turned and saw the Man who had appeared in his first dream, dressed now in the simple work clothes of a Southern farmer. Overcome at the brief sense of home and the presence of his companion, Will gathered himself before speaking.

"What am I to do?"

The Man smiled.

"Take the staff that is in your hand."

Will looked down to see the Enfield in his grasp.

"Is it true, what Evaline and I read? Are You with us even though we are only sparrows?"

The Man took one step closer.

"As I was with Moses, so shall I be with you. I will never leave you or forsake you."

Will hesitated for a moment.

"Even when we fall?"

The Man took one step closer and placed His hand on Will's shoulder, the expression upon His face that of a trusted friend.

"I am the Resurrection and the Life. If a man believes in Me he will live, even if he dies."

With those words the breeze began to sway the tops of the lofty pines, and Will closed his eyes and lifted his face to the sky to bask in everything that was home.

*****

Will was awakened by the sounds of a mockingbird, and the music startled him momentarily as he feared he had overslept. However, only the faintest of glows was present in the east as the darkness began to lose its foothold. Will checked his surroundings and found that all was as he had left it. The crude rope was still at his side, and the Enfields were still in their proper positions. His hunger gnawed at him, but the sensation had become such a common one that he hardly even noticed it. He looked skyward and noticed that the overcast had given way to clearer skies, and Will could see the morning star hovering above the eastern horizon. Seeing that everything was in its proper position, Will leaned back against the trunk of a nearby tree and contemplated his dream.

What a strange war this was. There were seemingly no absolutes, and nothing could be said with any certainty except as it pertained to individuals themselves. The North did not love the Black man, and the South was content for him to remain in his current position. Yet, here he was, in a forlorn forest defending the very people he had been accused of hating from the very people supposedly sworn to defend them. Nothing was as it appeared to be, nor could Will remember a recent time when it had been so.

Deep blue began to creep across the morning skies and vague shadows were now visible across the field. The stars, once clear as diamonds in an ocean of black, began to fade as they grudgingly gave way to their larger sibling. Will moved into position behind the poplar and placed his Enfield in the notch. Everything depended upon stealth, and Will determined to remain motionless in his position. Peering out across the field, Will felt his heart quicken slightly. Somewhere out there in the darkness was his adversary, and Will knew it.

Birds joined the morning chorus in ever increasing numbers as the light continued to increase. The sound was very familiar, and it reminded Will of many mornings when he had awakened to a very similar symphony as it wafted through his open window. The faces of his family appeared, and it amazed Will at how flawless they were in his memory. Before the war, he often let trivial matters at home bother him, yet, here in this place, those trivial things were what comforted him most. If only he could see them once more.

The far tree line was now visible across the field, but all that was beyond was still shaded in gray and black. Will estimated that the distance was around five hundred yards. A rustling in the branches overhead caught the soldier's attention, and Will slowly looked up to see a squirrel jumping from the top of one tree to the outstretched branch of another. He then felt a hint of inspiration and reached around to recover his Bible from the haversack. He opened the book to the last few pages, which were blank, and he began to write. Having finished his composition and proofreading it, he gently tore the page out, folded it in half, and placed it back in the Bible.

The sky was now distinctly blue, and a yellowish/orange glow became evident off to Will's left. Will could make out leaves on the distant trees as colors became increasingly more discernible. The Confederate's left hand grasped the end of his rope as his breathing continued in a rhythmic pattern. The time was near, and as soon as the first rays of light struck his position, the waiting would be over.

*****

Across the field, a dark and brooding pair of eyes peered out from beneath a dark green forage cap. A single piece of broom straw hung limply from the bearded lips, and the fingers drummed silently upon the stock of the Sharps rifle. From his lofty position in a beech tree, he had secured a full view of the woods directly in front of him. He was well aware that two other targets waited for him across that distance, and he grew somewhat impatient, as the young man had provided him his last shooting opportunity. However, he also knew that he blocked the only route to Fredericksburg and the fords across the river, and that it was only a matter of time before desperation set in and yet another opportunity would present itself. There was no regret for what had been done. The boy was a traitor and had served his purpose. The remaining two both represented undesirables, as had his first target. They were all merely fodder for his talent, and it was a talent that could never be satisfied. Inhaling deeply and then letting the air escape in a low growl, he propped his Sharps rifle upon a bracing limb in front of him and awaited the inevitable.

*****

The sun was peeking through the distant trees as Will intently scanned the far tree line, attempting to discern where he would be if the roles were reversed. He held the Enfield in place with his right hand and held the end of the rope with his left. The sun crawled agonizingly higher, and Will could now see that the tops of the trees above his head were bathed in a golden light. He flipped up the rear sight elevator and again estimated the distance to the other side. The distance was crucial to making his shot, and he might only get one chance to do it. Everything he knew, everything he had experienced, and all that he loved he mustered into this one final act. The sun had reached the point where it would just touch the head of the decoy when standing, and Will, still looking down the sight of his rifle, placed the slightest amount of tension on the rope.

"If you tickle us, do we not laugh?" Will quoted as he pulled the Enfield tightly into his shoulder.

"If you prick us, do we not bleed?"

Will cocked the hammer, finger gently on the trigger.

"If you wrong us, shall we not revenge?"

With a firm but smooth pull, Will saw his decoy rise from the obscuring grass, hesitate momentarily and then drop solidly into the support hole. Even from a distance, it was a surprisingly effective facsimile, and the golden rays of the sun made its sudden appearance even more striking. For a moment, the morning remained unchanged, and the chorus of songbirds continued unmolested.

*****

From far across the field, the sinister gaze scanned the field mercilessly for any sign of movement. The sunlight bathed the open space in a clear, yellow light but had yet to reveal anything of interest. The Federal sharpshooter felt his anger, like a smoldering ember, burst into flame anew. Did they believe that he would tire of waiting and simply vanish if they remained hidden long enough? Did they actually believe that there was a way of escape, and that their deaths were anything less than inevitable? They were cowards if they remained hidden and fools if they attempted escape. Movement caught his attention and his gaze shifted to see a gray-clad figure, his head covered with a typical slouch hat, rise from the grass near the point where he had shot the boy. Quickly adjusting his aim, he lined up his sights on the distant target.

"Fools," he growled as he squeezed the trigger.

Like the sudden striking of a pale serpent, Will saw the plume of white smoke appear about halfway up a distant tree. Will shifted his aim to accommodate, even as the distant bullet slammed into the decoy, placing a second bullet hole in the jacket very close to its predecessor. Aiming for the origin of the plume of smoke, Will felt the Enfield become an extension of his own arm and pulled the trigger.

Even as the projectile hurled across the open space, Will dropped his rifle and rolled to his left toward the next Enfield. Will's bullet sheared off several beech leaves as it hurtled through the branches and grazed the top of the Union sharpshooter's right shoulder and severed the strap to his haversack, which struck several branches as it plummeted to the earth. In shock, the Federal could feel the blood trickling down his arm, but his rage soon erupted once more as he observed the Confederate's plume of smoke. His Sharps could be reloaded much faster than his opponent's rifle, and he quickly shoved a new linen cartridge into the open breech. Quickly adjusting his aim to target the origin of the smoke, he fired off a second shot.

Will saw the second plume of smoke from his new vantage point and quickly centered his rifle on its origin, even as the Federal's .52 caliber projectile skimmed the top of the notch where his first rifle had been resting only a moment earlier. The distance was the same, his aiming point was the same, and the second Enfield bellowed fire as Will squeezed the trigger. The bullet crossed the grassy expanse at incredible speed and flew into the heart of the beech. The lead projectile fell from slightly above the Federal and shattered the front stock of the Sharps as it was being reloaded before striking him squarely in the chest. His body remained motionless as his breath escaped with a sinister hiss. Then slowly, like the felling of a great tree, he tumbled backward off of the limb. As he fell, the strap of his Sharps and of his cartridge box became entangled in the limbs of the great tree, and his body came to a sudden jolting halt, swaying gently from side to side. Will could see the devastating effects of his shot from across the distance and observed the lifeless body for some time before placing his head on the stock of the Enfield and closing his eyes.

*****

Evaline had heard the shooting and prayed after each distant

190

boom that it would not be the last that she would hear. She breathed a sigh of relief and remained where she was after hearing Will's last shot. Will did not return immediately, but she recognized his footsteps when he approached through the woods. She watched as he drew near and noticed that he appeared infinitely fatigued. He carried with him both his hat and the shell jacket with two conspicuous bullet holes in the back. He said nothing but assumed a sitting position across from her. After a moment, he inhaled deeply and looked up at Evaline.

"It's finished," he said with compassion.

"We free to go, den?"

"We are."

Evaline paused for a moment before responding.

"If it's all da same to you, can we just sit here for a minute?"

"Yes, for a minute."

*****

By midmorning, the pair had exited the woods and stepped out into the field. Will pointed to the beech tree in the distance, and Evaline shielded her eyes to focus on the motionless body hanging from its branches. After hiding for so many days, the pair felt vulnerable standing in the open without cover, and both expected a rifle to shatter the temporary tranquility. The pair walked side by side, enjoying the warmth of the sun on their faces. Little was spoken, but little needed to be.

Perhaps two miles from where they started, Will heard the music of water upon stones, and he knew that the river was near. The pair ascended a small ridge, and upon reaching the crest, they could see the running water below. John had been right, and the water was shallow and swift at that point. Scanning to his right, Will could see the two large stones jutting from the center of the river.

"The Sisters," Will whispered to Evaline as he nudged her arm to draw her attention to the landmark. Evaline nodded in response, but did not speak.

"Let's go down and take a look," Will continued, with Evaline again responding without words. Will took Evaline's arm to lead her down the incline, but as he did so, he suddenly became aware of the sound of voices coming from behind them. Will motioned for Evaline to stop. Turning around, at first Will saw nothing. Then, in a steady stream of blue, Will saw the first portion of a Union regiment crest a nearby ridge and move directly toward them.

"Oh, no," Will began. "Evaline, you have to go!"

"What is it, Will?"

"I believe some folks have taken an interest in my handiwork, and if they found our friend, they will be particularly unhappy with me. It looks like a Yankee skirmish line. Here, quickly take all of the food."

Evaline was suddenly overwhelmed.

"Will, wait. I done told you dat I can't do dis."

"You can, Evaline. You have to. You are not the same person you were when we first met, nor am I for that matter."

The voices grew steadily closer.

"Here, Evaline. Keep the Colt pistol. Time is very short. Remember what John told you. Avoid both armies and only make contact with the people on the Railroad. You'll only be safe when you reach Canada."

"Will, please…"

Will stopped for a moment and looked with compassion on the young woman who had become like a daughter to him.

"I know you're afraid, but this is all that I can do for you now. I must draw them away. Remember the sparrows. Home for you lies across that river."

Will then pointed toward the advancing blue line.

"Home for me lies that way."

Will lingered for a moment longer.

"Now go, Evaline, quickly."

The young woman was sobbing.

"I won't never forget you, Will."

The Confederate embraced her quickly and, without her noticing, slipped a piece of folded paper into one of the food bags. Evaline then turned and, unable to look back, ran down the hill toward the river below.

Alone, Will turned to face the long blue line. He was still concealed among the trees, but only a few steps forward would place him in full view. To lighten his load, Will placed one of the Enfields against a tree. He then quickly checked the second musket and made sure that the Spencer was loaded. Holding the Enfield at the ready with the Spencer across his back, Will inhaled deeply. Never looking back, Will took a step forward, the words of the Georgia poet sounding in his ears.

*"Out of the hills of Habersham,
Down the Valley of Hall..."*

Will cocked the Enfield and continued forward.
*"I hurry amain to reach the plain,
Run the rapid and leap the falls..."*

Will remembered his home in the coastal plain and wandering along the banks of the swift flowing waters.
*"Split at the rock and together again,
Accept my bed, or narrow or wide,
And flee from folly on every side..."*

The blue line was directly in front, and Will knew that he had been seen. He halted where he was and inhaled deeply, gathering every sensation as if it were his last.

*"With a lover's pain to attain the plain,
Far from the hills of Habersham,
Far from the valleys of Hall."*[1]

The blue line had halted in unison and stood observing the gray-clad intruder as if it did not know what to make of him. An uneasy stalemate persisted for a moment more before Will suddenly threw the Enfield up to his shoulder and took a random shot over the heads of the Federals before dropping the weapon and fleeing back to the woods. The Federals were only stunned for a moment before the entire line opened fire and Will could hear the bullets hissing by and thudding into the tree trunks as he dove for cover. Pulling the Spencer from his shoulder, he chambered a round as he continued to run to his right through the forest and away from Evaline.

"Get him, get him!" Will could hear the command shouted down the line as the Federals continued to take shots at him. Looking to his left, Will could see the entire line of blue rushing to close in on him and was dismayed to see some Federals closing in from ahead as well.

"Run, Will!" the Confederate's tired mind screamed to his

---

[1] Mary D. Lanier, *Poems of Sidney Lanier* (Charles Scribner's Sons, 1915), 24-25

exhausted legs. "Run! Everything depends on you!"

And so he ran. Starved, alone, and fatigued beyond all comprehension, he pressed on as death continued to rain all about him. The Virginia forest seemed somehow to understand the plight of its little brother and twisted and bowed as it absorbed the lethal blows meant for him.

"Send Johnson up! Send Johnson up!" the Federal call resounded. Ahead of Will on the hillside, a blue clad soldier wiped the glare from the front sight of his Springfield and eased into a kneeling position as he tracked the lone Confederate. He then took aim, carefully leading the man as he ran.

"You sure you got him?" a comrade asked kneeling alongside.

"Yeah, I got him."

"That's a tough shot."

"I said I got him. Just like shooting a running deer."

A moment later, the Springfield bellowed, and Will felt a heavy thud in his left side that completely knocked him off his feet and shoved him to the right.

"Get up! Keep going!" his mind continued to command him. Using every ounce of strength, Will grasped desperately at the greenery about him and pulled himself upright. Quickly looking up to his left, Will saw the man who had taken the shot. In an almost reflex action, Will threw the Spencer up to his shoulder and pulled the trigger. Johnson's head snapped back as his body flattened on the hillside and remained motionless.

The pain in his side was excruciating and breathing was labored, but Will pushed himself onward. Every step was a struggle, and the Confederate knew that he could not keep up the pace. The pressure from the men on his left was pushing him toward the thicker vegetation along the river, and Will knew that he would soon become trapped against the water. A blue-clad figure appeared between the trees only a few feet in front of him, with movement in the periphery off to his left indicating the presence of another. The Federal lowered his Springfield and aimed it directly at Will's chest, but the Georgian was faster and fired at point blank range. The blast knocked the man backward and sent the Springfield flying upward end over end. Quickly grasping the temporarily suspended weapon by its stock with his left hand, Will swung the lengthy weapon to the side and pulled the trigger. Fire and smoke engulfed all in its path.

But it was the last act of which he was capable. There was

nothing left as he could no longer drive himself forward. All of his love, all of his strength and might were completely expended, and he collapsed behind a large poplar tree, his back against the trunk and facing the thick forest to the front. Gasping for air and unable to lift the Spencer, he drew the LeMat and held the weapon against his chest. The sounds of the feet of innumerable men were clear and close as they churned through the leaves and closed on his position. He heard the voices, dripping with vengeance, as they called out in unison for his destruction. He studied the wall of green in front of him, knowing that it would be one of the last images that he would ever see. Forcing himself onto his knees, he took a last deep breath before turning to face the enemy but collapsed back as he lacked the strength to maintain the position. The sounds of the soldiers' feet were almost upon him, and he closed his eyes to await the inevitable.

"With a lover's pain to attain the plain…"

The leafy wall directly in front of him suddenly erupted in a wall of flame and smoke as the thunder of hundreds of rifles pounded his ears and the whistle of deadly projectiles flew past him. The volley mowed down the advancing men, and the blue line halted as it tried to ascertain what was happening. An eerie moment of silence followed the blast, but the tranquility was short-lived, as the forest was suddenly filled with the unmistakable sound of the Rebel yell. Blurs of gray and butternut burst from the woods and flew past Will as they swept the faltering Federal line back up the hill and away from the river. Dazed, Will sat motionless behind the tree, still grasping his Lemat revolver. He could still hear the sounds of firing behind him, but no one was apparently near until Will saw someone approaching him from his right. Looking up, Will was greeted by the confused face of a Confederate soldier as he studied the man sitting in front of him. He was a little older than Will, but his advantage in years had been magnified by hard labor and fighting. There was a scar on his left cheek and the brass belt buckle was heavily dented as if it had been struck by a bullet. He kneeled down next to Will, still studying the man in front of him.

"You all right, son?" the man asked with a thick, but familiar Southern accent.

Will nodded.

"You hit?"

Will nodded again.

"Where?"

Will pointed to his left side.

The man stood once again and moved around to Will's left.

"I don't see no blood," the soldier stated after inspection. "Must have winged ya."

"It doesn't feel that way."

"May have just broke some of your short ribs. Now, mind you, I never said it didn't hurt, but it won't kill ya."

The man then began to chuckle, his shoulders moving up and down with the emotion.

"I'm not sure what you thought you was doin', but I'll tell you one thing, I ain't never seen anything like that! You took on an entire regiment! Pennsylvanians, I believe." He then paused as he finished laughing.

"In any case, it's good to meet you. I'm James Franklin Bennett, 13th Georgia Infantry. My friends call me Frank."

Will smiled and extended his hand.

"William Mark Seymour, 3rd Georgia sharpshooters. My friends call me Will."

"I figured you had to be a Georgian. Ain't nobody else gonna be stupid enough to do something like that!"

Will nodded in agreement, forcing the beginnings of a smile.

"What exactly are you doin' out here anyway? You don't exactly strike me as the deserting type. You get separated from your unit or something like that?"

"Yes," Will responded. "And I'm just now finding my way back. It has not been easy."

"I can imagine," Frank responded, still sizing up the man in front of him. "We've been watchin' this Pennsylvania unit for a few days now, and it seems that they picked today to try to probe our flank. I guess we kind of helped each other out today. You brought 'em right to us, and we were able to get you out of a pickle in the end. In any case, we had better get you up and get back. You never know when there might be something bigger brewing. You think you can walk?"

"I'll be slow, but I can make it."

"Here, have some water before you give it a try."

After a few sips, Will felt a little stronger and was able to get to his feet. Most of the 13th was returning by that time, and Will fell in with his fellow soldiers as they returned to their lines.

*****

After returning, Will had to meet with the usual officers and authorities to recount his story as to how he ended up so far from his unit. Will retold the entire account as it happened except that he never mentioned his encounter with Evaline and Edward. At first, his account was met with some skepticism, but all of the facts of his story were verified through direct contact with the 3rd Georgia. After all, it was difficult to believe that a Confederate traveling north would be deserting, especially one brave enough to attack an entire Union regiment. When all was said and done, Will's account was confirmed, and he was told that he would be transferred back to the 3rd the following day. As he meandered among the 13th Georgia, he once again spotted Frank sitting with his mess mates around an inviting campfire. Frank motioned him over, and Will spent the last few hours of daylight retelling his adventure to eager listeners. Even though a natural story-teller by nature, Will still found it difficult to put much heart into the tale. Perhaps the reason was because everything was too fresh, and that he was still alive was too unbelievable. That may have well been the case, but Will also knew that the main reason was that his mind was preoccupied by the fate of his friend. He had spent such a short time with her, but the thought of her alone in the wilderness was almost more than he could bear, and he prayed that she had made it to the next safe house.

The other soldiers began to drift slowly away from the fire as they prepared for their duties or to retire for the evening. Soon, it was Will and Frank sitting around the fire staring into the flames and swapping stories of South Georgia.

"I wish I had your luck," Frank began. "You strike me as a lucky fellow, while on the other hand, mine ain't so good."

"Lucky? How do you figure that?"

"Well, I figure any man with two bullet holes in the middle of his back and another in his haversack who ain't dead yet has got to be doin' something right."

Will had not noticed the hole in his haversack, but at Frank's mention of it Will examined it and saw a perfect bullet hole in the middle of the fabric bag. Will explored its ragged edges gingerly as he recalled that it was hanging on his left side when he had been shot. Respectfully sliding his Bible from within, Will held the book out to the flames as the flickering orange light illuminated a round defect directly in the center. Carefully sifting through the pages, Will found that the bullet had been halted in the Gospels, and Will read the familiar words upon the final page of the bullet's flight.

"...*ye are of more value than many sparrows...*"

Will slowly closed the book and his eyes as well.

"That wouldn't be the first time that's happened to a fella," Frank commented.

Will did not respond.

"There is something else I wanted to ask you."

Will opened his eyes.

"You wouldn't happen to know anything about a young Negro woman crossing the river close to where we met up with you, would you?"

Will did his best to hide his concern, but the expression on Frank's face betrayed that he already knew more than he was admitting to.

"What did you do?" Will asked with trepidation.

"We let her go."

A pause followed.

"Why?"

Frank shrugged his shoulders.

"Kindness, I suppose. I don't fight and starve and bleed just to keep her as she is, and I expect I can say the same of you."

Will bowed his head and the emotions of the past few days came roaring over him, and his shoulders began to move rhythmically with the silent sobbing.

"It's all right, son," Frank said compassionately. "You let it all out if you got to."

Will then dried his eyes on his sleeve as he heard Frank's distinctive chuckle.

"Like I said, I ain't never seen anything like what you did before, and I don't expect I ever will again."

Inhaling deeply, Will looked up at the heavens and soon found Cassiopeia and the Big Dipper and, between them both, shone the constant gleam of the North Star.

Epilogue

For years I would sit in my parents' living room studying the old black and white photograph and the pale eyes that stared back at me from within its borders. William Mark Seymour was an old man in the picture, seated in a chair, his legs casually crossed and his hat pushed back on the crown of his head. As was the custom of the day, his face showed no emotion, and I have spent hours contemplating if his generation understood who he was any better than mine. It was after his time that we discovered that, because of what he had done, Evaline succeeded in crossing the border to the safety of Canada. He never knew that she learned to read and write, was reunited with her husband, and that her sons, William and Mark, had the privilege of listening to her tell in immaculate detail the story of a gray-clad warrior from Georgia, who risked everything that he loved to find her a new home. Whenever she spoke of him, emotion would often hinder her description of the man and she would simply respond with the words of the Bard:

"He was a man, take him for all in all, I shall not look upon his like again."

She would then inevitably retrieve a yellowed slip of paper that the Confederate had slipped into one of her food sacks at the time of his departure and, with trembling voice, she would begin to read.

Evaline,

My young friend, I wish that I had more to give you than the pathetic gratitude of a lowly teacher. I am indeed poor by the standard of worldly status and possessions, but my time spent with you has made me infinitely wealthy, both in this life and in the one to come.

As I write to you, I sit here in the darkness completely unaware of my fate over the next few hours. But I do know this. Regardless of whether I ever see home again, I sincerely hope that when I see you again my actions will cause me to be able to look you in the eye and know that I gave every last measure while I walked with you along life's path. You have become a daughter to me and, as painful as it is, I must now let you go and place you in the hands of the Father, who is infinitely more loving and kind than I could ever hope to be.

You are an answer to prayer. You will succeed. Listen closely to the great cloud of witnesses cheering you on. One of the voices shall always be mine. I shall never forget you.

Your humble servant always,

William Mark Seymour

I have resolved myself to the fact that, in this life, I will never be the man that Will was. Yet, his blood flows in my veins and I pray that perhaps there may be something of him that lives on in this inadequate descendant. Although life and circumstances have taken me away, when I return to my South Georgia home and watch my sons play among the lofty pines, I can close my eyes, turn my face to the sky, and hear the wind call my name.